Nan overbalan

She descended hea
floor, but into the
someone who pro
gentleman! And he promptly rewarded her
with a vigorous kiss on her shapely mouth. . .

Nan, usually so hardened to the proprieties,
so used to acting the part of the Rector's prim
eldest daughter, surprisingly found that her
first thoughts were not those of gratitude for
being caught, nor even of anger at being so
summarily kissed. Instead, she could only
think, Who in the world is he? And what the
devil is he doing here in the pantry? What she
should have said, of course, was something in
the order of, How dare you, sir? Unhand me
at once!

Paula Marshall, married with three children, has had a varied life. She began her career in a large library and ended it as a senior academic in charge of history in a polytechnic. She has travelled widely, has been a swimming coach, and has appeared on *University Challenge* and *Mastermind*. She has always wanted to write, and likes her novels to be full of adventure and humour.

NOT QUITE
A GENTLEMAN

Paula Marshall

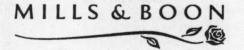

MILLS & BOON

DID YOU PURCHASE THIS BOOK WITHOUT A COVER?

If you did, you should be aware it is **stolen property** as it was reported *unsold and destroyed* by a retailer. Neither the Author nor the publisher has received any payment for this book.

All the characters in this book have no existence outside the imagination of the author, and have no relation whatsoever to anyone bearing the same name or names. They are not even distantly inspired by any individual known or unknown to the author, and all the incidents are pure invention.

All rights reserved. The text of this publication or any part thereof may not be reproduced or transmitted in any form or by any means, electronic or mechanical, including photocopying, recording, storage in an information retrieval system, or otherwise, without the written permission of the publisher.

This book is sold subject to the condition that it shall not, by way of trade or otherwise, be lent, resold, hired out or otherwise circulated without the prior consent of the publisher in any form of binding or cover other than that in which it is published and without a similar condition including this condition being imposed on the subsequent purchaser.

*MILLS & BOON, the Rose Device and LEGACY OF LOVE
are trademarks of the publisher.
Harlequin Mills & Boon Limited,
Eton House, 18–24 Paradise Road, Richmond, Surrey TW9 1SR
This edition published by arrangement with
Harlequin Enterprises B.V.*

© Paula Marshall 1995

ISBN 0 263 79303 6

*Set in 10 on 11 pt Linotron Times
04-9511-91466*

*Typeset in Great Britain by CentraCet, Cambridge
Printed in Great Britain by
BPC Paperbacks Ltd*

CHAPTER ONE

'Lord, what fools these mortals be!' Shakespeare.

MISS FIELDING, the Rector of Broomhall's eldest child, known to all her friends and relatives as Nan, stood on a tall stool in the Rectory pantry and cursed life. She was busy arranging the first jams of the summer of 1819 on a high dark shelf, away from the light. The oaths she was using were mild, but firm, discreetly intoned beneath her breath.

She privately counted the sum of her annoyances. Her hair was coming down, her old brown dress, despite the presence of an apron made from sacking tied round her waist, was streaked with fruit and syrup. She was perspiring, for the summer day was hot and not really suitable for jam-making at all. Worse, the top shelf was almost out of reach and the only ladder which might have helped her had been taken away by the carpenter who was busy repairing one of the Rectory's bow windows.

Worse still, and by far the most galling, the rest of her family was entertaining itself after the fashion which pleased it most. Her father, Caleb Fielding, was upstairs in his study teaching eleven-year-old Chaz, his youngest child and only son, Latin verbs. Her one remaining unmarried sister, Jane, was out visiting her friend Caroline at her home at nearby Letcombe's Landing, and was doubtless seated idly in the shade, under a cedar tree, a glass of newly made lemonade to hand, flirting with any pretty young fellow who happened to be sitting near by. Her mother, Lavinia

Fielding, who had proclaimed herself a helpless invalid after the birth of her last child, was lying on her bed being fanned by one of the undermaids. She was also being read to by Kelsey, once the Fielding children's governess and now by way of being a general factotum in the Rectory.

Only Nan Fielding was working, and suddenly, quite suddenly, Nan Fielding was tired of work, tired of being the dogsbody around whom the life of the Rectory and, yes, the life of the parish revolved. Tired of being nearly twenty-eight years old, past her last prayers, sensible plainish Nan Fielding with only a pair of fine eyes to recommend her to anyone. Although once there had been a young man to gaze into those eyes, and tell her that she was beautiful Anne, his own darling girl. . . but that young man had been dead and gone many years ago. . .

How long had this fit been coming on? she wondered, setting the last jam pot neatly at the end of the line. Was it the result of being the family's mainstay ever since her mother had realised how practical dear Nan was after Chaz's birth? Or was it that this morning she had found one of Randal's letters, its paper yellow and its ink brown, tucked away in a drawer and long forgotten?

Or was it the fact of her sister Jane's sheer inconsiderate selfishness, her belief that Nan existed only as some kind of automaton, such as eastern sultans in fairy-stories were reputed to possess, which once wound up was able, tirelessly, to look after their master's interests and fulfil their slightest wants? Her other two sisters whom she had chaperoned, cared for, and seen that they had made good marriages, had been grateful to her for what she had done, and sometimes continued still to do. Only Jane took everything for granted—

complained, even, that Nan did not consider her enough. . .

Above all Jane was intent on making a grand match, much better than any of her sisters, and thought that Nan was too practical, too dowdy to push her interests hard enough against those of girls who had a grander name than Fielding. Never mind that their father was the cousin and heir of Sir Charlton Fielding Bart, the whole world knew that Sir Charlton was only of mid-dling fortune, and being younger than Caleb Fielding was like to die after him. . .

Oh, damn, damn, double damn. To Gehenna with everything, cursed Nan as she touched ground once more. For there on the lowest shelf were two errant pots which she had quite forgotten. And now she would have to climb back on to the chair again, and range them alongside the others. Which only went to show that self-pity was a deluding and disgusting thing—and time-wasting into the bargain.

So, to save wasting any further time, Nan climbed back on to the chair, a pot in each sticky hand. But, alas, in the doing her hair had quite come down—but what of that, for who was there to see it? Which was another observation best not made, for as, invoking Satan and all the devils from hell, Nan leaned sideways on one leg to save having to climb down and move the stool along *again* she overbalanced, and fell, letting out a little scream as she did so.

But good fortune, for once, was with her for she descended headlong, not to the hard stone floor, but into the obliging waiting arms of someone who proved to be a rather large gentleman!

'Well, well, well,' he drawled, having arrived in the pantry in time to catch a nymph, falling, if not from the skies, from a high stool, 'what have we here? A divine armful sent down to me by Jove, no less. A happy portent to greet my arrival in South Nottinghamshire!'. And he rewarded the nymph with a vigorous kiss on her shapely mouth. . . .

Nan, usually so hardened to the proprieties, so used to acting the part of the Rector's prim eldest daughter—for her bad language was indulged in only in private—surprisingly found that her first thoughts were not those of gratitude for being caught, nor even of anger at being so summarily kissed. Instead, as her saviour continued to hold her tightly to him, stroking her right breast gently as he did so, causing the most alarming tingles to radiate all over her body, long starved of such affection, she could only think, Who in the world is he? And what the devil is he doing here in the pantry? What she should have said, of course, was something in the order of, How dare you, sir? Unhand me at once!

But before she lost her good sense completely and asked him that in those rude terms Nan looked him firmly in the face which was so near to her own. It was most disconcerting, to say the least, to discover that he was not only large, but extremely handsome. His eyes were so grey that they were silvery. His nose was long and dominant, his mouth long and shapely. His hair was fashionably cut and darkly glossy with a frosting of silver in it—borrowed from his eyes, perhaps. And what had brought that trope on? Admiring gentlemen's looks was not the habit of Miss Fielding. Most surprisingly of all, she who knew everyone in the village and the surrounding countryside had never seen him before.

'Pray who, sir, are you? And what are you doing in the pantry?' she finally croaked at him, something odd having happened to her voice as well as to the rest of her body.

The stranger still made no effort to put her down. Which proved that he was not only large, but strong, for Nan, although by no means plump, was a tall woman and well-built. The manly chest against which she was reposing was both broad and warm, and, to an elderly spinster who had not had a man's arms about her for some twelve years, oddly comforting. . . And she really must stop thinking in the prose of a Minerva Press novel, and start trying to make this unknown rake behave himself! But what with trying to wriggle out of his arms, and stop the jam pots she was still holding from falling on to the floor, she found herself unable to think clearly.

He answered her with a rumbling laugh, and the words, 'What am I doing in the pantry? Saving servant girls from breaking their necks, of course. You don't seem very grateful.'

Servant girls! Her hair, her clothes, her apron, and possibly her language as she fell, must have deceived him as to her true rank. To this humiliation had she come! No wonder Jane looked at her with distaste and the suggestion that even for a chaperon she was rather more of a plain dowd than she needed to be.

She opened her mouth to pour righteous indignation over him for holding her in such a familiar fashion, to inform him that she was Miss Fielding, the Rector's eldest daughter, but before a word could so much as pass her lips he bent his handsome head and kissed her again—full upon her half-open mouth!

It was a polite kiss, if one snatched from a servant girl could ever be deemed polite, and when it was over he took no further liberties with her. She opened her mouth again to inform him that she was not accustomed to being so treated, but the only result of that was that he misunderstood her, and murmured, 'Another kiss for further payment for rescuing you?' This time the kiss was full and lusty, his tongue gently probing her mouth, and touching hers before it retreated.

Hampered by a pot of jam in each hand, Nan could

do nothing to defend herself. He was obviously one of those predatory gentlemen who took their pleasure with the women servants of any house where they happened to find themselves. But that was not the worst thing of all. To her disgust Nan found herself enjoying the kiss, and the spicy aroma from either his hair or his linen which surrounded him, and wouldn't have minded if it had lasted longer. Most of the men whom she met smelled only of horses, and wouldn't have dreamed of kissing her; nor would she willingly have kissed them back. But that was no reason to welcome this stranger's advances.

The kiss over, he gently lowered her to the ground, where Nan carefully put the jam pots on the lower shelf and then turned to face him, to discover that he was not only tall but also well-built and beautifully turned out, from the top of his admirably dressed head to the tips of his shining boots. Wealth and power shone from him like rays from the sun.

So what was he doing in the Rectory pantry? She was soon to find out.

'My good girl,' he murmured negligently, 'you may perhaps be able to inform me where the Misses Fielding are this afternoon. Miss Jane Fielding distinctly told me when we met at Sampford Lacy two days ago that she would be at home to me here today and invited me to call. I rang the bell but no one answered. Seeing that the front door was open, and fearing that something was amiss, I took the liberty of entering. Only to find that no one was about. Growing a little alarmed, I took the further liberty of exploring the house—to find not Miss Jane but Beauty herself, working diligently in the pantry, and I just in time to save her from a dreadful fall!'

Speaking thus, he drew a fine cambric handkerchief from his pocket and, murmuring, 'Allow me,' gently wiped the mixture of jam and perspiration from Nan's right cheek.

Nan was suddenly and deeply aware that so far she had not, apart from the question she had put to him after she had fallen into his arms, uttered a word. Shock and surprise—as well as sensual delight—had kept her mute. It would, she felt, be too humiliating to confess that she was the elder Miss Fielding whose cold propriety was known throughout South Notts and North Leicestershire.

And 'Beauty herself, working diligently in the pantry'! How dared he come out with anything so preposterous? He was jeering at her; he must be. She had no idea at all how unlike the lively picture which she presented to her unknown visitor was from the prim one which she saw in the mirror and which as Miss Fielding, the Rector's spinster daughter, she usually showed to the world.

Her hair, whose collapse she had lamented, had fallen in long waves and ringlets about her face, softening it. Tawny in hue, scraped back into a tight knot, it usually looked a dull mouse-brown; loose, it shone with red and gold lights. Her face, normally pale, was rosy with the heat and exertion. Her lips, usually primly straight, were swollen, soft and tender as a consequence of both his kisses and his caresses—which, shamefully, she had made no attempt to resist. Her eyes, a deep turquoise, shone with indignation at being so carelessly handled, but the intruder was not to know that.

As for her clothing—well, it was how a fine gentleman exepcted to see a servant dressed, so he made nothing of it. He merely admired the clean lines of the long-limbed body revealed by the drab dress clinging damply to it. Those gentlemen who met Miss Fielding in her normal habitat had never had the opportunity to discover that she possessed a body at all, never mind a shapely one.

What Nan would have liked to do was to ring a great peal over him, to put him in his place, once and for all, but from what he had just said he was obviously one of Jane's beaux. And what would he think of the Misses Fielding if, dressed and dishevelled as she was, she confessed that she was the Rector's eldest and most proper daughter? With any luck he would not recognise her when they next met. She usually took good care to live in Jane's shadow when she was chaperoning her, and would make sure that she looked her worst for the next few weeks.

So, remembering charades taken part in long ago where she had played the part of a serving maid, Nan bobbed him a submissive curtsy, offering in a thick Nottinghamshire accent, 'Lor', sir, the young ladies be gone over to Letcombe's Landing for the day, and the rest of the fambly be engaged or out. Be there owt I can tell 'em? As to 'oo y'are, that is?'

She was a little afraid she might be overdoing things. The mischievous part of her which no one knew existed, and which had helped her to survive the years since her mother's withdrawal from the world after Chaz's birth, almost had her pulling her forelock. The large gentleman smiled his lazy and charming smile at her, displaying a splendid set of white teeth.

'Nymph, garlanded with jam and jam pots, if not with flowers, you may tell Miss Jane Fielding that Brandon Tolliver came to pay his respects to her. He is at present residing at Gillyflower Hall and will be pleased to entertain any of the Rector of Broomhall's family. He will also present his compliments to the Rector himself at a suitable date in the near future. You can remember all that?'

'Ooh, I'll try, sir.' And Nan bobbed an even lower curtsy, trying to hide her face as she did so.

'Good girl!' He rewarded her with another smile, and without the hint of patronising condescension which the gentry usually offered to servants. He hesitated a moment, and gave a soundless laugh before pulling a guinea from his pocket. 'That's for promising to remember my message, and my thanks for three splendid kisses—with my apologies to the lad you may be walking out with for stealing them from you.'

He closed Nan's disbelieving fingers over the guinea, made her an elaborate bow and took his bright self away. Nan had just enough presence of mind to give him time to leave the Rectory before she ran into the front drawing-room to watch him striding down the path which led to the gate where a spanking new curricle picked out in sky-blue and gold was waiting for him. His tiger, also picked out in blue and gold, stood beside it. Nan's recent visitor jumped up, took up the reins and bowled away, the tiger now clinging on for dear life at the back.

So that was Mr Brandon Tolliver, who said that he was the new squire of Gillyflower Hall, but who knew so little about his inheritance that he was not yet aware that it was known to one and all as Gilliver Hall. The locals invariably shortened it as they shortened the word gillyflower, or wallflower. But more to the point, who was he and where had he come from?

The whole world knew, or thought it knew, that when curmudgeonly old Bartholomew Tolliver had gone to his last rest his second, much younger cousin, Desmond Tolliver of Broomhall House, would inherit. So where had Mr Brandon Tolliver, silver-tongued seducer of plain servant girls, come from? And was that why Desmond had been called to London shortly after old Bart's death, and had not yet returned? Well, doubtless she would soon find out.

Another surprise was that Jane had said nothing about meeting the impudent Mr Brandon Tolliver, and would doubtless be furious that she had missed him—even if it was her own fault.

Jane was. 'He must have misheard,' she wailed that night after the Letcombes' gig had dropped her off at the Rectory, and she had arrived in time to partake of the tea which Kelsey had carried through for them, dinner at the Rectory having been over for some time.

'I told him that I would be at home tomorrow, not today. Oh, dear, and we had such a famous time together at Sampford Lacy, and he's most enormously rich, and he only talked to me; he wasn't at all interested in Charlotte Alden, Louisa Thurman or Caroline Letcombe, I could tell. Oh, what appalling luck.'

'No need to take on so,' murmured Nan gently. She had quite recovered her balance and her usual sang-froid and was trying to put out of her mind the memory of the shameless way in which she had allowed Brandon Tolliver to kiss and caress her. Brandon Tolliver, indeed, would not have recognised his 'Beauty', who was now wearing a shapeless dark dress, had scraped back her tawny hair beneath a disfiguring cap, and was speaking in her usual self-effacing manner. 'No need at all. He will doubtless be staying here for some time, now that he has inherited. He said that he would be calling again soon.'

'You met him, then?' queried Jane. 'Not that *you* could have had much to say to interest him,' she added a trifle scornfully. 'He's the most amazing quiz. Full of life and fun.'

'So Annie said,' Nan murmured. She was tatting

vigorously, an occupation useful for unconsidered spinsters—particularly one who was busy lying by omission to her rather ill-natured sister. At least Jane wouldn't question Annie about their visitor, so no risk that she would discover Nan's fib—that Annie hadn't met him at all! Not that this was the only, or the most important, fib to which Nan treated the family who took her so much for granted.

Jane refused to drop the subject of Mr Brandon Tolliver; she said, with self-satisfaction in her voice, 'I'm sure that his inheriting Gillyflower Hall will have put Desmond's nose thoroughly out of joint. He was always so certain that it would come to him.'

Nan felt a small pang of grief for Desmond, and also felt constrained to reprimand Jane a little for flightiness. 'A most unChristian comment for a parson's daughter to make, my dear, and not one which you ought to utter outside our family circle.' She ignored the face which Jane pulled, and received some small support from Kelsey, who, surprisingly, had never greatly cared for Desmond.

Kelsey murmured drily, however, 'I am sure that Mr Desmond will doubtless be feeling most disappointed, if not to say cheated. After all, the late Mr Tolliver virtually promised him Gillyflower Hall.'

Well, that was the correct thing to say, even if rather lukewarm, but for some reason Kelsey had taken against Desmond, even if he did visit the Rectory frequently, to play chess with the Rector and to talk books with Nan and the rest of the pretty sisters. It was not often that Kelsey took against people, but when she did there was no moving her. Nor could she say why she did. 'I feel it in my bones,' she had once told Nan, 'and very often my bones tell true.'

Which was a bit hard on Desmond, who had always

been unfailingly kind in his stiff way to the Fielding family, and to Nan in particular.

Nan briefly wondered what Kelsey's bones would make of handsome, airy Mr Brandon Tolliver who made so free with servant girls. Would she succumb to the charm which he had so carelessly ladled over the Rectory's supposed parlourmaid? And why should she be allowing Mr Brandon Tolliver to monopolise her thoughts?

So Nan shook herself mentally and said, in the most composed manner she could muster, 'I agree; it cannot but be distressing for poor Desmond to be passed over. And pray how did his cousin Brandon, if cousin he be, come to be at Sampford Lacy when you were there, Jane?'

Jane replied petulantly, for she always disliked being questioned closely about anything, 'I'm sure I don't know, Nan. All I know is that he's excellent company, not a bit like Desmond who is so grave and dull. He made us all laugh time and again.'

Now why was it that that comment should cause Nan to have a brief memory of a pair of flashing silver eyes and a curling mouth. . .? Oh, pooh to that! Those eyes would never flash for plain Miss Fielding. . .

In an effort to banish the unwanted memory Nan murmured repressively, 'I am sure that he need not be so remarkably witty as to be able to reduce you and all your friends to hysterics.'

Even Kelsey looked a little surprised as Nan came out with this barbed comment. Jane's response was to pout in Nan's direction before remarking cuttingly, 'One might expect you to talk like an elderly gorgon, Nan. I think that you have forgotten what it was like to be young. Who can be surprised that you refuse to read anything by the author of *Sophia*? Papa's books of sermons are more in your line!'

For some reason these darts from Jane, which Nan was usually able to ignore, hurt her more than a little. To steady herself she spoke even more quietly than usual. 'It would be as well to remember, Jane, that Mr Brandon Tolliver is almost double your age, that you know very little about him other than that he is a great flirt, and as a very young girl it might be as well for you to go slow with him.'

Kelsey and Jane both stared at her. Jane said, her pretty voice more cutting than ever, 'Now, Nan, how do you know all that about him? I was not aware that you had ever met him. You surely did not gossip about him with Annie?'

Now here was a facer, as young Chaz was often given to saying. For once, Nan's tongue, usually on a tight rein, had run away with her. She chose not to make any comment, merely shook her head and tatted away more vigorously than ever. Least said, soonest mended. After a brief pause during which they all drank tea, Nan finally said, to no one in particular, 'After all, we must always remember that real life is not at all like the life in the novels by the author of *Sophia*.'

'And what a pity that is,' sighed Jane, tossing her curly blonde head and flashing her bright blue eyes as she took from the little basket which she had carried with her from Letcombe's Landing the first volume of a three-volume novel, bound in pretty blue cloth, with an elegant label on the spine which read '*Amelia's Secret*, by the author of *Sophia*'.

'Only think, I have come away from Letcombe with Sophia's latest. Charlotte has lent it to me. She says it is even more exciting and more horrid than the last. One cannot guess what Amelia's secret is, she says, and I suppose I shall have to wait until the last volume to find out! You may have it when I have finished with it.

I have quite fallen in love with the hero, Mr Lancelot Beaumains.'

'Oh, I really haven't time to be reading novels.' Nan's voice was subdued. 'And you know how dear Papa disapproves of them.'

'Well, Sir Avery doesn't,' announced Jane. 'He reads each one of Sophia's as it comes out. He has read all of the Waverley novels as well, and so has Papa, for all that he says that he dislikes novels!'

'I shouldn't make too much of that,' retorted Kelsey, gathering up the tea things. 'What Papas do and what daughters do are two quite different things. But I must confess that I do enjoy Sophia's novels; there is a bottom of common sense in them, and they are so witty. You ought to read them, Nan. You would enjoy them.'

'No time,' Nan returned briskly.

'Lancelot Beaumains is very like Brandon Tolliver,' continued Jane, flicking over the pages of *Amelia's Secret*. 'Very handsome and great fun. He teases the heroine all the time.' She glanced sideways at Nan before taking the opportunity to stake her claim to the infinitely desirable Mr Brandon Tolliver. 'Charlotte Alden says that the *on dit* in London is that he is most immensely rich. He told her that he intends to settle at Gillyflower Hall and improve it. He has sent for an architect and a landscape gardener to begin work at once. He said that he will be attending the Assembly Rooms ball in Highborough next week. I am sure that you would wish me to attend also, seeing that he was *most* particular in his attentions to me—and he will surely expect me to be present.'

One might assume, thought Nan nastily, that from what I saw of him today Mr Brandon Tolliver is '*most* particular' in his attentions to anything female on two legs. Aloud she said, 'Well, that being so, I agree we ought to attend, so long as you promise to conduct yourself properly. I will prevail upon Papa to escort us so that we may all have the pleasure of being introduced to such a charmer.'

Jane chose to ignore the touch of vitriol in this last speech, and exclaimed with delight at the prospect of yet another meeting with the new owner of Gillyflower Hall. It was left to Kelsey to say to Nan, as she extinguished the candles in the drawing-room after Jane had gone to bed, 'Are you feeling a little under the weather today, my dear? I know that Jane was being her usual tiresome self, but it is not like you to bite back at her quite so sharply.'

What to say to that? That I have the most distinct impression of life passing me by and that whereas I was able and willing to shepherd Jane's older sisters about the county and in London because they were so sweet-natured and grateful I am coming to find Jane's little unpleasantnesses to me unbearable? That was the unsayable truth.

But it was not the whole truth. For had it not been Mr Brandon Tolliver's careless kisses which had reminded Nan Fielding that she had once been young, desirable, and desired?

CHAPTER TWO

'So, YOU mean to settle at last, Brandon?'

Brandon Tolliver bent his handsome head and said affectionately to his widowed sister, Mrs Lydia Bligh, who was keeping him company during these early days at Gillyflower Hall, 'Oh, yes, indeed, my dear. I think that I may have found exactly what I was looking for— a pretty, biddable young girl of good, if not great family who will make an excellent mother for my children.'

Lydia Bligh, who was engaged in stitching a fire-screen portraying a pair of rosy cherubs with their arms around each other and their tiny wings extended, gave a great sigh at this, and said shrewdly, 'And who is this paragon—who, I may remind you, will also be your wife, as well as the mother of your children? I take it that you will no longer be keeping the excellent Mrs Emma Milborne—or will you be holding her in reserve when you become bored with your pretty and biddable bride?'

Now this was naughty of Lydia, was it not? Particularly when he was contemplating doing what she had long asked him to do—giving up Emma in order to found a family.

'Oh, you misjudge me,' he told Lydia reproachfully, walking away from her to gaze out of the window across the neglected park, so that she might not see his face. Who knew what she might read there, seeing that she was as shrewd as he was? 'I have pensioned Emma off, and she is to marry her penniless suitor whom she has long adored, but could not afford. We parted on happy terms, I hasten to add.'

'No doubt.' Lydia's tone was satiric. 'Now you may tell me who your child bride is, and I will exclaim in suitable terms at your choice.'

'Unkind,' Brandon murmured, without turning round. 'You met her at the Ameses'. Miss Jane Fielding. She is, in case you don't know, the youngest daughter of the Rector of Broomhall, the living in my gift. He is by way of being the distant cousin and heir of Sir Charlton Fielding of Ryall in Northumbria.'

Lydia laid down her needle, frowned. 'I remember her. Remarkably pretty. Seemed very taken by you. No dowry, I suppose. Has the Rector any income beside his stipend, which I happen to know is a poor one?'

Brandon turned round, a somewhat mocking expression on his face. 'My dear girl, you know that I have not the slightest need to marry money. I am rich, and growing richer. The late wars made my fortune secure, and the India trade grows and is growing. One advantage of being a merchant first and a landed gentleman second is that I may add to my fortune, rather than throw it away.'

'True.' And Lydia smiled for the first time. 'For all your romantic looks, Brandon, you are the hardest-headed creature it has been my fortune—or misfortune—to know. Are you not being a trifle too hard-headed in contemplating this marriage? She will be your wife, Brandon. She struck me as a little shallow and somewhat selfish. Now you are very deep and confounded selfish—not a good mixture, I would have thought.'

'Oh, I think that you wrong her. She is young and will grow deeper as she moves into the world, I am sure.' Brandon frowned a little. 'My information is that the Rector is comfortably placed financially, and that there will be a small dowry. The story is that he wrote a theological book of great profundity some years ago

and made a tidy income from it. I must admit that I
found that a little surprising, but it is true that from
being the usual struggling poor relation of a cleric he
became very much richer some five or six years ago—
so I suppose that theology may pay more than I would
have thought!'

'Your information!' Lydia gave a short laugh. 'No
doubt you put some agent to the trouble of investigating
the family into which you think to marry. How exactly
like you. I suppose that you know everything that there
is to know about them. You really are the outside of
enough.'

Brandon threw himself down into a large armchair
opposite his sister. 'Knowledge is power, my dear. I
know that Miss Jane is a trifle selfish as well as you do,
but she is also shrewd, and determined to make a good
marriage, I am sure. I also know that she has a dowd
for an older sister, who acts as gorgon and chaperon,
besides a much younger brother, Charles, familiarly
known to all as Chaz. Her mother has retired from the
world as a semi-invalid, and the elderly dowd runs the
household, including Miss Jane, with a rod of iron,
even managing the finances for the Reverend Caleb—
he being, I'm informed, as befits a theological philosopher, totally unworldly.'

'Your agent earned his pay. I wonder that he has not
listed the contents of the pantry and the colour of the
Rectory curtains for you,' returned Lydia. 'From what
you tell me, marriage with the dowd might be an
excellent business proposition, if it is she who is keeping
the Rectory afloat.'

'I like the thought of a pretty face sitting opposite me
at breakfast, as well as a pretty face setting the table,'
announced Brandon with a wry smile. 'There's a
damned fine specimen of the female sex running round
the Rectory kitchens, to my certain knowledge. For

some reason my agent never mentioned her. As to business acumen, I hire clerks to help me with that. I need a wife for different reasons altogether.'

'No doubt.' Lydia took up her canvas work again, stabbing one of the cherubs in the eye. 'I hope that Miss Jane's sister will be at the ball next week. I like to meet ladies out of the common run, dowds though they may be.'

He was not to be put down, it seemed. 'Now, Lydia, you are not to be contrary. You seemed very happy in Miss Jane's company at the Ameses'. Try to be happy with her now that you know that I am seriously considering her as my wife.'

'And that's the rub,' said Lydia sharply, attacking the cherub's eye again. 'A pleasant companion at a house party is one thing, but viewing her as your prospective wife is quite another! Especially when you tell me that your roving eye alighted on some underservant when you made your visit to the Rectory to revive your friendship with Miss Jane.'

Brandon looked a little self-conscious as this barb struck home. 'Now, Lydia,' he expostulated midly, 'you know full well that, although I may have many faults, seducing servant girls is not one of them. . .'

'I never thought that it was. But it isn't kind to dally with them, Brandon. Oh, I know that when you see a handsome creature of any station you always wish to pay her your respects, but it is wrong of you to raise any kind of expectation in servants. You are a handsome and powerful man and you scarcely understand the kind of effect you have on such poor young things. It would be the height of unkindness to make them dissatisfied with their own simple-minded village swains. And if you are pursuing Miss Jane Fielding, make sure that you do so after a fashion which will not cause her distress if you change your mind.'

It was Brandon's colour which changed at this. He
sprang to his feet, exclaiming a trifle bitterly, 'I had no
idea that you entertained such a low opinion of me,
Lydia! I see that I have been living in a fool's paradise
so far as you are concerned.'

Lydia knew at once that she had hurt him and, little
though she had wished to do so, she thought that
perhaps it was all in a good cause.

'No, Brandon,' she said, as coolly and equably as she
could. 'It is not a fool's paradise in which you have
come to live, but a small country district where gossip
reigns as queen and where everything which you say
and do will be chewed over ad infinitum, where there
are few, if any, secrets. You have no notion of how
different you will find it from living in a cosmopolitan
society, where, with respect to you, a certain licence
reigned instead. I am only saying that it will be best for
you to go carefully, particularly at the start of your stay
here.'

She avoided looking at him while she threaded her
needle with some pink wool in order to pick out Cupid's
lips, and waited for him to reply. It would not do for
them to be at odds, if she was to live with him and be
his hostess until he married. Although he had always
been kind to her, she knew that in the world in which
he had lived for the last twenty years he had always
been known as a hard man. She did not want him to be
a hard man with her.

Brandon, taking stock of what his sister had said,
acknowledged a certain truth in it. He had heard of the
narrow-minded nature of country society, and it would
not do for him to gain the reputation of being a careless
rake before he had so much as settled in it.

He told himself firmly that he would behave himself.
After all, he was determined to settle down, was he
not? Why else had he pensioned off Emma and decided

to make his home in the house he had inherited from his second cousin? A wealthy man in his middle thirties owed it to himself to go carefully, to steady himself, marry a good little wife, and start a family. The time of flirtations, grand passions, confidential little suppers with opera dancers, the squiring of barques of frailty and the cultivation of little bits of muslin must be considered to be over.

It hurt him somewhat to discover that Lydia might suspect him of corrupting the innocent, when he had always been careful not to do so. If he saw the nymph from the Rectory again he must be sure to avert his eyes, ignore her, and think of the ladylike charms of Miss Jane Fielding. He knew that he would be seeing her at the Assembly Rooms ball at Highborough, where he hoped to be introduced to the Gorgon, as Jane naughtily nicknamed her older sister Nan, and also her elderly parent.

Another thought struck him. 'Do you think Cousin Desmond will be present at the Assembly Room ball next week? And, more to the point, ought I to call on him beforehand? He was very short with me when we met at the lawyers in London, which is not to be wondered at. The poor fellow always thought he was to inherit, and I gather that, while not exactly starving, he is not particularly blessed with this world's riches either.'

'I think that you ought to visit him,' said Lydia slowly, relieved that Brandon, good fellow that he was at heart, if a trifle selfish like all men, had not taken what she said too ill, 'if only that if you do he won't be able to say that you met him only to drop him. But from what I gather from Broomhall gossip he is hardly likely to attend the ball; he doesn't often go into society. He has something of a mild *tendre* for Miss Fielding, I understand.'

'Ah, Jane's Gorgon,' smiled Brandon, good humour recovered. ''Pon my honour, Lydia, I am quite agog at the prospect of being introduced to provincial society. It's a pity the Fieldings are merely comfortable—if Miss Fielding had possessed a large dowry, one might have encouraged Desmond to cultivate his *tendre* and to go so far as to offer for her. It would ease my conscience over depriving him of Gillyflower Hall, and set him up for life into the bargain. If I do marry Miss Jane, I shall have to see what I can do for him—tactfully, of course, and without making it look as though I am offering him charity.'

Lydia put down her canvas work, stood up, and impulsively walked over to Brandon to kiss him on the cheek.

'I must never forget,' she told him, seeing that he looked surprised at receiving such sudden and unprovoked affection, 'what a thoroughly good fellow you are at bottom. Such a sentiment does you great credit. Now if you would only stop calling poor Miss Fielding the Gorgon I should feel so much happier. I know that you have caught the habit from Jane, but it does neither of you credit.'

She paused. 'It is one of the reasons why I am not completely certain that you ought to think of making her Mrs Brandon Tolliver—but she is young, and doubtless her manners will improve with age and experience.'

'Doubtless,' echoed Brandon optimistically. 'Well, the next few weeks should reveal all, I trust.' He smiled his charming smile at her. 'One thing, my dear; I am determined to enjoy country peace after enduring town bustle.'

Afterwards he was to laugh at himself for this piece of presumption. Country peace, indeed! He had lived so long in cities, among the bustle of a corrupt commercial world, that he had come to see the country as an Arcadian place where the only passions present were those of happy shepherds and shepherdesses dancing in the smiling fields. But poverty existed there, as well as in the back alleys of London—aye, and jealousy, hate and revenge too. As he was soon to learn.

Nan, dressed soberly, was seated in the Rectory drawing-room on the same afternoon, writing at a desk which stood in the window and looked out over the front lawn. Kelsey was chaperoning Jane on a visit to Gillyflower Hall, where they arrived shortly after Lydia and Brandon had concluded their conversation.

She was happy to be alone. There were times when she wished herself free of being the Rectory's indispensable guardian and today was one of them. Chaz had peered round the door a moment ago, pleading with her to join him in flying his new kite. He had looked so happy and eager that for a moment she had almost thought to indulge him. And then she had thought of how tired she was, that she had, for various good reasons, not retired to her bed until well after one in the morning, and that this would be the only time of day that she might sit down for a few moments.

'Come on, Nan,' Chaz had urged her. 'You know you like flying my kite, and this is a new one, a stunner—there's no one else to go with me. Please. . .'

'Take Roger,' Nan had said. Roger was their boy—or rather youth—of all work. Refusing Chaz anything always made her unhappy. From his birth he had been a handsome, biddable child—clever too. In face and body he didn't resemble any of the Fielding men, who were all tawny-haired and big-bodied; even her sedentary father had the build of a bruiser. Instead Chaz was dark, slender and intense, with a pair of flashing hazel eyes shot with green.

'Roger doesn't make up exciting stories about what the kite is doing and where it's flying to like you do,' he told his sister. 'It's forever since you came out with me.'

'I've been so busy lately,' Nan excused herself.

Chaz was possessed of a brand of practical logic foreign to his father and most of the Fieldings apart from Nan. He said, almost angrily, 'Then why can't Jane do some of your work and help you? Instead she's always out jaunting. She's jaunting again this afternoon. At Gillyflower Hall. Why couldn't you have gone over there with Kelsey and left Jane to do whatever it is you're doing?'

'Copying Papa's new book,' Nan told him. 'Jane couldn't do that.'

Chaz's logical mind supplied him with no answer to that incontrovertible statement. He gave something between a grunt and a groan and shot out of the door, crying ungraciously, 'Very well, if you won't come I suppose that Roger will have to do. And if it's Papa's new book you're copying, you'll do that forever. He changes it every day, as well you know!'

Nan resumed writing, although her wrist ached and her eyes were tired. A noise outside disturbed her. She looked up to see that Desmond Tolliver had arrived on horseback and that Jackson, who trebled as coachman, butler and groom, was leading the chestnut which he had been riding round to the mews at the back of the Rectory. Desmond himself was striding smartly to the Rectory front door. He didn't, Nan noticed with a sinking heart, look very pleased with life.

So she wasn't surprised, when Annie ushered him in, that he didn't appear to be his normally equable self. As usual he was tidily, if not exactly fashionably, turned out. Also as usual his manner was severe and slightly aloof. He didn't in any way resemble his wicked cousin

Brandon, as Nan had come to think of him since the episode in the pantry.

True, Desmond was tall, but his hair wasn't dark or curly, being an indeterminate lank brown, *not* cut à la mode. His face was tanned and lean, but possessed nothing of the mobile charm which had distinguished Brandon's. He had no naughty look or charming smile for Nan Fielding—and no wonder, thought Nan disconsolately. Here I am in dull dark grey again, a turn-out years old, and my hair is dressed to be out of the way, not to be fashionably dangling around my ears and neck. On top of that, truly on top, I am wearing my duenna-cum-spinster's cap, which quite extinguishes me and makes me look forty.

A thought struck her. Did Desmond also accost housemaids, kiss them vigorously, and stroke them until they were helpless jelly in his strong arms? Did all men, when they were not in drawing-rooms being polite and exceedingly proper, either to pretty young ladies like Jane, or plain old ones like Nan, have that certain look in their eye when they dealt with those who were plainly not ladies? What would it be like to be a 'not lady'?

And why am I thinking such dreadful thoughts, and have been doing so since I met *him*? Nan banished Mr Brandon Tolliver to the dungeons of her mind and concentrated on listening to Mr Desmond Tolliver, who was, as usual, being as proper as proper in everything which he said to her. Would he have been improper in the Rectory pantry if he had thought her a housemaid?

'I am so happy to find you in,' he was telling her earnestly after she had made him sit down and rung for Annie to fetch them tea. 'I feel most desperately in need of your cool common sense.'

My cool common sense, thought Nan wildly, while nodding gravely in his direction. And what has happened to that, seeing as I am constantly thinking of the dissolute roué who invaded the pantry and very nearly invaded me?

'I am sure,' Desmond was continuing, still earnest, 'that I need not tell you of the thunderclap which struck me down after my cousin's death.' He paused, then continued in melancholy vein, 'It was not that I looked forward to cousin Bart's death, but I own that the thought that after it my own monetary cares would be over did feature in my thinking. I am, after all, only human.'

This came out after the fashion of a man who needed what he had just said to be contradicted, but Nan was only equal to nodding again. It seemed, in the circumstances, the most tactful thing to do.

'So. . .' and Desmond dropped his voice mournfully '. . .you may imagine what a blow it was for me to find myself passed over for a cousin whom I was not even aware existed, but whom the damned—— I beg your pardon, my dear Anne, but I am most overset, as you see.'

More nodding from Nan seemed to steady him. Yes, perhaps nods *were* better than words in certain circumstances. If she had nodded at Mr Brandon Tolliver would he have stopped kissing her? She must truly be going mad, and now she had lost one of Desmond's long-winded and lachrymose sentences. She really must stop wool-gathering.

'Cousin Bart had told his lawyers, it seems, to find his true next heir, and the property was to go there. They had to trace back three generations—*three generations*—to find this man whose grandfather took precedence over mine, and the result was that this upstart, who is no gentleman, has inherited.'

'Upstart,' echoed Nan. 'And no gentleman. Forgive

me, but if he is truly a Tolliver, how does that come about?'

'His father had no money and it seems that Brandon was articled as a clerk straight from a country grammar school! A clerk! He rose in the merchant's house where he was employed, saved money, invested it during the late wars, or so I am told, was taken up by the Rothschilds or some such, and made himself a fortune large enough for him to cut loose and start his own house. The war continuing made him richer still, and on the two occasions when the market fell, and others were broken by it, he gambled in the right direction, won, and is now as rich as Croesus. The devil of it is. . . oh, do forgive me. . .he has no need of Gillyflower Hall or Bart's estate, whereas I. . .'

Desmond fell silent. Yes, it really was, thought Nan, full of pity for him, a truly terrible story. On the other hand. . .yes, on the other hand, how strong a character must Brandon Tolliver have been to have made himself a fortune after such a poor beginning. It all went to show that there was much more to him than she might have thought if all she had known of him was the encounter in the pantry.

But she really must say something sympathetic to poor Desmond whom Bart had treated quite abominally, allowing him to think, from when he was quite a small boy, that he was the Tolliver heir. All Desmond now possessed was an impoverished estate, a small country house, Brandon Hall, named after Brandon and Desmond's great-grandmother's family, and the home farm, which had come to him through his mother, the only daughter of a poorish country gentleman. Desmond's father had been one of those who had lost money in the late wars, not gained it, which Nan knew must make his cousin Brandon's successes seem the more galling.

'Not quite a gentleman,' repeated Desmond sadly, when Nan had commiserated with him, made him drink a cup of tea and eat some of the Bosworth Jumbles which were the speciality of Grace, the cook from Leicestershire.

'There is something I really ought to say to you,' he continued slowly. 'When Bart died my first thought was that now I might realise one of my dreams. That is, to marry. And when I thought of who I would like to make my wife my thoughts immediately turned to you.' He was standing now, one hand behind his back, tea and Jumbles alike forgotten.

'After all, Anne, we are both old enough to know that we are beyond passion and its traps. We are both creatures of great common sense. I cannot but admire your housewifery and the businesslike way in which you run the Rectory. The whole world is aware that you are the mainstay of the house and the parish. I felt that we would really deal well together, and that I would gain a wife of whom I, and my mother, would be proud. But, alas, situated as we are, prudence dictates that this marriage cannot be. But I thought that you ought to be aware of the high esteem in which I hold you.'

What sort of kisses would high esteem provoke? was Nan's unruly thought. She supposed that she ought to be flattered by what Desmond had just said. But 'beyond passion', and the confession that he was marrying her to acquire a housekeeper. . .! Dreadfully, tears pricked at the back of her eyes.

If Mary Tudor had said that when she died the word Calais would be inscribed on her heart, then when Nan Fielding died the words common sense ought surely to be found there.

Desmond was waiting for her to say something, the kind of half-smile on his face which told her that she ought to be profoundly pleased by what he had said when all that she really felt was the deepest depression. For if he had truly loved her, then he would not have allowed such considerations as he had listed to come between them. He might be poor as the wealthy counted poor, but many poorer than he had married, and fathered children. And even if she did not love him he had been a good friend, and she might have been tempted to end the barren years, to let others, as Chaz had suggested, do their share of the Rectory's duties, and marry him for that alone.

But this passionless recital left her gasping. Nevertheless she rose, and said, her voice shaking with a kind of grief, and not, as Desmond easily assumed, gratitude, 'You do me too great an honour, sir. I shall always remember and treasure what you have just told me.'

He took her lax hand and kissed it. 'Oh, I knew that you would understand, Anne. You will also understand, I am sure, when I tell you that I shall not be going out into society for the next few weeks. I feel that I cannot face the world. . .the curious and greedy eyes of those who must know what a blow this has been. I mean to take my misfortune like a man, but I must retire for a little. I intend to keep up my connections with you and the Rector, whom I hope to see before I leave, but I shall not be at the Assembly Rooms ball to dance with you.'

'Oh, Papa is at the church this afternoon,' Nan told him. 'He is meeting the verger and the churchwardens to inspect the tower, which he fears is in need of repair. If you care to look in, I am sure that he would be happy to see you.'

For some reason which she did not quite understand Nan wanted him to be gone. She wanted to say, I am Nan, not Anne, and have been since I was a child—only Randal was ever allowed to call me Anne—so why do *you* always call me Anne? More, it would have been better for you not to tell me that you intended to propose if you were not actually going to do so. And I dislike the fact that you took it for granted that I would have agreed to marry you if you *had* proposed!

None of which could conceivably be said aloud. Instead she was left to comfort him gently, which by his manner he plainly expected her to do. So, as usual, Nan, not only exercised her common sense, but did her duty.

It was only when he had left that, to her utter astonishment, Nan began to cry. For who was there to comfort her, the plain spinster sister who had not received a proposal, only the information that she might have done so if the potential proposer had inherited the property—which in all honesty he had done nothing to deserve, but which he had counted on since he was a small boy?

Worst of all, it was not only for herself that she was crying, but also for the knowledge that a man whom she had respected and esteemed had revealed himself as a hollow straw, who at the first set-back had collapsed into maudlin self-pity.

And all this because charming, heedless but apparently deep Mr Brandon Tolliver had walked into their lives. What else could they expect to happen? The serpent had arrived in Eden.

CHAPTER THREE

HIGHBOROUGH was a pretty little market town on the banks of the River Soar in North Leicestershire, near to the boundary which divided it from South Nottinghamshire. It was the centre of social life in the region, boasted a large set of Assembly Rooms and had once contemplated turning itself into a spa, but the landowner who had dreamed up the notion had died before he could launch it. Alas, his son was more interested in spending his money on himself in London rather than on the natives of the town from whence a large portion of his rents were derived.

Nevertheless it remained both lively and attractive and on nights when the moon was full there were not only balls at the rooms, but also musical recitals and meetings of the Highborough Literary and Philosophical Society. One of the most ardent contributors of papers to this group of gentleman amateurs was Nan's father, who took an interest in matters archaeological and topographical as well as theological. Occasionally a group of strolling players graced the small stage, and Nan had seen Romeo and Juliet portrayed by ranting thespians over twice their age, but had been so entranced by the music of Shakespeare's words that they had filled her mind for weeks afterwards.

Fortunately today had been fine, the sky was clear and the moon would be high when the time came to drive home from the ball, so that all but one of the inhabitants of the Rectory's ancient coach were in high

35

spirits when they left for Highborough in the late afternoon.

The exception was Nan. She had put on the oldest gown which she had dared to wear, so old and dowdy that Jane had screamed at her when she had walked into the entrance hall ready to leave.

'Pray, Nan, what could possess you to wear that? That is the most monstrous turn-out it has been my misfortune to see you in. You look exactly like the housekeeper on her way to have tea with the lady's maid!'

Nan could almost forgive Jane for her cruel words. Dreadfully, for some odd reason the sight of herself in the long glass in her room had made her want to laugh; she looked such a fright that she was almost a parody of a dowd. She could only murmur, 'Well, Jane, if you wish to shine tonight, you will surely do so even more, seeing that you are getting no competition from me. . .'

Jane had rewarded this piece of nonsense with a disdainful toss of the head. It hadn't so much as occurred to her that plain Nan could ever present her with any competition, but for once had she held her tongue.

What Nan had chosen to wear in an attempt to prevent Mr Brandon Tolliver from recognising her was a dun-coloured brown day dress with some ageing and coarse saffron-coloured lace about its high neck and around her wrists. No one, seeing her in it, could guess that she even possessed a body, let alone a shapely one. She had even found a cap of the same depressing material to wear on her plainly dressed and scraped-back hair. Its saffron lace frill fell forward over her eyes, hiding their beauty. The whole ensemble extinguished her quite.

Yes, there seemed small chance that Mr Brandon Tolliver would identify her as the nymph in the pantry.

She supposed that sooner or later he would have to discover his mistake, but the later the better. In a few weeks he might have forgotten the encounter. Doubtless it had been a commonplace one for him!

Nan wronged him in that. Not that he had thought much more about it, and certainly it was the last thing on his mind when he entered the ballroom, Lydia on his arm, looking modish in apricot, to discover that the Fieldings were seated not far from the group of musicians arranged on the small dais.

Jane, who had been waiting for his arrival, fretting and worrying that perhaps the whole occasion was such small beer to him that he might not even turn up, threw him a dazzling smile. The Letcombes were seated next to the Rectory party, and she and Caroline had pulled their chairs together and were quizzing the company over their raised fans when Brandon's entrance drove everything unconnected with him from their heads.

Nan was seated at the back of the room, between the Ladies Alden and Letcombe, both of whom were more than twice her age, but she privately thought that she looked older than either of them.

'And how is your dear mama?' asked Lady Letcombe, more from the need to say something to poor Nan rather than from any real desire to know. 'Still unable to go out? Do you think it possible that we shall ever see her in society again? Caroline!' she commanded in a severe tone, not doing Nan the honour of waiting for an answer. 'Do stop staring quite so hard at Mr Tolliver. Patience is required from you until the Master of Ceremonies brings him over. Is not that so, Miss Fielding?'

Nan, who privately thought that the greatest patience on such occasions as these was shown by unfortunates like herself, who were condemned to spend most of the evening watching others enjoy themselves, gave a cool assent. She would not even have the dubious pleasure of Desmond asking her for at least one dance, as he was keeping to his intention not to attend the ball.

Most of the men in the room were not seated, but were leaning against the walls or the pillars of the hall. Another room, where tables containing cold food and drink were set out, opened out of the ballroom and was reached through a large classic arch. Statues of half-clad nymphs, gods and goddesses stood in niches around the walls of the room.

Jane and Caroline's excitement grew apace. The MC was talking to Brandon and his sister. 'I vow I shall die if he does not come over soon,' Jane announced dramatically. Her card for the evening would have been full by now if she had not insisted on leaving several spaces open for Mr Tolliver. What if he never came over at all? Surely he would, for had he not been *most* particular? He must have meant *something* by that. Jane thought that she would burst, and all that tiresome Nan could do was to tell her to sit still, and not to wriggle or laugh too loudly.

And then the dance was over, the musicians were quiet, mopping their brows, and the MC was bringing Brandon and his sister over towards them. The Letcombes and the Fieldings all stood up together, even though the MC was gallantly waving the ladies down again. Even the Rector, who was heartily bored by the whole business, and who considered dancing barbaric, but was compelled to attend the ball to do his duty by his youngest daughter, found himself pleased to meet again the new owner of Gillyflower Hall.

Brandon Tolliver found the whole business of a provincial assembly ball so quaintly charming that everything enchanted him. His sharp and curious eyes took in Jane and Caroline's pleasure at seeing him again. He also registered the rector's other-worldly but

friendly greeting of the man with whom he had talked
knowledgeably of the necessity to repair Broomhall's
church to speak to him after entertaining the Rectory's
housemaid. He recognised Sir Avery and Lady
Letcombe, to whom he bowed, and also Kelsey whom
he had met a few afternoons ago.

The fright in the hideous brown dress with the ugly
cap hiding most of her doubtlessly plain face must be
Jane's Gorgon, and so the introduction to her, made
across two rows of chairs, proved. It was not surprising
that poor Jane complained so much about her. The
wonder was that such a pretty little charmer could have
such a plain creature for an older sister.

In return the Gorgon bowed, murmured something
unintelligible. Never less than polite, Brandon bowed
in his turn, and murmured, 'Charmed to meet you,
Miss Fielding.' He could not resist adding in a slightly
satiric tone, of which afterwards he was a little
ashamed, for he was a kind man at heart, 'I have heard
so much about you from Jane.'

If she had not been determined to say as little as
possible, Nan might even have retorted, Indeed, and
very little of it pleasant, I suppose! As it was she said
nothing at all, and by good fortune her father's touching
Brandon on the shoulder to remind him that he had
promised to recommend a builder who would be sure
to do an honest job on the tower ended their
conversation.

One by one members of Nan's party departed to
enjoy themselves. To her great delight, Brandon led
Jane on to the floor. Caroline was claimed by George
Alden, the son of the neighbouring landowner,
Viscount Alden. Sir Avery, gallantly squiring his wife,
followed Brandon and Jane, while Caleb Fielding,
without so much as a murmured word of apology to
Nan, wandered off to the supper-room to exchange

notes with the Rector of Elmdon, the neighbouring
parish to Broomhall, leaving her alone, sitting symboli-
cally with her back to the wall.

The music rose and fell. Brandon twirled Jane around
by her uplifted hand. Her pretty face was all aglow. He
looked up to see the Gorgon watching them. He
frowned and looked away. Something about the elderly
dowd sitting there, deserted by everyone, upset him a
little—and for what unaccountable reason?

He found himself looking in the Gorgon's direction
when the dance brought her into his line of sight again,
but this time a middle-aged man whom he recognised
as Sam Stone, the local lawyer whose services he had
already engaged, had walked across the room to greet
her. Before he turned again, and she was lost to his
view, Sam Stone had seated himself by the Gorgon and
was talking earnestly to her.

For her part Jane was talking earnestly to him and he
had not heard a word she had said, but since all that he
was being favoured with was sweet nothings about the
flowers, the pleasant nature of the music, and how
charmed she was to have met his sister Lydia again, he
was not missing very much. To all this Brandon made
the most correct of answers—which had her smiling
back at him.

'Practising for marriage,' he later told Lydia wryly.
At the time he wondered what Sam Stone and Miss
Fielding could find to talk about with such close and
obvious interest.

Annoyed by his preoccupation with her, Brandon
tried to dismiss the Gorgon from his straying thoughts,
and, in reply to Jane's question as to whether he had
yet read the latest novel by the author of *Sophia*, told
her that so far he had not, but that he hoped to. 'She,'
he acknowledged, 'if the author proves to be a she, has
a sly wit often missing in such works.' Jane discovered

that she liked Brandon even more. She would be sure to tell Nan that Mr Tolliver apparently did not find reading novels a waste of time.

Nan, who would have been astonished to discover that Brandon Tolliver, a little conscience-stricken as a result of his unkind words to her, was thinking about her, was talking business with Sam. She had known him since she was a child, and he was the only person in Nan's life from whom she had few secrets. For the last ten years, since her mother had retired into invalidity and the Rector had manoeuvred himself into such a muddle that he had been near to bankruptcy, she had run the Rectory finances.

'Your father is needed to sign some papers, my dear,' he was telling her. 'I shall bring them to the Rectory on Monday. It is one responsibility he cannot slough on to you.'

Nan nodded. 'And the other business?' she asked him cryptically.

'Accomplished,' he said with a rare smile. 'I received a letter today which assured me that your latest. . . offering. . .is more than acceptable, and that what they are prepared to. . .give. . .for it is beyond anything which they have suggested before.' He had been choosing his words with care, lest they were overheard. He paused, then asked, 'And your father, my dear? He still suspects nothing?'

'Nothing.' Nan's smile was a little twisted. 'Which we agreed was the best thing. He, being so unworldly, believes that it is his great work on the nature of the Trinity which is responsible for our recent affluence.'

'And when you have finally succeeded in settling Jane, what then?' And Sam Stone gave a meaningful look at Jane, who was now talking animatedly to Brandon on the other side of the room, laughing up into his handsome face, and tapping at him with her fan when he laughed back at her.

For some reason the sight of this gave Nan the strangest pang. She lost kind Sam Stone for a moment, before remembering that he had asked her a question.

'And then nothing,' she answered him almost shortly. 'I have my duty to my parents, you know.'

He shook his greying head at her. He had been a handsome young man and was now a handsome middle-aged one, widowed since his beloved wife had died in childbirth some fifteen years earlier.

'No, I don't know.' He was almost abrupt. 'You have a life of your own, and ought to be able to live it. Only I and God know how hard you have worked these last years, and all unacknowledged by anyone. None of your family is grateful for what they know that you do, let alone what they *don't* know that you do.

'I had not thought to say this here, in such circumstances, but I feel that I must. I honour you above all the women I have ever met. You are unselfish and kind, you hide your light so as not to extinguish Jane's. No, do not deny that,' he told her, raising a hand as she tried to deny what he was saying to her. 'Looking at you tonight I know that to be true, and because I have come to care for you, as well as to admire you, I am asking you to marry me as soon as you are free— when Jane marries, that is. I will see that the Rector and your mother do not suffer as a consequence of your marriage.'

Nan was so shocked by this unexpected proposal and the expression of earnest love on his face that all that she could do was open her mouth and shut it again. For a moment, at the end of his proposal, the world had seemed to stop. Now it was turning again, the dance had ended and her party and that of the Letcombes, together with the two Tollivers, were making for where she and Sam sat.

Sam, seeing this, said rapidly, 'No, do not try to answer me now, my dear. Think over what I have said to you. I love you as well as honour you, and would like to free you from the trap which life has created for you. You may give me an answer when you please, but for both our sakes do not be overlong in your consideration.'

He rose and bowed. 'You will forgive me for moving on. I am supposed to be talking business tonight with Lord Alden, and although the surroundings are not suitable I cannot oppose him, he is such an old friend. You will present my compliments to your father, as I shall leave after speaking to m'lord.'

He had gone. Jane was sitting by her and was talking excitedly about Brandon, and how he had made her laugh, and how much he liked reading the novels of the author of *Sophia*. All this, for once, flew over Nan's head. She was quite overwhelmed by what had happened to her. In one week she had received two unexpected proposals—albeit that the first, from Desmond Tolliver, had not really been one at all!

But this second one from Mr Stone—perhaps she ought to think of him as Sam, was her dazed inward comment, seeing that he was considering her as a possible wife—was indeed a facer. 'Facer' was another of Chaz's favourite pieces of slang which seemed particularly suitable applied to Sam Stone's proposal, which was a genuine one—even if he was also proposing delay to satisfy her sense of duty, she supposed. It was, unlike Desmond's, also very flattering. She had no reason to believe that it was not sincerely meant. And if Sam had spoken only of admiration and care, rather than love, he had not chosen to demean either of them by insisting, as Desmond had done, that they were beyond passion.

Who would have thought it? In effect, elderly spinster past her last prayers though she was, she had already accumulated three more proposals, counting Randal's, made so long ago, than Jane had yet managed. The thought made her laugh to herself. The rest of the evening passed in a haze. Mr Brandon Tolliver continued to be *'most* particular' to Jane, dancing with her again, and taking her into supper.

Nan went into supper with the Letcombes. Lydia Bligh, seeing how isolated she was, took it upon herself, in her kind way, to talk to her, but Nan found herself barely able either to eat or to speak. Her throat seemed to have closed. As she finished her meagre meal she saw Brandon and Jane coming towards her, but the thought of trying to speak to him without giving away her—and his—secret was too much.

She dodged away from them behind one of the pillars and went through a side-door into a long corridor where she sat alone on a stone bench trying to make sense of what was happening to her.

The only thing was that every time she tried to do so the picture of Mr Brandon Tolliver laughing at Jane came into her mind and would not go away. And pooh to that, was her desolate thought. What I really ought to be contemplating is becoming middle-aged Sam Stone's second wife. At least he would be kind to me. . .if I were free to marry him, that is. . .

Sitting in the carriage on the way home, being talked to by Lydia about the events of the evening, and in particular about Miss Jane Fielding, whom Lydia was coming to agree might make him a suitable, if rather young and flighty wife, Brandon said abruptly, 'You were right to reproach me the other day, Liddy.'

It was a long time since he had used her childhood pet name when speaking to her. 'About what, my dear?' Lydia replied gently, looking out of the chaise window at the peerless moon sailing above the clouds.

'About not being unkind and careless. I was unpleasant to that poor drab creature, Jane Fielding's older sister, and it has been on my mind ever since. I cannot even apologise to her, for to do so would be to demean her further. I was being as frivolous and thoughtless as Jane herself, and there is no excuse for me at my age.'

Well, here was a turn-up, was Lydia's startled inward response. 'You conversed with her, then?' she thought fit to ask.

'No, indeed, I said but a couple of sentences to her, and the second intolerable. Should I marry Jane she will be my sister-in-law and I shall owe some kind of duty to her. Bad for me to begin such a relationship by distressing her as I am sure I did.'

'Oh, she allowed you to understand that?'

'Not at all—or not in words. I could tell by her stance, what I saw of her mouth—which was all that I could see of her face beneath that dreadful cap.' He wriggled restlessly. 'Lord, Liddy, I am turning Methodee, as they say, to trouble myself about such a thing. Never mind; I will try to make it up to her later when. . .well. . .when. . .you know.'

'No, Brandon, I don't,' replied his sister forthrightly, 'and I don't think that you do. Consider. This might reflect badly on Jane as well as on yourself.'

'She's but a child, Liddy, and will learn, I'm sure. . .' He was restless again. He laughed a little, and said, with an attempt to recover his spirits, 'Do you think that it is associating with the Rectory party which is bringing on these thoughts, or is it living in the country? I never seemed to have them in the old days.'

Lydia made no reply; the chaise was turning on to the front sweep at Gillyflower Hall and footmen and lackeys were running towards them. It was no time to be dissecting one's conscience, she thought; the matter would have to wait until tomorrow—or never, perhaps.

CHAPTER FOUR

'Nan, why has not the hem of my blue evening gown been mended? I most particularly asked that it should be seen to immediately.'

'Miss Fielding, the butcher has forgot to send the meat which I ordered; pray will you have words with him? This is not the first occasion on which this has happened.'

'Nan, my dearest girl. You are quite the best reader of novels in the Rectory, but somehow these days you never seem to wish to entertain your poor old mother by treating her to a chapter or two. I beg that you will find a little time this evening to read me some more of the author of *Sophia*'s novel.'

'Daughter, I know that you have been a trifle busy lately, but I did ask you, most particularly, to copy out the latest chapter of The Nature of Grace. At this rate it will never be ready for the printers. . .'

'Nan, dear, I know that you have very little time to yourself these days, but I would like you to assist me to decorate the church, ready for this Sunday. Mrs Aske, who promised to do so, has taken a fit of the ague and cannot leave the house. You have such a neat hand with flowers. This afternoon would be a most suitable time.'

'Dear Nan, I know that you are busy but I have lost my new kite; the wind whipped it out of my hands, and I last saw it flying in the direction of Gillyflower Hall. I should be most obliged if you would come and help me to look for it this afternoon. . .'

Nan put her hand to her head and wailed at poor

Chaz, 'No, no and no! I have spent the whole morning being badgered by everyone in this house, and it is beyond me to satisfy everyone. You should have taken more care of your kite.'

'Oh, have a heart, Nan. Why, once you were only too happy to fly kites with me.'

'Chaz, take Roger and go and look for it yourself.'

'But I have Nan, I have.' Chaz's face was a picture of misery. 'Oh, why are you such a crosspatch these days, Nan? You used not to be.'

'I used not to be many things,' Nan replied fiercely. 'But time changes us all, Chaz, as you will find out when you grow up.'

'Grow up! Well, if growing up means becoming like you then I don't want to.' And Chaz ran out of the drawing-room where Nan had been busy copying out the Rector's latest treatise.

She put her head down on the desk before her and cursed God and what her life had dwindled down to— the Rectory dogsbody for whom no one really cared, but whom everyone expected to see that life ran easily and sweetly for them.

She sat up again and humbly begged God's forgiveness, and thought instead that Sam Stone was offering her a way out. But did she want that way, and would her parents allow her to take it? She looked out of the window; the sun was shining, a little breeze was blowing. It really was the most delightful summer's day. And she would be unable to enjoy any of it; she was bound to a wheel of tasks.

'No,' she said aloud, to no one at all. She threw down her quill pen, ignoring the string of blots it made on the white paper. Why should she not enjoy the sun? She stood up, pulled on her shawl which she had draped over the back of her chair and walked out of the drawing-room and then the Rectory front door without a backward glance.

Why should she not spend the afternoon in the scents of the woodland around Gillyflower Hall and look for Chaz's kite while she was doing so? Someone was calling her name as she crossed the front lawn. For a moment she hesitated, and turned to see who it was. Kelsey was standing at the front door waving a basket of flowers at her.

Duty almost overcame her, but then rebellion took over. No, Kelsey could manage on her own quite well. She merely wanted Nan's company in order to gossip to her about village affairs, and by the end of the afternoon the only result of it would be that Nan would have acquired a few more chores.

Well, a fig for everything and everybody! She took herself through the wicket gate at the side of the Rectory's paddock where an old grey donkey grazed, and walked along a rutted path through the scrub and woodland.

And I have not even put my bonnet or cap on, she realised. For her cap had irked her by its reminder of what she had come to, and she had flung it off in the middle of copying out the last page before Chaz had interrupted her and sparked off this minor revolt. If only someone would thank her, or show her some affection, then she might feel a little better.

Nan shook herself. It was too bad of her to wallow in such self-pity. She really ought to be looking for Chaz's kite. To find it would give this walk some justification, if justification were needed. She meandered happily along, thinking of nothing, looking up into the trees although she was sure that she was on a wild-goose chase—though a better name for it might have been a wild-kite chase!

She had walked quite a long way towards the Hall

when she saw Chaz's lost treasure. It was high in the
branches of a somewhat rickety tree, its tail dangling
forlornly down. Now the common-sense thing to do
would have been to go straight back to the Rectory, tell
Chaz or Roger where it was to be found, and they could
then have come along and recovered it.

But the spark which had ignited Nan's rebellion had
also ignited something else in her. Looking up into the
tree, she remembered happy childhood days when she
and Randal had shouted and played in a similar woodland and had, between them, climbed every tree in
sight. Why should she not climb this tree and take
Chaz's kite home as a trophy?

Her skirts would be a nuisance, but what of that?
There was no one about to see her and she could hitch
them up with the help of her shawl. To climb to the
forking branch where the kite was caught and release it
would be the work of a moment. No sooner said than
done. Almost twenty-eight she might be, but her body
had lost none of its agility, and she shinned up the tree
as though Randal was still with her, cheering her on,
and not lying dead in foreign soil, leaving behind only
memories. . . .

She reached the forking branch where the kite had
become entangled, and carefully began to disentangle
it. Easy, something sang inside her, but, as always,
pride went before a fall. The tree was old and inwardly
rotten, and even as her fingers began to loosen the kite
Nan heard, to her horror, an ominous creaking in the
branch on which she was perched.

'Oh, hell and all its devils!' Nan's oaths were always
theological, as befitted a parson's daughter, and this
flew out as the creaking grew louder, the branch broke,
and Nan found herself falling without any hope of
salvation and without even having liberated Chaz's kite.
And this time she was falling not from a high stool, but

from a high branch, with the hard ground below. She had no time to be frightened, only to recognise that she was lost and falling. The wages of sin were truly deathly, as well as certain!

Mr Brandon Tolliver had decided that the fine day demanded more homage from him than merely sitting in the house and admiring it through a large window. He had asked his sister to accompany him, but she had pleaded tiredness.

'You really are the most energetic creature,' she had told him forcefully. 'Always on the go. Go and be energetic on your own. I confess that simply to see you there radiating determination makes me feel quite weak. I can only imagine what you think "a little walk" entails!'

He had laughed at her, picked up a stick and set out on a tour of exploration of a part of his property which he had not yet visited. He could see Broomhall and its church in the distance, and perhaps he might even decide to visit the Rectory, talk to Miss Jane, and find some way of being pleasant to the Gorgon. . .

Yes, it was quite delightful to quarter the countryside knowing that it was yours, and that everything that you saw was new and consequently interesting. The track he was following led him to a clearing, where he paused for a moment to look around him. . .to discover that the countryside held more surprises than one.

For a lively young female had climbed one of the taller trees and was sitting astride a branch, showing a fine pair of legs. Her hair had come down and her splendid arms were upraised for she was freeing what appeared to be a kite from the tree's upper branches.

By Jove, it was the servant from the Rectory again! And what a superb specimen of womanhood she was! He had seldom seen a finer pair of female legs, and he had seen a few of them in his time! Brandon stood back the better to enjoy the sight of such a charming nymph. All his good resolutions to his sister and to himself about not pursuing servant girls were flying away at the sight of this one. What a hoyden she must be! By the looks of her she had no doubt given the village lads some pleasure in her time. They hardly deserved such a splendid pair of calves and ankles!

His happy contemplation of the female form divine in action was interrupted by the creaking which had distressed Nan, and was the harbinger of her fall. He started forward to assist her, for such an enterprising nymph deserved more than a broken neck. . .and for the second time in three weeks Mr Brandon Tolliver caught the falling Miss Fielding in his strong arms.

Only this time she came down with such force that although he was able to break her fall she took him to the ground with her, knocking the wind out of the pair of them as she did so. . .

For a moment Nan had no idea of where she was, or what had happened. She was still held in Brandon's arms, and he was beneath her this time, lying flat among the woodland flowers and herbs, surrounded by their scent. It took a little time for them to recover. Brandon was to discover later that he was bruised. Nan was merely shocked, Brandon's body having protected her from the worst consequences of her fall. His hand still resting on her arm, he sat up as she rolled a little off him, to sit up in her turn, so that they were now side by side, staring at one another. Turquoise eyes met amused silver ones.

'*Again*!' exclaimed Brandon, once his breath was back. 'Do you make a habit of falling from on high, my fair nymph? If so, you must beware. I shall not always be present to save you.'

Yes, it was he, her nemesis, Mr Brandon Tolliver,

always about when she was doing something unladylike! And whatever would he think of her? Her skirts were up to her knees, her hair was down, her bodice was torn by her descent through the tree so that Brandon could see the shape of one creamy breast tipped with rose.

It was only too plain what he thought of her! Of its own volition his arm went around her and he heard himself saying, his voice hoarse, 'And does not your rescuer deserve a reward?' And Nan Fielding found herself flat on her back being thoroughly kissed— *again*!—by the desirable Mr Brandon Tolliver who was being '*most* particular' to Miss Jane Fielding.

He was also being '*most* particular' to her elder sister, believing her to be quite other than she was. The devil of it was that Nan Fielding liked behind held and kissed by the strong man whose warm body was so close to hers, who was plainly roused by her and the sight that she presented—so roused that he was doubtless about to try to have his way with her among the greenery of the woodland, the birds calling about them, and Chaz's kite high overhead. . .

It was the thought of Chaz which restored Nan to sanity—that and the knowledge that she would not be able to keep her true identity secret for very much longer—and what would be the result of that? The mind boggled. Even the author of *Sophia* might find it difficult to suggest a way out of this predicament.

But oh, it was hard to say the words which would stop him as their kisses, caresses and sighs grew ever more urgent. And I don't really know him, and he doesn't know me at all, and what sort of man carries on like this with a servant girl, chance met? she thought wildly. And if he really wants to marry Jane, I shouldn't be allowing him to take all these dreadful liberties. . .

And why am I able to ponder moral problems with

my brain while my body is busy letting Brandon Tolliver undo it? There being no answer to this, Nan cried, 'No, certainly not,' and pushed Brandon away as strongly as she could, her whole body aching with the desire to clutch him to her rather.

For a moment he resisted her, and then, his head clearing, he rolled away from her, aching himself. What in God's name had come over him? He had never done such a thing before. His love-affairs had always been with willing females well-known to him. He had never been, as he had truthfully told his sister, one for passing dalliance with servants and underlings.

Even as they fell apart they heard footsteps crashing through the undergrowth. Both of them sprang to their feet, rearranging their clothing. Nan undid her shawl and threw it around her shoulders to hide her ruined dress. She could do nothing about her hair. Brandon was in better case, although she noticed, with wry amusement, that a certain amount of buttoning up of his breeches flap was going on. She had, it seemed, stopped him in the very nick of time.

They were thus almost respectable when a small boy, one of the village children, galloped into the clearing to stare incuriously at them. They were the great ones of his world, and what they got up to was always mysterious.

He immediately said the fatal words which Nan had dreaded. 'A fine arternoon to you, Miss Fielding. I've come a-looking for Master Charles's kite.'

Nan heard Brandon's breathing change at this revelation. She tried not to look at him, and said to the child as coolly as she could, 'It's up in that tree, Jem, the one with the broken branch. Run and tell Master Charles where it is, and ask him to bring Roger with him to free it.'

He pulled his forelock at her and ran off, after saying respectfully, 'Yes, Miss Fielding.'

Nan pulled her shawl tightly around her shoulders. Despite the warmth of the day she had begun to shiver. She said formally to Brandon without looking at him, 'Good afternoon to you, Mr Tolliver,' and began to walk away in the same direction as the boy.

Only to be stopped by a strong hand on her arm dragging her around to face a grim-faced man who was staring at her with an expression of profound astonishment on his face.

'Oh, no,' he told her ruthlessly. 'You don't escape from me as easily as this, madam. What game were you playing with me?'

Nan could not resist answering him in kind. 'Why, the same game that you were playing with me, Mr Tolliver, and it reflects little credit on either of us.'

'And that statement, at least, is the truth,' he rasped, his mouth now as straight as it had been smilingly curly until he had discovered who she was. He continued to hold her in such a grip that Nan thought that she would be bruised by it. He was taking in every detail of her present disgraceful appearance, which was so unlike that of the prim Gorgon he was used to seeing, sitting at the back of every room which he had entered in the last three weeks.

Then, as though he were uttering an oath, he came out with a single explosive word, 'Why?' And then again, 'Why?'

'Why what?' demanded Nan, trying to pull away. 'Pray do release me, sir. I have many duties awaiting me at the Rectory.'

His smile was almost ugly as she came out with this. 'Oh, indeed, madam, so I understand. As you must understand the import of my question. Why the double masquerade? You caught me nicely with them both, did you not? The upright spinster lady and the serving maid with a glad eye for the main chance where gentlemen are concerned. With how many men have you played the latter part?'

'Oh, for shame!' exclaimed Nan, still trying to pull away. 'It was you who set upon me in the Rectory pantry, and I was only saving you embarrassment by not informing you that you were like to ravish one of the Rector's daughters while courting the other!'

'Ravish, madam, ravish? You joined in the game so lustily, I thought that you had pleasured half the village.'

Brandon knew that he was being disgraceful, but shame at his own bad behaviour was somehow being transferred from him to her. Even as Nan slapped his face with her free hand he was full of remorse.

He held and clasped that hand too, mastered himself, and began to remember who and what they both were, who a moment ago had been nymph and satyr celebrating their passion in the time-honoured way.

'No,' he said. 'No. I should not have spoken to you as I just did, and you will forgive me. But consider your appearance, then and now. Consider the condition in which I found you—up a tree! Am I to believe that you occasionally grow tired of propriety and abandon it so that you may adventure, unknown and secure in your mode of servant?'

Shame was gripping Nan as well as Brandon. Her walk in the woods, which had begun in what now looked like wicked defiance, had ended even more badly than she could conceivably have expected.

'Believe what you please,' she told him. He was still holding both her hands, but in the lightest clasp so that she could have broken away without a struggle—but somehow she did not want to release herself from him.

More than that, they were both beginning to understand that if they were to meet again in the small society in which they lived they must somehow manage to come to terms with what they had both done after a fashion that would enable them to do so without embarrassment.

Brandon began to allow his intellect to dominate his reasoning, and not his passions. And about time too, he thought dismally. Twice, not once, but twice, I have set upon a woman I have never met before and treated her like a whore. Reason might say that she had responded like one, but what chance had he given her to do otherwise? And who would, or could, have guessed that she was Parson Fielding's prim and proper daughter?

'My sister says. . .' and this time his voice was low and calm, not high and angry '. . .that you are much put upon. Is it possible that occasionally you need some sort of release from the call of duty?'

This was so exactly what Nan had felt earlier that afternoon that she began to tremble. Brandon felt it and drew her slowly towards him, so that they were face to face and breast to breast again, but strangely passionless—as though, Brandon thought afterwards, they had actually achieved consummation and were quivering in the aftermath of it. Strangely, for a fleeting moment each felt that they had known the other forever.

'I have frightened you,' he said, his voice as gentle as he could make it. 'I apologise to you for that. It was neither gentlemanly nor kind of me to speak and behave to you as I did. My sister Lydia frequently tells me that I am no gentleman and I fear that she may be right.'

He took in Nan's white face, her quivering lips. She felt as though everything that she had suffered and endured since the news of Randal's death had all fallen on her together. The attraction which Brandon had for her, and which she surely could not have for him, seemed not only a reproach to her, but a weight she must carry.

And she was being so unfair to both him and Jane. For if he was honest in his pursuit of Jane for a wife, what was she, Nan, doing, to come between them in any way, however unintended?

'If you will allow me to leave,' she told him, her face slightly averted lest it reveal to him more than she wished him to know, 'I will try to find my way back to the Rectory without being seen. It was foolish of me to climb the tree to release Chaz's kite, but I so seldom allow myself to do foolish things that perhaps we can both forgive me for doing this one.'

Her whole mien had become so humble and defeated that Brandon felt himself to be the most utter cur. He let go of her hands and stood back.

'You will permit me to escort you to the Rectory paddock?'

'If you must,' Nan told him simply, 'but I would rather you did not.'

'Oh, I think that I must. I have disgraced myself sufficiently for one day. You must allow me to do some small penance, although,' he could not prevent himself from saying, 'escorting the nymph who lives behind Miss Fielding's mask of propriety is no penance.'

For a moment the passion which had flared up and burned so brightly between them was revived. Nan gave him a half-smile of such sweetness that Brandon almost blinked at it. How could anyone have called her plain? How could he have thought her plain, even when she was the Gorgon?

But then, he had not seen the Gorgon up a tree, her shapely legs in full sight and her superb body outlined by the dress which was strained tautly around her. And what was he doing to allow his thoughts to stray in such a wanton manner when he had just told himself that he owed it to her to forget all that had passed between them and remember only that she was Jane's elder sister and the Rectory's overworked factotum?

As for the Gorgon herself, she was a mass of seething embarrassment. Walking alongside Mr Brandon Tolliver, allowing him to take her grubby hand, scratched as a consequence of trying to free Chaz's kite, she was only capable of the deepest shame as he kissed the back of it gently. The beautiful eyes which looked up at him were full of tears.

'Come, my dear Miss Fielding,' he said, his voice as kind as he could make it. 'You must not repine too much over what is now past and gone. Try to think of it as an amusing episode from one of the works of the author of *Sophia* and all will be well.'

He was hardly prepared for the result of this well-meaning attempt to lighten what had passed between them. Nan dragged her hand from his violently, put it to her mouth, and exclaimed, 'Oh, no!' Then she turned to half run across the paddock towards the Rectory as though the devil himself were behind her.

'The devil!' exclaimed Mr Brandon Tolliver aloud. 'I shall never understand women, never!'

CHAPTER FIVE

'AN INVITATION,' exclaimed Jane, waving a splendid sheet of cream writing paper at Nan, 'for us all to attend Mrs Bligh's open day of fruit and flowers at Gillyflower Hall! Papa has just given it to me to pass on to you. The whole family, save for Mama, of course, is invited, including Chaz, and we are to stay over for three nights. Is not that monstrous kind of them? For sure Mr Brandon Tolliver is behind this invitation.'

'To stay over,' repeated Nan distractedly. She had just come downstairs after changing out of her ruined dress and tidying up her equally ruined hair. 'We only live a bare mile away. Why should we stay over? We could walk the distance between here and Gillyflower Hall in no time. And what will Mama do while we are away?'

'Oh!' Jane was determined to show her impatience at Nan's backwardness and her equal determination to be a guest at Gillyflower Hall. 'There is to be a ball on the middle night, and a musical recital on the last one. Dear Mrs Bligh has arranged for some musicians to come over from Leicester to play for us, and half the county will be there. We cannot be forever rushing backwards and forwards between the Rectory and Gillyflower Hall every five minutes, as even you must acknowledge! And Kelsey will look after Mama for us. She has already agreed to do so.'

She tossed her pretty head. 'Besides, Papa is quite determined that we shall go. Mr Tolliver is proving *such* a benefactor to the parish, he says, what with providing extra funds to repair the church tower and to replace the pews which have woodworm, as well as giving an endowment to the old women's almshouses. It will be only right and proper, he says, to support him and his sister in their enterprises.'

The last thing which Nan wanted was to be brought into intimate contact with Brandon Tolliver again, but she could hardly allow her own whimwhams to interfere with Mrs Bligh's kindness, whether Brandon was responsible for them or not. She took the letter of invitation from Jane and read it through, while Jane rushed on excitedly about the benefits which Mr Tolliver and his sister had conferred on the district by coming to live in it.

'I have known that this celebration was proposed for some time,' she announced. 'When Mrs Bligh was at the Letcombes' the other week she raised the prospect of some such enterprise with Lady Letcombe and asked her advice on whom to invite and whom to employ to make a small stage for the musicians to play for the ball, and for the recital the next evening. Only think, Desmond is quite reconciled with them, and has agreed to attend! I would have thought that you, of all people, would find that monstrous agreeable.'

Why me 'of all people'? wondered Nan, putting down the letter. I suppose Jane thinks that Desmond may have a *tendre* for me—the sort that elderly persons have for one another, I imagine! For some odd reason this thought was so amusing that it drove the dismals away a little.

Further excitement ensued. The door was flung open as Chaz rushed in crying, 'Oh, what a brick you are, Nan, to go looking for my kite! It was too good of you after I spoke to you so scurvily. Jem came and told me that you had found it, and his papa helped us to fetch it down from the tree. Was it you or Mr Tolliver who found it? Jem said that he was with you when he met you in Gillyflower Woods.'

Was it Nan's imagination or did a strange silence suddenly fall as Chaz ingenuously threw this grenade into the Rectory drawing-room? Jane stared at her sister, as did Kelsey, who was busy darning Chaz's everyday woollen socks.

'You did not,' said Jane, in the voice of a prosecuting counsel, 'tell us that you went walking in the woods with Brandon! Pray how did that come about? I distinctly understood you to say that you were too busy to mend the hem of my dress, or to read to Mama! And why should you say nothing of it when you came home?'

Harassed, Nan came out with, 'I suppose, Jane, that it is allowed for me to have some private life of my own? I was in the middle of copying out Papa's latest book when the beauty of the day decided me on a walk into the woods to look for Chaz's kite. I found it by chance, just as Mr Tolliver came upon me on *his* afternoon walk. We exchanged politenesses and he escorted me to the paddock gate. I understand that he could not stay to visit as he was expecting a visitor of his own.'

Now this last was pure fiction, particularly the bit about exchanging politenesses, but something had to be said.

'Oh!' Jane was mollified, but not completely so. Chaz looked at both his sisters. He was beginning to question a little many of the foundations of Rectory life, one of them being that Jane had all the fun and Nan did all the work.

'Why should not Nan walk with Mr Tolliver if she wanted to?' he asked Jane belligerently. 'He is not your property yet, nor Caroline Letcombe's either. And Nan's conversation is always a deal sight more interesting than either yours or Caroline's, I can tell you. Nan knows about kites and fishing, and the battles of the late war, whereas all you and Caroline talk about is your clothes and balls and how to do your hair.' He roared relentlessly on. 'If I were Mr Brandon Tolliver I know who I should want to marry——'

'Charles Fielding!' exclaimed Kelsey, as though she were still his nanny-cum-governess. 'Hold your tongue. You are not to speak to your sister after that fashion.'

He would not be silenced, and roared back at her, face scarlet, 'Why ever not? *She* never chooses her tone when she talks to Nan.'

It was Nan who stopped him this time. 'No, Chaz,' she told him. 'You help neither me nor yourself by speaking so. Apologise to Jane.' She added this hastily, because she could see that Jane was about to throw a fit of the hysterics, and she knew that if Jane did she would be compelled to slap her, and she was fearful that if once she began to do so she wouldn't know how to stop.

'That I won't,' began Chaz furiously, only to have Kelsey rise to her feet, take him by the arms, and say,

'Go to your room, Charles, and only come down when you have recovered your temper. You must learn that it is not always wise to say exactly what we think.'

He pulled away and ran towards the door, to turn at it and shout into the room, 'That may be so, but you are all jolly unfair to Nan, and I am not much better.'

He left behind a silent room until Jane began to speak. 'Papa ought to give him a beating for his insolence to me. Why should I not ask Nan about her meeting with——?'

'If anyone says Mr Brandon Tolliver's name again I shall scream,' announced Nan in ringing tones. 'I am going to my room to enjoy a little peace and quiet. You may fetch me down for supper,' she told Kelsey, 'and perhaps by then we shall all have recovered our tempers.'

But she was still trembling when she opened the door to her bedroom which doubled as her sitting-room and which was her only refuge from the cares of the household. It was a large room at the back of the house, on the second floor, and looked out across the paddock towards Gillyflower Hall and its park, and the winding path on the left which led to it through the wood.

The room contained a big four-poster bed, two elderly armchairs and a small table which had come from her mother's home years ago, and which had been passed on to Nan when she was a girl. In one corner stood a large wardrobe, in another a small and elegant walnut bureau which her parents had given to her long ago when she had still been young enough to be petted, before her more conventionally pretty sisters had begun to occupy their hearts and minds.

The bureau had a little top which could be let down so that one could write upon it, and also had the advantage of small but strong brass locks on the top and the drawers below it. Nan always wore the key to it on a ribbon around her neck below her dress.

She walked over to the bureau, pulled out the key, unlocked it and let down the top to reveal an ink-well, quill pens, a penknife and a small box of fine sand. Next she opened one of the drawers, lifting from it a pile of paper, some of it written on, some not, which she placed on the top.

She sat down, picked up the quill pen, and sharpened it with the penknife before dipping it into the ink-well. But instead of writing with it she put the pen down, rested her head upon her hands and willed herself to forget everything which had happened that afternoon.

When her heart had stopped bumping and her breathing had returned to normal she picked up the pen again, pulled a blank sheet of paper towards her, and for the next hour wrote steadily and surely, until she heard the bell for supper sounding in the Rectory hall.

She did not want to stop working, but knew that she must. Not to partake of the evening meal would be sure to be remarked upon, and she didn't think that she could stand either Jane's reproaches or Kelsey's solicitude. Far better to break off, go downstairs and, even if she found eating difficult, try to join in the conversation, if only to help poor gallant Chaz.

Besides, Sam Stone had said that he would look in after supper to speak to her father about signing documents relating to the business of the church. She and Sam had already gone over them, and all her father would have to do was append his signature, secure in the knowledge that his lawyer and his daughter would not let him down.

Nan re-locked the bureau and examined herself in the small mirror which hung above the wash-stand. Yes, she looked pale, but not unduly so. Her cap was a little awry, but that was soon straightened. She sighed, smoothed down her skirts and prepared to go downstairs, the very model of propriety who would never, ever climb a tree or lie willingly in Mr Brandon Tolliver's strong arms being made love to!

Nor, she discovered regretfully as she talked with Sam over the tea board, which had been brought in on his arrival shortly after supper was over and Chaz had been sent to bed, did she wish to marry Mr Samuel Stone. She had thought of him as a kind and helpful uncle for so long that the idea of being his wife was odd and strange, and she knew now that she could not accept him even if it was possible for her to free herself from the prison of servitude which her life had become. To do so would be fair neither to him nor to her. For he would want of her what she could not give him. She was not so innocent as not to know that he would require of her more than friendship, and friendship was all she had to offer. She did not look forward to telling him so.

Over the teacups, before he retired to do business in the Rector's study, Sam mentioned that he too was invited to the house-warming at Gillyflower Hall. 'I have been doing some business for Mr Tolliver,' he announced, holding his cup out to Nan for another offering. 'I expect that you will all be there?'

'Indeed, indeed,' replied the Rector before Jane had time to assure him eagerly that yes, of course they would. 'I am not over-partial to such jauntings as these, but it would not be fair to Jane and Chaz to deprive them of such a pleasant outing.'

'And Nan,' remarked Sam drily, looking at her over the rim of his cup.

'Oh, yes,' said Nan's papa vaguely. 'She will be going too—to look after Jane and Chaz and see that they behave themselves,' he remarked, smiling at her. 'I am sure that she will enjoy the recital on the last evening. The rest of the programme is designed more for the youthful members of the party, I believe.' And his benign smiled encompassed them all.

Sam put down his teacup and saucer with a disapproving rattle while inside Nan something shrieked, Oh, Papa, do not consign me to the almshouses yet. For that, she knew, was where poor parsons' unmarried daughters went, if none of their brothers or sisters wished to offer them a home. Would she go to Gillyflower Hall as the elderly maiden aunt if Jane married Brandon? The very idea made her shudder.

Her trembling start was noticed by no one except Sam, who, looking a little alarmed, asked gently, 'Are you feeling quite well, Nan? You are very pale tonight.'

'Nothing,' lied Nan. 'It was nothing. Someone walked over my grave, perhaps.'

'Oh, what a horrid saying that is,' Jane said, and later, when Sam and the Rector had retired to his study to do business, she remarked a little acidly, 'From the way that Mr Stone looked after you and his "Are you feeling quite well, Nan?" one might think that you had an elderly beau there.' And she gave a scornful little laugh at the mere idea.

A great blush swept over Nan; she could not help herself. Jane laughed harder than ever at the sight of it. 'Oh, never say so! What, Nan, are you eager for the privilege of being the second Mrs Stone?'

Even for Jane this was rather more spiteful than usual. Nan stood up. 'Better perhaps than being the only unmarried Miss Fielding, Jane, and now, if you will excuse me, I shall retire for the night. I have had a long and arduous day.'

She heard Kelsey begin to reproach Jane for her rudeness to her sister as she left the room, and missed Jane's answer: 'Lord, Kelsey, what a fuss about nothing. She must know as well as the rest of the parish that she said her last prayers long ago. I sometimes wonder if Nan was ever young.'

'So happy that you were able to come—and that the day is so uncommon fine!'

Lydia Bligh had said this or some variant of it so many times on the first day of her small fête, as she chose to call it, that she began to wonder how sincere she sounded.

She had invited what looked like the whole of the district, and the whole of the district had chosen to attend. They were processing by her as they arrived in the large drawing-room at Gillyflower Hall, whose tall glass doors had been opened on to the terrace which

overlooked the park where her earlier guests were
already taking a turn. A cold collation was to be served
on the upper lawn, and the servants were already laying
it out.

Brandon, who stood beside her, looked particularly
fine in a charcoal-coloured jacket, cream pantaloons,
black silk socks—just showing—and light black shoes
decorated with silver rosettes. His cravat was a miracle
of his valet's art, it having taken the man, Brandon had
declared, half the morning to achieve such perfection.
His hair was fashionably wind-blown—another magic
trick of his valet's. He was being charm itself and no
one would have guessed that he had spent the morning
looking out for the Rectory party and one member of
it—Miss Fielding—in particular. He was, he knew,
supposed to be looking out for Miss Jane Fielding—or
that was what the world and his sister Lydia thought.

Just as he had begun to wonder whether they were
going to cry off—perhaps Miss Fielding was ill, or the
parson—he saw them ushered through the double doors
by the butler, and heard their names cried aloud, so
that Lydia swung round to greet them, before passing
them on, one by one, to him.

Who was he looking for? Again, most supposed Miss
Jane, who appeared absolutely enchanting in a cream
silk gown decorated with rosebuds. Little silk rosebuds
ran along the neckline of her dress, and one was tucked
into the pale blue sash around her waist, another
nestling among her golden curls. She had never looked
so lovely, so ethereal, and she knew it. Beside her,
Chaz had been wrestled into a youthful imitation of the
clothes which Brandon was wearing, and it was plain
that he was a handsome boy who was going to be a
handsome man. Behind them, as always, Parson
Fielding was his usual vaguely charming, flyaway self,
and beside him. . .

Yes, beside him was Miss Anne Fielding, wearing a deep purple gown with a high neck which looked, Brandon thought, as though it might have done duty for the mother who was never seen. This judgement merely confirmed his percipience, for it *was* an old gown of Mrs Fielding's, cut and trimmed to Nan's size. Even Nan's cap, whose frill drooped on either side of her face, had been her mother's. Thrift was a necessity, as well as a virtue, at the Rectory. Any spare money went to buy Jane's clothes, and ultimately, it was hoped, a husband.

If anything, Nan was more extinguished than ever. No strand of her glossy tawny hair could be seen, and her eyes were hidden in the shadow of the dreadful cap. Worse still, the ugly dress hid the beautiful body. So how was it that Mr Brandon Tolliver, surveying the Rectory party, felt a dreadful spasm of desire, not for the elegant fairy on the front row, but for the elderly dowd at the back? A dowd who was trying to avoid looking at him.

And he must not look at her. He bowed over Jane's hand, held it a little too long, told her how pleased he was to see her again and how charming she looked. Jane was always at her best when being admired. She sparkled prettily at both him and Lydia, saying everything that she should on such an occasion.

Chaz was greeted with the words, 'And how are you, old fellow? Did you manage to recover your kite? Does it still fly?' Brandon showed such genuine interest in Chaz's doings, complimenting him on being a member of the village cricket team at such a young age, that Chaz thought what a splendid fellow he was, who surely deserved better as a wife than an empty-head like Jane or Caroline.

Talking to the Rector, Brandon changed tack again, referring knowledgeably to his book *The Nature of the*

Trinity, of which he had taken the precaution of reading the first few chapters and skimming the rest. Nan's father was duly left with the impression of what a well-informed man Mr Brandon Tolliver was, for all that he was a mere merchant who, the Rector understood, had not been brought up as a gentleman. Nevertheless he possessed a splendid presence and was obviously learning to conduct himself as a gentleman should. Parson Fielding was very conscious of his own claims to gentility.

Lydia was busy doing the pretty at his side to yet another guest when Miss Fielding was finally presented to Mr Brandon Tolliver. She could not help but note that he looked more superb than ever. More handsome, too. He strongly resembled the portrait of his great-grandfather, Adolphus Tolliver, who had been a good-looking as well as clever man. In that, Nan thought, Brandon was the first of his descendants to resemble him. She could only wish that she had similar claims to be remarked upon.

He bowed. She bowed. He took her unwilling hand, bent over it and kissed it, saying, 'A pleasure to meet you at last, Miss Fielding,' as though he had not seen her several times in various drawing-rooms as the Gorgon, and twice as a nymph whom a wanton shepherd might pursue.

Nan tried to remove her hand quickly, but he hung on to it, and turned it over gently, to reveal the marks of the many different tasks which she did upon it. There was a little callus on her second finger which her quill pen had placed there as a result of constant use. Brandon frowned a little at the sight, and reluctantly surrendered the damaged paw. Both parties were only too well aware of the frisson of pleasure which went through them whenever they touched. Nothing like that ever happened when he had held Miss Jane

Fielding's hand, was Brandon's thought, while Nan's
was, I haven't felt *that* since Randal left me to go to
the war.

'I am pleased that you saw fit to accept our invitation,
Miss Fielding. Jane thought that you might refuse it.'

Nan could not resist saying, 'Jane is not always
correct in her suppositions, Mr Tolliver.'

Equally, Brandon could not help replying, 'Indeed,
Miss Fielding, nor am I always correct in mine, as you
well know.'

Nan flushed scarlet, and said in a low voice, 'I
thought that we had agreed to forget the past, Mr
Tolliver, and start anew.'

His eyes on her were frank. 'I have to inform you
that I have a problem, Miss Fielding. It is difficult for
me to do so.'

'Then perhaps I should not have come.'

Brandon was suddenly remorseful. 'No, indeed; I
should have held my tongue. You have little enough of
amusement in your life, I understand. Try to enjoy the
next few days, I beg of you. You deserve a taste of
pleasure.'

The silver eyes were so kind and serious as he said
this that Nan had difficulty in repressing a sudden gush
of tears at such unwonted consideration. Goodness,
what can be happening to me? she thought. I am
turning into a regular watering-pot. I must remember
that he cannot be sincere, that he probably still sees me
as. . .prey. After all, I behaved so loosely with him that
he may conclude that that is my true nature. . .and that
he may yet profit from it. . .

'I ought to move on,' she told him, for Lydia was
passing the next guest on to him, and reluctantly
Brandon allowed her to go.

She walked across the terrace, down the steps and
into the garden, to be greeted by Jane with the words,

'Why, Nan, whatever was Brandon finding to talk about that he should engage you at such length?'

To which Nan's only answer was a repressive and totally untruthful one. 'Oh, I suppose that he means to make all his guests feel wanted, Jane, and as, so far, we have exchanged so few words, he doubtless thought to make sure that I felt as welcome as those whom he had already favoured with many.'

Which left Jane thinking yet again how elderly and pompous Nan was beginning to sound, but which also reassured her that for Mr Brandon Tolliver the younger Fielding sister must be the one in whom to take an interest. A belief which was reinforced when presently Brandon made his way into the garden to inform her that he was to be one of her partners at the luncheon table, Lord Alden's son, George, being on her other side. The servants had finished their work and the food was waiting for their masters to eat.

Lydia, Brandon thought, had excelled herself. Besides cold ham and beef, good bread, Stilton and Red Leicester cheese, and great slabs of newly churned butter from the dairy which was part of the appurtenances of Gillyflower Hall, there were huge bowls of strawberries, as well as peaches, and dishes of whipped cream. The peaches had been brought from the hothouses of Lydia's new friend, Lord Alden, who lived at nearby Alden Hall, Gillyflower Hall being without a proper hothouse, although Brandon had great plans for one.

To eat with the fruit and cream there was a variety of cakes and biscuits, including a large Madeira cake, Threadneedle biscuits, a speciality of the Tollivers' cook, and Jumbles, a Leicestershire delicacy often called Bosworth Jumbles—presumably because of the battle fought there! The recipe for it had been acquired from the Rectory's cook. Lemonade for the ladies and

Cambridge milk punch for the gentlemen were carried from the house by the footmen at the last moment so that they arrived cool and fresh.

The guests stood around exclaiming at the feast. Nan found herself alone for a moment; Jane was on Brandon's arm, and Chaz had found a new friend, Tim Alden, while her father was in earnest conversation with the Rector of the neighbouring parish about the necessity of putting down the hedge priests who were attracting the local villagers to their impromptu open-air services.

'This is all very fine, is it not? And, I dare say, required a great deal of Cousin Brandon's money to fund it,' hissed a gloomy voice in Nan's ear as she took in the splendour of the tables. It came from Desmond, who then remarked, 'Remiss of me, Nan. I should have greeted you formally, I suppose, but as such old friends. . .' And he let the sentence die. He was dressed in dark, slightly outmoded clothing, and his cravat was a drooping modest thing. Was it Nan's imagination or did he look more faded than ever as a result of his cousin's being so completely à la mode?

He smiled wryly, and added, 'I should not speak so. It was good of him to invite me, offer me an olive-branch, but I had much rather I had not needed one.'

Unspoken were the words, Had I inherited then I would have been giving this house-warming party and not him. Instead he went on briskly, 'I am to take you in for luncheon, Nan, or so my cousin Lydia informs me.'

Desperate to say something, anything, to lighten the occasion for them both, for the sight of Jane hanging on Brandon's arm and laughing up into his handsome face was doing strange things to Nan's temper, she remarked coolly, 'How does one take a person *into* luncheon when it is held *outside* in the garden,

Desmond? And how will our hostess to be able inform us that it is served?'

Before Desmond had time to reply, the answer itself appeared. A round-faced youngster whom Nan recognised as the elder brother of Jem, who had come across Brandon and herself on the day on which she had found the kite, came out of the Hall. He was wearing a brilliant page's uniform in scarlet and gold, rather like a miniature guardsman, and he was carrying a large brass gong which he banged several times with a huge drumstick before piping shrilly, 'Luncheon is served, m'lords, ladies and gentlemen.'

Lydia offered her arm to Lord Alden, Brandon took in Lady Alden and one by one the guests processed in rough order of rank around the luncheon table. Rough, because Brandon took the view that appropriateness in one's partners at meals, so far as enjoyment was concerned, took precedence over everything else—so Lydia had placed him between Jane and Lady Alden, while Nan had been given Desmond and sat opposite them.

She thus had the agonising experience of watching Brandon being '*most* particular' to Jane. It did not ease her sore heart to consider that if she had judged Mr Brandon Tolliver correctly those merry eyes of his would be looking at pretty women like Jane, not plain ones like herself. She did not consider the compliments which he had paid her on the two occasions in which she had lain in his arms to be anything more than lures designed to trap a poor girl into letting him have his way with her.

For some reason the mere idea of Brandon having his way with anyone had Nan going hot all over. Desmond, who was busy haranguing her about the folly of local manufacturers in bringing in the new weaving machines, which resulted in so many men being laid off, provoking radical dissent and violence, looked keenly at her and remarked, 'Are you well, Nan? Your colour seems very high today.'

The other day it had been her pallor which had caused remark, Nan remembered acidly. Presumably these days she never possessed the correct complexion. She replied, her voice trembling slightly, 'I fear that I am feeling the heat today, Desmond. It is not usual for me to sit in the open in order to eat.'

He might have appeared to be carrying on a conversation with Jane which occupied his whole attention, but for all that, to his secret annoyance, Brandon had also been sharply aware of Miss Fielding and her conversation with his gloomy cousin Desmond.

He could not prevent himself. He leaned forward, remarked solicitously, 'If being outdoors is too much for you, Miss Fielding, then I am sure that Lady Alden and your sister will release me so that I may escort you into the shade of the Hall, and send for some cooling drinks.'

Lady Alden might have agreed to his suggestion, but Jane didn't want to; that was plain. Nan stammered, 'Oh—oh, no, I am not so troubled that I need you to disturb yourself, Mr Tolliver.'

'No disturbance,' Brandon told her, at the same time that Desmond, looking annoyed, came out with, 'No need to put yourself out, Cousin; I will escort Nan into the Hall.'

'But I neither require nor need anyone to escort me indoors,' almost wailed Nan at the improbable sight of the two cousins glaring at one another over a dispute about which of them should have the honour of looking after the dowdiest creature at the party.

Lydia Bligh was staring at all three of them in disbelief, particularly at Desmond's angry scarlet face. Sits the wind in that quarter? Well, who would have

thought it? was her inward comment. And as for
Brandon, well, who would have thought any such
unlikely thing as that he would be taking note of plain,
upright Miss Fielding—who was not quite so plain when
one took a good look at her?

Had Brandon been taking a good look at her, and if
so, when?

Matters were not improved by Jane saying angrily, 'I
am sure that there is nothing wrong with Nan. She is
never ill, you know. Why, even when the whole
Rectory was laid up last winter with the shivering ague
she was still on her feet looking after us all. She is as
strong as a horse.'

This unflattering last sentence had Brandon looking
in astonishment at the little fairy whom he had thought,
like all pretty girls, to be 'sugar and spice and all things
nice', as the nursery rhyme had it. And even if she was
not quite like the little boys in the same rhyme in being
made of 'slugs and snails and puppy dogs' tails' there
was still more than a touch of bile, he was beginning to
grasp, in most of Jane's remarks to her sister.

For her part, Nan felt like shouting aloud, Why, you
selfish ninny, I was as ill as the rest of you, but *someone*
had to stay on their feet and see that the house was
warm, the sheets and nightwear changed, medicines
doled out, and that drinks of water and hot lemonade
were in constant supply. How dare you compare me to
a horse?

'Please,' she said in agony, aware that the whole
table was staring interestedly at her—her at whom no
one ever looked, but always took for granted. 'I am not
in the least discommoded. Pray allow me to continue
my meal at table.'

'If you are absolutely sure,' both men began together,
Desmond now glaring at Brandon, who was looking
daggers at him.

'Yes,' she told them, while Lydia, aware that as hostess she should have nipped this in the bud, but had been too shaken by the reaction of both Desmond and Brandon to think straight, announced in a firm voice, 'I am sure that we must all allow that Miss Fielding is the best judge of her condition. May I suggest, Miss Fielding, that instead of lemonade you take a glass of Cambridge milk punch? I am sure that will set you up wonderfully.'

She signalled to the nearest footman, who ran to do her bidding, placing before poor Nan a huge glass cup, foaming to the brim with a concoction of which one of the major components was brandy!

And there was nothing she could do but drink it! She dared not demur, for Lydia's intervention had brought her end of the table to its senses, and they all began to eat the delicious food before them as though nothing out of the ordinary had occurred.

'What the devil is that fellow to you?' whispered Desmond in Nan's ear once the meal was over and they were walking along the terrace, ostensibly admiring the view towards Leicestershire. 'Why should he be so particular towards you?'

Nan was feeling the effects of two glasses of punch for Lydia had insisted on her drinking another. She said, with a light laugh, finding her words a trifle difficult to articulate, 'Why, Desmond, don't take on so. He's particular to all women, as I'm sure that you must have noticed.'

'Only to pretty ones,' returned Desmond unfortunately.

The devil got into Nan, or the Cambridge milk punch was talking out of turn.

'Then he must think me pretty,' she announced defiantly.

Desmond, who had just realised the insult he had put

upon her, replied a trifle uncomfortably, 'Then you are admitting that his behaviour towards you has been——'

'Has been nothing.' Nan's voice was as hard as she could make it. 'Forgive me, Desmond, but I don't propose to put up with your inquisition any longer.' Before he could open his mouth again, she was striding away from him, past the swing which Brandon had caused to be erected and on which all the pretty young things were taking turns to be pushed by Brandon and the unmarried men.

She was seeing the beautiful garden through a blur of tears. Shame and embarrassment had prevented her from enjoying the excellent food which the Tollivers had provided. She did not see Brandon look after her as she walked blindly on, towards the tiny lake with its small pavilion where the Tolliver women had, for two centuries, sat to admire the view and sketch or do their canvas work.

Oh, to be away from everyone forever and ever. But even an hour would do. No one would miss her. She was out of everyone's sight, and she could half recline on the marble bench in the shade and close her eyes, maybe doze a little. She had written far into the night because she was going to be unable to carry out her self-appointed task while she was at Gillyflower Hall, and not for the first time she wished that she had been left at home on her own. That would have been perfect bliss.

Doze she did—to be wakened by the sound of someone walking along the gravelled path which led to the pavilion. She shrank back, determined not to be discovered. A man stood in the doorway which was merely an open arch, and the man was Brandon Tolliver, the very last person whom she wished to see.

CHAPTER SIX

BRANDON almost didn't see her, but he must have heard the rustle of her dress, for he moved forward so that his dark silhouette was sharp against the bright blue late afternoon sky behind him.

'Miss Fielding?' His voice was tentative, questioning, then sure, as his eyes adjusted to the gloom and he saw her, huddled into a corner of the marble bench. 'Ah, there you are. Are you ill? May I assist you in any way?'

As earlier his solicitude distressed rather than reassured Nan. She sat up straight, and her voice betrayed nothing of the inward agitation which shook her every time she met him.

'No, indeed, Mr Tolliver, although it is kind of you to ask. I came here to enjoy the water and the sun, and in the half-dark I fear that I dozed off.' And then, anxiously, 'Have I been missed?'

Brandon walked further in, and waved Nan down as she began to stand up, sitting down himself on another bench set into the wall opposite Nan, after asking her for her permission to do so.

'Alas, no. You have not been missed, although you have sat here for some time. I say alas because it pains me to see that none of your party appears to show you any real consideration, although Chaz did ask me a little time ago whether I knew where you were. But he barely stayed for an answer. I saw you walk to the pavilion and realised that I had not seen you return. The rest of my guests have gone to their rooms to prepare for the evening.'

79

He paused, wondering at his own solicitude for the upright woman opposite to him who was allowing no shadow of emotion to cross her face. He was not usually wont to worry about such unconsidered creatures as Nan Fielding seemed to be.

So why was it that he was feeling anger that no one *did* consider her? He did not pause to answer his own question, but merely went smoothly on—Nan had already noted that his voice was a beautiful one, deep but not too deep.

'I took the liberty of sending one of the footmen to your room with a fresh bowl of flowers and a message. He came back to inform me that you were not there. I met your father on his way to the library—he told me what a splendid collection of books I possess, but appeared to have no idea of where one of his own possessions was!' He stopped, allowing Nan to enjoy this small joke—which she did with a slight nod of her head.

'Growing worried, because you seemed both ill and tired today, I decided to search for you myself—so here I am.' He looked around the pavilion, then asked, 'And do you like this building as well as the view?'

'I have always,' replied Nan truthfully, 'liked everything about Gillyflower Hall, but I had never seen very much of it until today. Your cousin Bart was quite the recluse, as I suppose you know.'

'So my lawyers told me. I am pleased that it pleases you, though.' He hesitated. 'I suppose we are breaking all the canons of etiquette by remaining together alone, in such a confined space.'

'I should not let it trouble you.' Nan's tone was earnest. 'I am so remarkably elderly and respectable that no one would think that anything was untoward if we were found together.'

Brandon made a short vexed exclamation and

jumped up. Nan had already learned what a very vigorous person he was, and that she had annoyed him by what she had just said was betrayed by his bodily movements as well as his speech.

'No!' he exclaimed violently. 'Just because the whole world chooses to demean you—including my cousin Desmond, for all his supposed admiration of you—it does not mean that you must demean yourself. It is time someone took a little care of you, instead of you spending your whole time caring for others. Are you never let out of prison? Was that why I have twice found you climbing on to stools and trees—to free yourself?'

'How very melodramatic of you, sir.' Nan tried to keep her tone as light as possible, but he could see that she was shaking, and he could not guess the cause.

He was the cause. He and none other. The shuddering became worse when Brandon walked forward to take her by the arm, exclaiming, 'Earlier today you were overheated, and now you are cold! No wonder that you are shivering. Come, let us walk you back to the house, and you must allow your maid to put you in a warm bath to restore you.'

It was not the cold which made Nan shiver, but his nearness. That and the weariness which had overcome her ever since she had reached Gillyflower Hall. Paradoxically, it had not been while she was pursuing her labours around the Rectory that she had felt tired, but at the moment when they had ended, and she was supposed to be enjoying herself, with servants around to satisfy her every whim.

Unresisting, Nan allowed Brandon to take her arm and walk her back towards the house. 'Suppose someone sees us?' she ventured, only for him to reply robustly,

'Nonsense, my dear Miss Fielding; you have just

informed me that your sober presence must disarm all criticism—I will not have you change your mind ere five minutes have passed. That would be to make you too like most of the other women in society!'

This sally made Nan laugh, and, encouraged, Brandon began to talk idly and lightly to settle and soothe her. 'As you may imagine,' he began, 'when the tea board came around, shortly after luncheon we all began to discuss the author of *Sophia*'s latest offering. Discuss, of course, is the wrong word, because we were all in agreement. The very young ladies, Jane in particular, could not sing her praises loudly enough.' He stopped, laughed a little under his breath.

'And you, Mr Tolliver?' Nan could not prevent herself from asking. 'Were you in agreement, or do you find novels such as *Sophia*'s frivolous and rather tiresome?'

'Oh, no, not all.' He shook his handsome head. 'Far from it. My trouble was that the rest of the company was busy praising her for the delicacy of the romance, saying, and I am quoting others, how sweetly pretty her writing is, how charming; whereas I, on the contrary, admire her for her astringency, the delicate irony which suffuses all that she writes, the insights which she displays into the darker sides of our nature. I must tell you that I hope that she does not come to live near me! I should not like that cool, probing eye turned on me and my doings. I say she, but, of course, she may be he—although I do not think so. What is your opinion, Miss Fielding? I should value it.'

Nan was silent for a moment while she debated on how to give this difficult question an honest answer. She finally came out with an equivocation. 'Jane will tell you that I do not read novels, so I fear that I cannot enlighten you.'

He looked at her sharply, and found that to do so

had the oddest effect on him. He wanted to tear off the disfiguring bonnet, dress her in something more suitable, and hope to see again the nymph who had sat astride the tree branch. All this havering about the author of *Sophia* was a blind to try to disguise from himself the strong and strange impression which the rector's eldest daughter had on him. It was Jane he was supposed to be fixed on, not Nan!

He found himself murmuring, 'Then you should read those by the author of *Sophia*; you would enjoy them. And despite what I have just said I should very much like to meet her, but one conjectures that she might be ninety. . .'

He rolled a comic eye at Nan and had the pleasure of hearing her laugh before she added gravely, carrying on the game he had begun, 'And carries a huge green umbrella and has a poodle called Pericles, which never behaves itself in company.' They were laughing together at the picture this presented when they reached the gravel path which led to the hall.

Brandon stopped, and released Nan's elbow which he had been lightly grasping, a touch which was helping to render her delirious and was doing no less for him if he were to be honest with himself, and said gravely, 'Whatever I may have hinted earlier, Miss Fielding, I am only too mindful of the need to preserve your reputation. I suggest that we part here, and that you go into the Hall alone. If any should be so bold as to question you, you may tell them the truth: that you were tired and fell asleep in the pavilion, awoke, and found your way home. No need to start any gossip by adding that you were with me.'

He bowed, before he left her with the words, 'I look forward to seeing you at supper. We are informal again this evening. That is Lydia's way and one which I too prefer.'

To tell the truth, even if it was only a part of the whole truth, appeared to be a habit of Mr Brandon Tolliver's as well as hers, was Nan's thought as she walked into the pleasant room which was to be hers during her stay at Gillyflower Hall. She had hardly sat down before there was a knock on her door. A little maid stood there, saying, 'Excuse me, ma'am, I'm Mary. I've been sent by the master to look after you while you are at the Hall. He said that you would be needing a bath. The footmen will be following shortly with the warm water, and meantime you must allow me to prepare you for it.'

Mesmerised both by Mr Brandon Tolliver and his splendours, Nan made no demur, but sat quietly on a large sofa ranged at the bottom of her four-poster bed as a procession of servants made the big, free-standing bath in the adjoining room ready for her.

Downstairs, Mr Brandon Tolliver, who was beginning to wonder if he was running slightly mad, because he had never felt like this about a woman since he was a green boy first discovering the opposite sex, was speculating on what kind of nymph Miss Nan Fielding most resembled when little Mary helped her into the warm water he had so thoughtfully provided for her!

However, tempting she might be supposed to look with her clothes gone, her dress for supper was no better than that which she had worn for lunch. While Jane was wearing amber gauze floating over amber silk, Nan was sensibly dressed like the chaperon she was in puce—another of her mother's cut-down dresses. Her cap was the saffron horror which she had worn at the Assembly Rooms. Lydia had mixed up her guests for supper, and Nan was now seated at the far end of the table. Fortunately her partner was Sam Stone, who had arrived a little earlier. He had told Brandon that business might prevent him from arriving before luncheon.

What a dismal turn-out! had been Sam's internal comment when he had greeted Nan in the drawing-room before supper. If she accepted him he would make sure that Mrs Samuel Stone had some new clothes. They might not be able to rival Lydia Bligh's luxurious and fashionable amethyst silk gown, enhanced by the diamonds which her late husband, an India merchant, had bought for her, but she would not be ashamed before the world as she was at the moment. The money going into the Rectory was being spent on everyone but Nan, apparently. Well, that would have to stop, preferably once Jane married this personable youngish man Tolliver, who was not, Sam decided, quite a gentleman, but none the worse for that.

The port which was circulated after the women had left was first rate, though. The Tollivers knew how to set a good table, was the universal comment. The cigars were first rate too, and the talk wasn't bad either. They were discussing shooting, about which Brandon was knowledgeable, when he threw into the conversation something which had happened to him in the previous week.

'Have some careless shots around here, do you?' he asked, swirling his port around in his glass, holding it against the light and admiring its ruby-red. The county had already discovered that he was a discriminating rather than a heavy drinker.

Lord Alden, one of the heavies, drawled, 'Not so you'd notice, Tolliver. Why?'

Brandon, making little of it, replied, 'I was walking in the woods near to your land, Alden, when some damned fool nearly took my head off. Took my new hat instead. Frightened himself as much as me, I suppose. I heard him running off, but couldn't catch a glimpse of him.'

'Might be some Luddite, of course, loosing off a shot at one of us,' offered Sir Avery Letcombe. 'Not that there's been much of that round here lately—not since Cullen was hanged at Highborough eighteen months ago.'

'That was the man who shot and killed Mason, the manufacturer, was it not?' offered Brandon, trying to make light of what had happened to him. 'I thought that after his death his gang of Luddites had all been rounded up and their weapons confiscated.'

'True,' said Alden, 'but one never rounds up *everyone* on these occasions. Besides, your cousin made quite a few enemies on the Bench. He was a harsh sentencer, and they might be taking it out on you.'

Brandon thought this improbable, preferring to believe that it had been an accident, although not quite the kind of accident he liked. His main worry, which he didn't confide in the others, was that he couldn't imagine what the shot had been meant for, if it hadn't been meant for him. None of his fellows seemed to take the matter very seriously. Even Parson Fielding remarked in his gently hazy manner, 'That sort of thing has probably happened to most of us at one time or another.' He blinked at the company and they all nodded polite agreement.

In the world in which Brandon had made his fortune one took nothing on trust. One minded one's back, and he had come to believe that few incidents of this kind ought to be lightly passed over. But he was a new man in this part of Nottinghamshire, and was well aware that he was not yet considered to be quite a gentleman for all his old name and his ownership of Gillyflower Hall. They knew that he had started life as a clerk. That he had been more than that in his time, had worked before the mast while on the way to his fortune, they might guess, but couldn't know. He had no mind to antagonise them by making heedless accusations.

But his values weren't theirs, and however much of a veneer he had acquired, and was still acquiring, they never would be completely. His cousin Desmond, who had seen Brandon shoot, remarked in a friendlier tone than he had yet used to him, 'They're not all as careful with their weaponry as you are, Brandon, nor are they such good shots. Whoever it was was probably ashamed of what he had done, and made off before you could reproach or reprimand him.'

More nods followed, and the matter was forgotten by everyone except Brandon—and Sam Stone, whose wise old face was thoughtful.

The arrival of the gentlemen after their post-supper drinking was eagerly awaited by all the ladies, none, surprisingly, more eager than quiet Miss Fielding, seated in a straight-backed chair in the corner among the other older women, watching the young girls playing spillikins to while away the time until the interesting part of the evening began. Chaz had left with the ladies and had gone to his room some little time before. Nan's eagerness related to the appearance of Mr Brandon Tolliver.

The conversation around her was abuzz with excited speculation about which of the Royal Dukes would marry next in order to give the throne an heir, now that the Prince Regent's only child, Princess Charlotte, had died giving birth to a stillborn baby. All the Dukes had large families by their various mistresses, but none of these was, of course, eligible to succeed to the throne.

The next source of mild uproar was the latest fashion in dress, and the new hairstyles, which were somewhat longer, Lady Alden said knowledgeably, than those which had been popular for the last twenty years.

Nan could not take part in any of this. She knew little or nothing of the doings of the Royal Family, and was hardly likely to be able to afford new toilettes or a new coiffure. On the other hand, the foibles of those around her always engaged her interest, so she was, if silent, never bored. 'So restful, Nan Fielding,' was the common cry. It was fortunate that they had no notion of what she was thinking!

In came the gentlemen in various stages of sobriety. Either, Nan noted, Brandon Tolliver held his drink well, or he had not been drinking heavily. He walked over to the table where the young misses were engaged in spillikins and naughtily reduced them to hysterics by his antics. Young George Alden, Lord Alden's heir, again made a dead set at Jane, and various other young men engaged themselves with various other eligible young females. Only Jane had two ardent courtiers.

And only Nan was left to sit alone and composed, her hands clasped together on her unbecoming puce knees. Sam Stone, who had been caught by Sir Avery Letcombe for advice on some legal pother he was engaged in, cut short Sir Avery's maunderings as quickly and politely as he could in order to make his way over to her.

'You are enjoying a break from your labours, my dear?' he asked her, solicitude in his voice.

Mischief glinted in Nan's eyes. Whatever happened to her, she thought, cheerfulness would always break in. 'What would you say, sir, if I answered that I am most uncommonly bored?'

'That it is the kind of answer I can imagine the author of *Sophia* giving one of her characters to say, but not yourself.'

Nan's eyesbrows—beautiful ones, Sam always

thought—rose slightly. 'You are able to make a distinction, then?'

He laughed at that, causing a few heads to turn. What *could* severe Miss Fielding be finding to say to amuse that old stick Sam Stone so?

'It is of that which I must speak to you, and immediately. There is a rather fine picture gallery opening out of this room. We could take a turn along it, and I could speak to you in some privacy without causing comment. You will allow?'

Nan nodded, and rose. She put her hand on Sam's arm, and he led her from the room, through the double doors, and into a corridor which ran the width of the house. Assorted Tollivers looked down their haughty noses at them, among the views of Italy and the paintings by Salvator Rosa which a mid-eighteenth-century Tolliver had brought back with him from the Grand Tour.

Sam stood in front of a view of Vesuvius in eruption, and said softly, 'It is your publisher, Mr Murray, my dear. He is no longer happy, or I may say willing, to keep the identity of the author of *Sophia* secret. He thinks that the mystery has gone on long enough. He is hinting that to reveal who the author is would enormously increase sales which are already large.'

'He would not think so if he *were* aware of who the author of *Sophia* is,' remarked Nan irrepressibly. For the truth was that some six years ago, using Sam as an intermediary, she had sent the manuscript of *Sophia* to Mr John Murray, the publisher who had helped to make Lord Byron both rich and famous. It was the earnings from *Sophia* and the novels which had followed it which were saving the Rectory from penury, not Parson Fielding's dim piece of outdated theology.

And all of them had been written at her little bureau, either at dead of night when the Rectory had gone to bed, or early in the morning when only the servants were up. The first, *Sophia*, had dealt with the adventures of a parson's daughter in the great world, after Nan had spent her first season in London, chaperoning her younger sister Madeline, and observing the passing show with a cynical eye.

She and Sam had insisted on the secret being kept, and at first Mr Murray had been willing to oblige them, but now he had apparently changed his mind.

'He is talking of sending one of his employees to Broomhall to meet me, and to try to winkle the truth out of me. Mr Murray is apparently certain that his author is a son or a daughter of a clergyman, and I suppose his man will spy out the land, after trying to wheedle me into revealing all.'

Nan suddenly became agitated. 'No,' she said, her hands rising to cup her scarlet cheeks at the mere idea of being unmasked. 'No. On no account must you give me away. It is of all things necessary that I remain anonymous. Think of the scandal, the distress Papa would feel if he knew what paid for his bread and butter.'

'It is high time that he did know,' riposted Sam, his kind face alight with anger. 'To work as you do on top of everything else, and to receive nothing in return, but to be neglected and passed over for those who are not worth tuppence beside you.'

Passion suddenly rode on his usually impassive features. He put out an impulsive hand to grasp one of hers. 'Give me the answer I wish for now. Marry me, Nan. Let me free you from the wheel of servitude to which you are bound. I would allow you to continue to write, if you so wished, but not as you do now, before and after a hard day's work.'

Nan disengaged herself gently. 'Oh, Sam, I have thought long and hard of your kind proposal, and my decision is that it would be unfair to you for me to say yes. I should be marrying you out of gratitude, friendship and, yes, a desire to escape the trap which my life has become. But you deserve better than that. I value you, that's true. But not in the way in which a wife should value a husband.'

She knew that there was another reason why she ought not to marry him, or any other man, but she could not tell him of it.

He turned a little away from her, to mutter, 'You are an honest woman, Nan, and I knew what your answer would be. Why cannot you be like the rest of your sex, looking only to the main chance? Then you would accept me. If I thought that you would ever find a man who wished to marry you, and would value you as I do, then I might feel a little happier at your refusal, but as it is. . .' He pulled out a large handkerchief and blew his nose vigorously. 'As it is, I fear that you may live and die exploited and unconsidered.'

Nan closed her eyes against his pain. She did not want to lose a dear friend, and said, 'We may remain friends, I trust?'

In a gesture such as she had never seen him make before he took her hand in his again to kiss it, and to say, 'Always, my dear. We have been friends since we first met, have we not? I could not relinquish my chaperonage of the author of *Sophia*. That would be to make my life even duller than it is.'

His faded eyes were twinkling at her as he spoke. There were many, Nan knew, who thought him a prosy man, a stick, but she knew better, and was only sorry that she could not give him what he most wanted: herself.

'And,' he continued, relinquishing her hand, 'if you wish me to help you retain your anonymity, I will do so—although I warn you, you will not be able to keep it forever—secrets can never remain secrets permanently.'

'I know that,' Nan told him. 'Nevertheless I wish to keep this one as long as possible.'

'What Sir Walter Scott could not do will be beyond you, I think,' he said—for Scott had wished to be known only as the author of *Waverley*, but in the end had been, in Sam's words, 'smoked out'.

'I will leave you now, my dear,' he said. 'I will ask you to consider Murray's wishes again, but the other business is dead and buried. Friends we are, and friends we will remain, I hope.'

Nan watched him go. To compose herself she turned towards the landscape again. Yes, Vesuvius was still bursting into flames.

She was seeing it through a blur of emotion. Not tears, but something else was moving her. A voice from the rear of the gallery said, a touch of mockery in it, 'I see that your elderly admirer has left you. For a young woman who makes little effort to attract, I judge that you are being uncommonly unsuccessful. I gather from something that my cousin Desmond has said that he has some vague aspirations towards your hand as well.'

'You are ungentlemanly, sir—particularly if you have been eavesdropping on our conversation.' For Nan was a little worried that the secret of the author of *Sophia* might no longer be a secret to her host.

'I do not need to overhear anything, my nymph in disguise,' Brandon drawled, his eyes hard on her. 'The looks your middle-aged swain casts in your direction tell all.'

Nan's face told him that she thought that others might have seen what he had done. He laughed softly. 'Oh, no, my dear. Your friends and family are blind when you are concerned. They take you so much for granted that if you danced a hornpipe on the front lawn they would assume that it was someone else they were seeing!'

Nan could scarce repress a laugh at this unlikely picture. She managed to return earnestly, 'Your absence will be remarked on, sir. You are the host, and you should not dally here talking with the least considered of your guests.'

'All my guests are considered,' he told her, as irrepressible outwardly as Nan was inwardly, 'and no one will miss me, for I have supposedly left to arrange some matters for my guests' convenience tomorrow.'

'Jane will miss you,' Nan could not stop herself from saying. His presence had the most dreadful effect on her. Her heart had begun to beat rapidly; a strange quivering swept over her body. Moths had invaded her head. She knew what all this meant, and oh, she ought to stop herself from feeling it, but could not.

He said something under his breath which sounded uncommonly like, 'Oh, damn Jane,' but he couldn't have said that. She must have misheard.

'Some of your guests might wish to visit the portrait gallery,' she informed him.

'What, and desert the pleasures of the drawing-room?' he retorted. 'They are all on fire over some child's games with counters, the men inspired by drink and the ladies by excitement.'

He was now so near to her that the silver eyes seemed to be filling all her world. Nan had nowhere to retreat to. And she needed to retreat, for he put up a hand to tip her cap up, causing it to fall backwards to the floor, revealing her tawny locks, her waves and curls which were trying to escape from their tight confinement.

'Sir, you are no gentleman to do such a thing.' Nan was vigorous, not complaining.

'I know.' His voice was as lazy as he was. 'I have never claimed to be one, and I don't like most of those whom I meet.' And he put both hands on the wall to hold her there without touching her, while he leaned forward to kiss her oh, so gently on the lips.

Oh, what bliss! She had forgotten what lovemaking was like. How sweet it was, how dear. Nan closed her eyes and he saw straight away, for his own were open, that she was not resisting him but welcoming him.

Oddly, at the sight of this surrender, the conscience which his sister claimed that he did not possess began to reproach him. He must remember that he was dealing with no flirt, no lady who was, behind a mask of virtue, as much of a lightskirt as the whores and courtesans she affected to despise. Instead he was in the despicable position of assailing a virtuous and untried woman who was unversed in the art of coping with double-dealing men.

He released her, which was difficult, for he had discovered to his surprise that to be with Nan was temptation itself. She looked at him with great eyes, and half whispered, 'I repeat, sir, your behaviour is most ungentlemanly. You are supposed to be "*most* particular" towards my sister Jane, and here you are being "*most* particular" to me. That is a scoundrel's part.'

'Oh, I am a scoundrel,' he assured her, and despite all his good resolutions he kissed her again—determined to prove that what he had just said was true, he thought afterwards, a little bitterly.

Nan was trying not to kiss him back, an almost impossible task. Somehow she managed it, somehow she pushed him away, just at the moment when his conscience pricked him again.

She found that she was panting, but composed herself sufficiently to move away from him and pick up her despised cap, as he pulled away from the wall, leaving her free to go. During the whole short episode he had touched Nan only with his mouth; his hands had remained on the wall and his body away from her. For some reason this had aroused him more than if he had been free with her. But that small contact had been enough to do its work on him.

When he looked up again Nan was gone. She was back in the drawing-room, with only one thing on her mind. And that one thing was that not only had she fallen in love with Mr Brandon Tolliver, who was most decidedly not meant for her, but that she desired him with a desire beyond anything which she had made her heroines feel for the heroes whom they desired!

What Brandon Tolliver had on his mind was that yes, he truly was running mad. But after a somewhat sane fashion, he recognised ruefully, because he had already started to cool his manner a little towards Jane Fielding. But nothing could mitigate the distressing fact that he was being '*most* particular' to two sisters at once—something which no gentleman should ever be.

Nan had hardly sat down again before Desmond, who had been stationed in a corner, watching the goings-on around the big table set aside for games, with a supercilious expression on his face, came over to be supercilious to her.

Nan knew that expression. It had seldom been directed towards her, more usually towards her flighty sisters, and anyone of whom Desmond disapproved—and he disapproved of many. Its presence this evening meant that she was his target.

He began without preamble. 'Where have you been, Nan? I have been unable to find you. Your father thought that you might have retired to your room. Did you?'

This abrupt and rude questioning angered Nan almost more than she would have credited if she had thought about it beforehand. 'You are neither my husband, my father nor my chaperon, Desmond. You have no right to submit me to such an inquisition. What I care to do is my concern not yours.'

'It is my concern when I have seen the fashion in which my cousin looks at you. I understand that he is a dangerous man where women are concerned. You would do well to avoid him. He cannot be after you other than to deceive you. I am informed that his marriage plans are fixed on Jane. You are supposed to be advancing her claims to him, not competing with her and putting both your reputations at risk.'

Nan rose to her feet. 'I am going to my room now. If all you can do these days, Desmond, is rebuke me for my conduct, then I would rather that you did not address me at all. It is also unkind of you to speak of your cousin as you do, when you are a guest in his home.'

'Which should be mine, if we all had our rights, as you well know.'

'No, I don't know, Desmond. Pray release me.' For as he had bitten out the last sentence at her, his face furious, he had also taken her by the arm to detain her.

'No,' he said, 'you will hear me, Nan. . .' His voice tailed off, for Brandon had returned from what Nan suspected was his purely imaginary errand, invented to track her down in the picture gallery and make love to her when Sam had gone. The cousins were a good pair, she thought disgustedly, both bent on embarrassing her in their different ways.

'Everyone happy?' queried Brandon cheerfully, as though he were slightly foxed—a ploy which didn't fool Nan, seeing that he had been stone-cold sober only a few moments ago. 'Shouldn't like to think that you had only come here to be miserable.' And his silver eyes, now shrewd and hard, were on Desmond's hand, which was still incontinently clutching Nan's arm.

Desmond let go of it, and Nan, to preserve the proprieties, for she didn't want the cousins warring over her twice in one day, bowed to them as formally as she could.

'You will both forgive me, I am sure,' she announced, 'but if I am to be happy I must retire to my room. Jane does not need me to chaperon her with so many others present, and I am not used to experiencing such excitement as I have encountered today.'

Both men followed the progress of her straight back across the room as she left it. Desmond met Brandon's eyes again, and knew without being told that his cousin's intervention had been quite deliberate. He said, his voice as harsh as Brandon's had been genial, 'You understand, I suppose, that Nan needs protecting. Her experience of life is that——'

'Of a parson's daughter,' Brandon finished for him. 'Yes, I do know, Desmond, but I thank you for reminding me of it. Now, I understand that you are quite a whist player, and my sister, being aware that the senior members of the party have had their fill of childish games, is making up some tables to please them. Your presence there would be valued.'

There was nothing for Desmond to do but go and play whist, and watch Brandon have the most disgusting good luck, while his own remained poor, as usual.

Brandon was watching Desmond, and his face was inscrutable as he did so. What had surprised him was the overwhelming desire to knock the fellow down on the spot which had come over him when he had seen Desmond bullying Nan. His own share at bullying her after a different fashion had stopped him from doing anything rash, as much as his wish to maintain the proprieties of polite life. Yes, he really was fit for Bedlam, and all since he had arrived at Gillyflower Hall!

CHAPTER SEVEN

'A BOATING party! How excessively delightful. And what ought I to wear, my dear Mrs Bligh? For one would not want to be other than exactly *comme il faut*!'

Well, thought Nan acidly, the next morning after breakfast, even if Jane was not a member of the *haut ton* she was certainly making a good fist of giving Lydia Bligh the impression that she was! Her one short season in society in Nan's company, with their father's cousin, Lady Fielding, had undoubtedly given her confidence, if not genuine polish.

'Something simple, my dear, will be all that is required from you and your sister.'

'Oh, Nan? Will you want to come too, Nan?' was Jane's reply to that, in a voice which suggested that Nan certainly wouldn't.

A slight frown crossed Lydia Bligh's face, and Nan, who had been busy deciding that a boating party on the Soar was the last event which she wished to attend, found herself saying, in as cool a voice as she could manage, 'Of course I shall wish to go, Jane. I have never been on a boating party before. "Excessively delightful" seem to me to be quite the correct words to use.'

This earned her a sharp look from Lydia Bligh. Cool though Nan had been, the touch of mockery which she had not been able to prevent herself from betraying when she had echoed Jane's fulsome tone had not escaped her hostess. I must be more careful, she thought. Splendid nullity is my line, not comments *à la* author of *Sophia*. I must save those for the book I am writing.

Jane's self-satisfaction was so great that she, at least, heard nothing amiss, although she did frown a little when Brandon strolled towards them, because it was to Nan that he spoke after bowing politely to her sister first.

'And will you enjoy a morning on the river and an alfresco picnic afterwards, Miss Fielding?'

Nan answered him as calmly as she could, aware that, as usual, the mere sight of him had set her heart beating wildly—something which she must never betray to him or to anyone else.

'I am not quite sure, Mr Tolliver. I was thinking that perhaps, after all, a quiet morning seated in one of the arbours in the garden, with the author of *Sophia* for company, might be a happy alternative.'

'Oh, no, it wouldn't,' he assured her rapidly, with as much vigour as politeness would allow him when contradicting a lady. 'I won't have you shutting yourself away. You are not yet ninety, don't own a poodle and the weather is such that a green umbrella is not obligatory. . .and——' He paused, his eyes on her merry.

'And. . .?' prompted Nan, astonished to hear that he had taken such note of what she had said to him yesterday evening—and beginning to flirt with him in consequence, much to his pleasure.

'And. . . Cinderella shall go to the ball with the other young ladies; I insist. Isn't that so, Lydia?' he called to his sister, raising his voice a little. 'Miss Fielding must not play truant this morning, must she?'

Lydia looked up sharply, as did Jane and several others present, Lydia because she had never heard that tone of voice from Brandon before, Jane and the rest astonished that an unconsidered and elderly chaperon should be engaging so much of their host's attention.

'Only if Miss Fielding felt unwell could I possibly recommend her to miss this morning's fun,' was Lydia's obliging answer. She knew that that was what Brandon wanted to hear, and wondered again what his game was with poor, downtrodden Miss Fielding. He could surely not be acting out of simple kindness—could he? Not that Brandon could not be kind, but it was rare for him to attach himself to other than the more obvious beauties in any company he was in.

'So, there it is,' Brandon announced triumphantly. 'Both your host and hostess demand your company, Miss Fielding; you cannot possibly refuse it.'

For the first time Nan became fully aware of the glares which the young women of the party were turning on her. Jealousy, the green-eyed goddess, was having a field day at Gillyflower Hall. She muttered something indistinct, which the brother and sister took as agreement, and Lydia, whose powers of management seemed to be as great as her brother's, announced that Nan would be in the leading carriage with herself, the one which Jack Coachman would be driving. Desmond would also be a passenger. Chaz would go in the gig with young Tim Alden and equally young Jack Letcombe, with Tim's tutor, Mr Figge, to keep them in order.

Jane, who already knew that she would not be travelling with Brandon because he had arranged to go on horseback, was to be George Alden's passenger in his curricle. They had been friends since childhood, and familiarity in this case had certainly bred a little contempt: Jane took his adoration of her for granted.

This decision of Lydia's to seat her with the other most eligible male catch had the effect of raising Jane's spirits at the expense of depressing those of every other young woman in the party. After all, thought Jane triumphantly, if she could not be driven by Brandon, then to partner George was certainly the next best thing! It would be very much more fun than to have to sit with Lydia Bligh and make polite conversation, so Nan had not really gained very much after all by travelling in the first carriage.

And she would be sure to call Brandon over to her when the party set off, thus ensuring that both her beaux would be dancing attendance on her at once.

Consequently, when all was decided, she retired to her room to dress herself with care, putting on her most attractive straw bonnet with the daises, and demanding to borrow Nan's only good shawl. 'For I take cold so easily, you don't, and Mrs Bligh says there might be quite a breeze on the water, so do let me have it,' she said, thus making sure that she looked as fetching as possible—at her sister's expense.

Nan handed over the lacy thing, one of her few pretty possessions, with an inward sigh, but if she wished to secure a husband for Jane as soon as possible, then some sacrifice must be made. So now she had to make do with her second-best, worn beige wool wrap about her shoulders. Her dress was second-best too, another cut down from one of her mother's, but it was rather better than her usual turn-out, being high-waisted, in cream muslin, trimmed with some rather pretty lace on the neck and sleeves. Her cap was not quite so disfiguring either; it was lighter and finer than usual, in a cream lace which matched the muslin.

Altogether she did not feel too unhappy as the party set off, with a great deal of laughter and chatter from the young people, and a great deal of decorum from their elders, including Nan. The Tollivers' big old-fashioned coach in the rear carried the servants and the food which the party would require after an arduous morning spent amusing themselves on the water.

Once or twice on the ride to Highborough Brandon

pulled level with their carriage to converse with them, and Desmond unbent enough to point out the landmarks of the country round about, which was now Brandon's adopted land, or so he said.

The boatyard where small pleasure- or rowing-boats could be hired was on the edge of Highborough, just where a rash of white-fronted villas had recently sprung up, built by the newly rich manufacturers who were spending their profits from the mechanical looms. A group of sturdy men stood about hoping that the gentry might choose to hire them, rather than take on the burden of rowing themselves. They had been alerted beforehand, by a messenger from Gillyflower Hall, that the Tollivers' party would be arriving that morning, and Brandon decided on seeing them that everyone's pleasure would be enhanced if the local oarsmen were used.

He was also keenly aware, having been poor himself, that, given the poverty of the area, his money would be highly welcome to men whose own source of livelihood had disappeared.

One of the men approached him and offered his barge as a source of transport for 'my lord', as he insisted on calling Brandon, and some of his party.

It and his horse were ready, he said, and perhaps, if 'my lord' didn't want to hire him for his own use, then his servants could be taken on board, along with the party's food and drink. The carriages and horses were to be left behind at some stables near by.

Nan was delighted by the whole business. The freshness of the sunny day, the breeze arising from the river, the smiling faces of the boatmen who were only too pleased to oblige 'my lord', and the cheerfully competent fashion with which Lydia and Brandon organised their pleasure, entranced her beyond words.

One sturdy youth handed her into a rowing-boat in

which Desmond and Lydia already sat; another took up the oars. Brandon, who had decided that he must stop being '*most* particular' to Nan—in public, that was, in private being another matter—had put himself in a boat with Jane and George Alden. Consequently Jane was on her highest ropes of pleasure, with George looking daggers at 'that old man', as he privately called thirty-five-year-old Brandon.

Brandon, for his part, was alternately amused and appalled by his own duplicity, for he found himself looking ahead for a glimpse of Nan even while he was engaged in flattering Jane and annoying George.

Sleepy cows stared at the noisy throng as they were rowed downstream towards the Trent into Leicestershire. Rails, ducks, geese and swans sailed around them, the swans stately and the ducks busy. Nan trailed her hand in the water, wishing that she had a parasol with her—one like Lydia's, a confection of pink and white lace—to shield her complexion. I shall be a milkmaid's brown on top of everything else about me that is unfashionable, she thought ruefully, but oh, what a dream of a day!

The terrain through which the river meandered had grown increasingly wild and woody, and was a place where it seemed that no man had set foot, since it was uncultivated, with natural stands of trees and tall hedges everywhere. Unimproved by Capability Brown and his followers it might be, but it had the beauty of the natural, and so Nan told Lydia and Desmond. 'One might imagine fairies and elves treading among the undergrowth, and Oberon and Titania waiting to greet us when we reach journey's end.'

Desmond stared at her. How unlike practical Nan to be so romantic and poetic, his expression said, but Lydia Bligh, who was beginning to find the eldest Fielding daughter both intelligent and witty behind her façade of dull modesty, murmured appreciatively, 'What a charming thought. And Bottom, will he be there, Miss Fielding, or shall we find the Duke and his bride?'

This further reference to *A Midsummer Night's Dream* passed over Desmond's head, he being more used to reading books on political economy than poetry, but Nan smiled at it, and continued the game she had started.

'Or shall we,' she went on gaily, 'if we stay here until night falls, come across the lovers and help them to untangle themselves before Puck can confuse them by his tricks?'

She was aware that she was giving herself away a little to all her hearers, and when Lydia laughed appreciatively at what she had said she coloured a little, and decided to be silent in future. She had an important secret to keep, and to betray her own flights of fancy too often might be to reap a harvest she did not want! It was of all things necessary that the author of *Sophia* remain anonymous.

Anonymity, therefore, must be her own refuge. She fell silent, and remained so until the party reached its destination, whereupon she forsook the boats and the barge to watch the swans from the safety of the bank. Desmond, again by his expression, obviously preferred the dull, silent Nan to the witty, talkative one, which almost had her talking again, but wisdom kept her dumb.

Jane was not dumb. Her charming voice could be heard as she tried to hold both her admirers' attention at once. Eating the splendid cold collation, which was set out on damask tablecloths spread out on the grass, with bottles of white wine and lemonade tied with cords to nearby bushes, swinging gently in the river water to keep them cool until the party was ready to drink from them, she managed by some art to have half the men, both young and old, hanging on every light word she uttered.

And very light they were, thought Nan grimly. She sat between Sam Stone and Desmond, both of whom, in their different ways, tried to entertain her. But, alas, nothing could keep her thoughts away from Brandon.

He was as splendid as ever in his fashionable turn-out, which was absolutely all that it should be for a boating party in summer. He was wearing light nankeen breeches, light boots, a tan-coloured jacket of the finest wool with brass buttons, a cream-coloured shirt, to match the breeches, presumably, and a cravat which was just short of extravagant, as befitted a day in the country. He was, Nan decided savagely, much prettier than she was.

He certainly made all the other men, even the younger ones, look dull by comparison. His conversation sparkled too. He was telling Jane, Caroline and Charlotte of a visit he had paid to Macao, years ago, when he had been only a lad and had worked before the mast. Listening to it, punctuated by the girls' ready laughter, Nan suddenly became aware that he was cheating. He was embroidering a story from a book of Eastern fairy-tales which she had read long ago, and pretending that the adventure had happened to him.

'And the Sultan,' squealed Jane, entranced. 'Did he really promise you any bride you wanted because you had brought him the golden cup which he had coveted? Whatever did you say to that?'

'Oh——' Brandon was equal to anything '—that I had a bride at home, and that my religion did not allow me more than one. To which his answer was that that seemed to him to be a poor sort of religion, and that I ought to convert at once to his and have as many as I pleased, as soon as possible. He would personally arrange it for me. . .' He paused tantalisingly.

'And what did you say then?' asked Caroline Letcombe, her eyes as large as saucers.

'Only that it was as impossible for me to break my vow to be faithful to my one wife as it was for him to break his vow not to be faithful to any of his many wives.'

Nan, who had been trying hard not to listen, and to keep her face impassive, broke down as this ingenious and lying tale reached its witty and untruthful ending, and began to laugh helplessly. Desmond hissed angrily in her left ear, 'I am disappointed at you, Nan, that you are amused by such a flibbertigibbet as my cousin is proving to be. One wonders how he ever made a fortune. He seems formed only to keep silly young girls entertained.'

Having no answer to make to that which would please Desmond, Nan said nothing. Sam whispered in her right ear, 'For my part I find Mr Tolliver's efforts to keep his younger guests entertained quite charming. He appears to have an imagination to match your own.'

There was no answer that she could make to that either. Brandon, his tales over, rose from where he had been sitting and made his way to his sister's group, just as the footmen arrived with glasses of white wine and lemonade. Offered a choice, Nan for once accepted the wine, only to meet Desmond's disapproving eye again.

It must have attracted Brandon's notice, for he sat down on a tree stump near by to stretch his long legs and remark, 'So happy to see that you are enjoying yourself, Miss Fielding. You are, I hope, pleased that you obeyed my orders and joined our little jaunt?'

'We are all enjoying ourselves,' remarked Lydia a trifle severely. She was again put out by Brandon's making such a dead set at Nan. He had spent the morning behaving himself, but perhaps it had been too much to expect that he would go on doing so once the afternoon had arrived.

'I was about to propose,' she went on, 'that after we have recovered from our meal we should take a short walk into the country. The young man who rowed our boat here——' she waved a hand at him where he sat enjoying his luncheon with the servants who had begun to eat theirs '—tells me that there is a very pretty little green lane behind us, which in spring is edged with bluebells. It is shady, so we may be out of the heat of the afternoon sun.'

'Whatever you wish, my love,' smiled Brandon lazily. 'Were the ground a little more open, I would have suggested that we might bring along a cricket bat and ball, and enjoy ourselves with them, but I was informed that there was very little flat land round here. On the other hand, what could be better than to enjoy a country walk after a country meal and a country row downstream?'

And so it was arranged. The party lay back, dozed and prosed—even Jane and her friends eventually fell silent—until Brandon decided that they had all been sedate for long enough, and mustered everyone for the walk except Lord and Lady Alden and Sir Avery and his wife, who cried off for their various reasons. The two women preferred to sketch; they had brought their books and crayons along with them. The two men preferred to stay behind to drink Brandon's good wine, although that was not the reason they gave for doing so.

The lane and the views from it were pronounced as charming as the young boatman had said. Chaz and the other boys ran on ahead, Mr Figge panting after them—*they* were not interested in views, pretty or otherwise. Nan, walking along between Sam and Desmond, who seemed to be having a silent struggle as to which of

them was her cavalier, found their combined presence
oppressive, until Lydia Bligh removed Sam, asking him
very prettily to be her escort. 'For,' she told him, 'I
need a strong arm to help me over the stiles, and Miss
Fielding does not need two!'

The real reason was that encouraging Desmond to
pursue Nan might result in his winning her for his wife,
which would neatly remove her from Brandon's orbit.
Much though Lydia liked Nan, Brandon had begun by
favouring Jane, was still doing so, and Jane must
therefore properly be considered to be the young
woman he ought ultimately to propose to. If he would
not behave himself, then she must arrange matters so
that he did.

Jane, unaware that Nan was any sort of threat, was
unwisely provoking Brandon by encouraging George.
That, she hoped, might bring him to a firm decision to
make Jane Fielding his wife. Caroline and Charlotte,
her two best friends, had not given up hope of securing
Brandon for themselves. Like Jane, neither of them
saw Nan as any sort of threat. George Alden was
pursuing Jane in the hope that she would come to her
senses and realise that Brandon was far too old and
passé for her.

Nan was trying to hide from herself the fact that she
was strongly attracted to Brandon to the degree that
she could not stop thinking about him. Brandon was
equally drawn to Nan, and to his horror was finding
more and more that merely seeing her roused him,
whereas Jane, while superficially even more desirable,
created no such urgency in him.

Desmond and Sam were at last aware that they were
rivals. In his head, Desmond was composing reproaches
to Nan along the lines of, You surely are not serious
about accepting that jumped-up attorney's attentions,
Nan? He is old enough to be your grandfather!

Sam for his part, was thinking, It is devoutly to be hoped that Nan does not favour this sour puritan of a man who would make her life a misery if she were ever to marry him. He would never forgive her for being the author of *Sophia*, let alone consent to allow her to go on writing her novels if she were his wife.

All this seething emotion was, of course, neatly hidden under the good manners of the party. Only Chaz, Tim and Jack were free to express their high spirits, along with their desire to find a suitable place to fly Chaz's kite which he had thoughtfully brought along with him.

Mr Figge was not sharing in their joy. He had not thought, when he had been an undergraduate at Oxford, that life would condemn him to shepherding small boys, trying to teach them Latin grammar and escorting them around the countryside. Earlier he had enjoyed an all too brief conversation with Chaz's elder sister, the commonsensical Miss Nan Fielding, so he too was sharing in the general gloom, but was hiding it as successfully as everyone else.

What made matters worse was that it was as though they really were walking through Arcadia, that happy rural country where everything grew in abundance without anyone having to do any work. The only member of the party besides Brandon who knew that this was an illusion was Nan—but she, like him, was not sharing her knowledge with anyone.

Unaware that the sunny afternoon might hold unexpected perils for them, the little party walked on. It gradually straggled over some distance, with Lydia, Desmond, Sam and Nan at the front, and the others strung out behind them. Lydia was about to call a halt, judging that they had gone far enough, when her little group reached a small clearing where Mr Figge and the boys were waiting for them.

At the far end of the clearing was a kind of tent made from a grey blanket draped over several poles of wood. In front of it were the remains of a fire. Above it a rusted iron cauldron hung from a tripod made from tree branches. Before the tent stood a woman, at the sight of whom the bright afternoon and their idle pleasure was dimmed.

The woman was filthy. She was a caricature of a woman, her face hollow, her body gaunt. She cradled a dirty baby in her arms, and the sour smell of poverty hung about them both. She held the baby towards Lydia and said one word, which at first was not understandable, but which Nan suddenly interpreted as 'Mercy'.

Shocked, no one moved or spoke. The woman cried out again, this time moving towards Lydia, who said faintly, 'Poor creature, what are you doing here?'

Desmond, pushing Nan, Chaz and the boys behind him, exclaimed harshly, 'Away with you, woman! Begging is an offence, as well you know, and squatting too,' for he had correctly interpreted what the presence of the makeshift dwelling meant. To squat on land for more than a certain length of time gave you certain rights over it, much to the annoyance of more orthodox landowners.

The woman cowered away from him. Lydia, more sympathetic to her misery than Desmond, repeated gently, but almost reproachfully, 'What are you doing here, so far away from any village? You should have applied to the parish for help.'

It was not that Lydia meant to be unkind but the comfortable life which she had lived for so long had sheltered her from such sights. She received no answer, the woman merely letting loose another harsh cry, so that Nan, who had originally been shocked into silence and immobility, gave way to her own deepest feelings at the sight of the woman and her neglected child. More, of all of them, she alone could see that the woman was near to collapse, so that she was not surprised when her eyes rolled upwards and she fell slowly to the ground.

It was now Nan's turn to exclaim, to push by Desmond, to run forward and bend down to rescue the baby, who had rolled away from its mother to lie among the rough grasses and weeds by the side of the lane.

Nan picked it up. It appeared to be under six months old, was unhurt, and had set up a feeble wailing. She clutched it to her bosom to comfort it. Desmond, with a look of disgust on his face, joined Lydia in bending down to examine its mother cursorily.

He straightened up, to say, 'She has only fainted; she appears to be still alive,' almost as though he regretted the fact. Lydia gave a little exclamation at the harshness of Desmond's words and, sitting down on the ground, cradled the woman's filthy head on her knee.

Nan, while cuddling the baby, had grown aware of how cold it was; its pinched features were blue despite the warmth of the day. She thrust it at Sam, saying, 'Here, hold it for me a moment, please.' The baby's crying grew louder still as Sam took it clumsily from her, which allowed her to strip the shawl from her shoulders, before reclaiming the child in order to wrap the shawl closely about its shrivelled little body.

'Oh, really, Nan!' exclaimed Desmond, unmoved by the tender way in which she was hugging the baby to her, and the entranced expression on her face, which was holding Sam in thrall. 'Whatever do you think that you are doing? For all you know it is suffering from some foul disease. Put it down.'

'If hunger is a foul disease,' retorted Nan, 'then that is what is wrong with it, and I shall certainly not put it down until its mother has recovered and we have found

some means of feeding it.' For the baby had seized the
forefinger with which she had been stroking its cheek
and had begun to suck it vigorously, until a wailing cry
announced that it had found no sustenance there.

No one thought fit to answer her. Lydia had managed
to get the woman, who had regained consciousness, to
sit up, and just as Desmond began to expostulate with
Nan again Brandon and the rest of his party, who had
been dawdling and picking wild flowers on the way,
arrived in the clearing. He took in the situation at a
glance and said in his pleasant voice, 'Squatters?' And
then, 'Deserted by the husband?'

But talk was not all he did. He joined his sister in
examining and questioning the woman. They spoke in
low tones together for a moment, then both stood up,
Brandon announcing, 'It seems that her husband, who
was a weaver, turned away because of the new
machines, has either deserted her or is lost, or injured,
for he has been gone for several days, and she has no
food left, and she fears that the child is dying.'

'But that,' Desmond remarked stiffly, 'does not mean
that Nan needs to risk contagion by nursing it, as I
hope that you will tell her, cousin.'

Before Brandon could reply, Chaz forestalled Sam
Stone, who was about to protest at Desmond's discour-
tesy to the woman he loved and respected, by crying
firmly, with a baleful glare at Desmond, 'Hoorah for
Nan, I say. The Bible tells us, or so my papa says, that
the Good Samaritan should not pass by on the other
side, and Nan is the best Good Samaritan I know. Why,
she even found my kite when no one else would trouble
themselves to look for it. If she's not allowed to hold
the baby, then I will. Although I don't like babies
much,' he finished glumly.

This brave declaration lightened the mood of the
party wonderfully, the only member of it who remained

unhappy besides Desmond being Jane, who muttered audibly to Caroline, 'I must say I wonder at Nan for wanting to hold anything quite so dirty.'

Giving her a sharp look, Brandon strode across the clearing to Nan, saying, 'My dear Miss Fielding, you will allow me to take the baby from you for a moment.' When she began to protest at losing it, he added, with his most dazzling smile, 'You may have it back, I promise you.'

He held the baby as carefully as she had been doing before fulfilling his promise and handing it back to Nan. 'Nothing seems to be wrong with it but hunger, I dare say,' he offered in his usual cheerful manner. 'No need for us to wrangle. I suggest, Mr Figge, that you return to the river with the boys and ask two of the footmen to make an impromptu stretcher, and bring it here so that Mrs Blagg and her baby may be carried back to the barge and thence to Gillyflower Hall. She tells me that she is a sempstress, and I am sure we can always find room for another at the Hall.'

Desmond's answer to this was, 'Your kind heart does your credit, cousin,' said after a fashion which suggested that it didn't. Then he added, 'But such indiscriminate charity will mean that you will find yourself at the mercy of every bold beggar in the district.'

'No, indeed.' Brandon's tone was equable. 'I have no intention of housing or caring for every beggar in the district, only this one poor woman and her child whom we have come across today.'

Chaz, who had been about to leave with Mr Figge, said approvingly, 'Nan is not the only Good Samaritan, then, Mr Tolliver. Neither of you passes by on the other side.'

Brandon answered him a little wryly. 'I think you flatter me, Chaz. But yes, on this occasion I cannot let my sister and yours be the only ones to offer succour to the needy.' He cast a glance at Nan as he spoke. Something in her transfigured face as she held the poor starving baby to her touched him so deeply that he was compelled to turn away from her. In doing so he found Sam Stone's eye on him, and knew that he had in some sort betrayed what he was beginning to feel for Nan Fielding.

But what *do* I feel for her? he asked himself as they all walked soberly back to the river. Such a strange mixture of compassion, friendship, admiration and lust. Whatever can it be? He dared not admit to himself that it might be love, for had he not decided that that emotion did not figure in his calculations as to his marriage and his future life? He was not even sure that he thought that it existed outside the haverings of poets and inside the covers of Minerva Press novels.

CHAPTER EIGHT

SECURE in the knowledge that poor starving Mrs Blagg had been fed, put to bed in the servants' quarters at Gillyflower Hall, and that a temporary wet nurse had been found for the baby by Lydia in the shape of the butler's wife, whose own baby was in the process of being weaned, Nan felt able to attend the ball that night.

Not only the guests at Gillyflower Hall were to be present, but also many from Highborough, and a few of the villages round about. The night was serene, the moon was high, the musicians from Leicester, who had arrived while they were on the river, were gifted, and the ballroom had been decorated to perfection with flowers from the gardens under Lydia and the head gardener's supervision.

Nan made her way downstairs some time after Jane had burst into her room and demanded to accompany Caroline and Charlotte, who were both being chaperoned by Caroline's elderly aunt. 'You surely do not need to stand guard over me all the time,' had been her ungracious comment. Nan had not argued with her. She was feeling a strange sort of satisfaction after having persuaded Brandon and Lydia to allow her to carry the baby all the way back to Gillyflower Hall—much to Desmond and Jane's disgust.

There had been one untoward incident on the way home which had frightened Nan more than it should—for what was Mr Brandon Tolliver to her, other than someone who was occasionally briefly kind? After their first passionate interchanges, that was. Brandon's horse, Nero, had been brought round to him when they were all assembled in the carriages again. Mrs Blagg had been put in the servants' coach, a little to their disgust, she being so very dirty.

Brandon mounted with his usual athletic ease. He was one of the few men Nan knew who did not possess the beginnings of a paunch through over-eating and indulgence in strong drink. Even Desmond, she had noticed, had begun to put on weight. The sight of Brandon on horseback was almost enough to make her forget her joy in having a real live baby to herself for a few moments, or rather the joy changed and centred on Brandon and his attractive presence. . .but her pleasure in his athleticism was not to last long.

A dog belonging to one of the boatmen ran out and frightened Nero. He gave a snorting plunge and for a moment Brandon fought to control him. He had just done so when one of the girths snapped—and Brandon was then fighting desperately to stay on board Nero and not to be thrown. A battle he was doomed to lose. He was thrown headlong, to land face down on the ground, and, for one heart-stopping moment, to lie quite still.

Heart-stopping for Nan, that was. One moment she was secretly drinking in the sight of him mastering Nero with such power and grace, and the next moment he was—what and where was he? Only the baby in her arms, she realised afterwards, had stopped her from disgracing herself by leaping from the carriage and going to his assistance. All the other women began to wail and exclaim while George Alden, who had been about to take his seat in his curricle, ran over to where Brandon lay and was the first to reach him and examine him to find out what damage had been done.

Fortunately not much. For Brandon was already stirring by the time that George bent over him, and George helped him to sit up.

'How goes it, old fellow? No bones broken, I hope,' he enquired anxiously.

'I don't think so,' muttered Brandon. He was both shaken and winded, aware that he had been fortunate in not pitching on his head. 'I shall be A1 at Lloyd's in a minute, I hope.' And he put his head down as a wave of faintness swept over him.

Meantime one of the attendant grooms had caught Nero and was inspecting his saddle, which had slipped sideways.

'His girth snapped, sir,' he announced, running over to where George and now Desmond were helping Brandon to his feet.

'Best not ride back,' George told him. 'There's room in one of the carriages, I'm sure.'

Brandon wanted to say no, but common sense prevailed. He allowed himself to be walked over to the Letcombe's carriage and take his place with them. There was a great bruise starting up on one side of his face, his fine coat was covered in grass and his breathing was still disturbed.

From where she sat Nan gazed at him, agonised, unaware of what her eyes were telling poor Sam, who, having had Brandon's inner feelings revealed to him, was now witnessing Nan's. He knew at once that she had not accepted him because her heart was given to the charming rogue which he suspected Brandon to be. No one who had made such a great fortune at such a relatively early age could, Sam was sure, be other than hard and devious beneath all the surface attraction.

But Brandon was a strong man, and Nan was a strong woman. Sam was old and wise enough to know that like called to like. Whether like would get like was quite another matter. The odds were that Brandon would marry for reasons of prudence, or of prestige, and neither would lead him to lay his heart or his name at Nan's feet. What was important was that Nan should not be hurt.

His admiration for her grew as she kept her composure while Brandon lay back against the cushions of the Letcombes' carriage and slowly regained his senses. After a few moments he had recovered enough to assure his travelling companions that he had suffered no permanent damage.

'Which was just as well,' he told Lydia cheerfully, when they were safely back at the Hall. 'Just think of the brouhaha it would have caused if you had been compelled to cancel everything tonight if I *had* broken my neck and was laid out in state in the big drawing-room ready for the undertakers!'

Lydia shuddered. 'Never say so, my dear. Even to think of it. . .' And she shuddered again. 'You are sure that you will be able to attend the ball tonight?'

'Quite sure,' he told her. He had, she was pleased to note, regained his normal cheerful manner. 'Oh, I'm bruised, but nothing fatal, thank God.'

'You should reprimand the grooms.' Lydia was energetic. 'Quite wrong of them to allow you to start out with a frayed girth.'

'Oh, yes.' He seemed a trifle abstracted, she thought, which was perhaps not surprising in the circumstances. He did not tell her that he had gone round to the stables shortly after his return to the Hall and had asked to examine the broken girth.

Ned, the head groom, had looked steadily at him and said gravely, 'I thought that you might ask that, maister,' and had taken Brandon over to where the saddle lay on some staging at the back of the stables.

He had said nothing more, but stood back while Brandon examined the girth. His expression had remained impassive until Brandon had stared him straight in the eye and said, 'Now, Ned, do you see what I think I see?'

Ned had pursed his lips. 'I did think as how I might be mistaken, but I see that I am not. . . I think. . .' He had paused, not wishing to say the unsayable.

'That the girth was three-parts cut through, quite neatly, so that it was only a matter of time before it parted and I was thrown,' Brandon had finished for him.

'Aye. But who would do such a thing and why? You might have been killed. I do know that there was nothing wrong with the saddle when I put it out. I always check the girths, and have taught all the lads to do the same. Sim swears that it was whole when he saddled Nero, and I do not think that he was lying.'

Brandon had thought a moment. He didn't think that either Ned or Sim was lying, and said so. 'Which leaves us with this. That the girth was cut deliberately while it was at the stables by the Soar, during the time we went upriver.'

'Aye, maister—but who would do such a thing?'

'Who indeed? Malcontents, Luddites, Jacobins angry at all gentlefolk and landowners—happy to see one pitch on his head and not get up again.'

He had not added that he was not quite satisfied with this as an explanation, even though Ned was nodding his head in agreement. After all, this was the second time since he had arrived at Gillyflower Hall that an odd accident had happened to him. He was thinking of the shot which had so narrowly missed him. More prudent, perhaps, not to dwell too much on them. Coincidence might be at work, but for some reason Brandon's intuition, which had helped to make him a fortune, told him that there was more to his run of misfortunes than that. Meantime he must watch his back.

He was not watching his back when he stood among his guests at the ball. He didn't think that here, among his own people, coincidence would strike again. Above his head, on the painted ceiling, Jove rode in the clouds, a thunderbolt clutched in his right fist, to remind mortals that one might plan one's life, but one could not command life to follow the plan.

Apparently Mr Brandon Tolliver could not even command that Miss Nan Fielding would be present at a ball in his own mansion. He took a rapid look around the big room to see that Jane was the centre of a circle of playful young men and women, and that most of the house party were present as well as those guests who had come from Highborough and round about to take part in the ball.

But no Miss Fielding. He turned to Lydia and said, as apparently aimlessly as he could, 'I don't see Miss Fielding among the chaperons, Lydia. Is she unwell, do you think? She seemed cheerful enough on the way home when she was holding Mrs Blagg's baby.'

How like Brandon to remember Mrs Blagg's name, and how unlike him to trouble over Nan Fielding.

'She seemed well enough when we returned home, Brandon. Perhaps she is feeling a little tired and is resting in her room. Why do you ask?'

'Oh,' he offered, as vaguely as he could, 'the poor woman seems to have a dull time of it. She is not so very much older than Jane and the rest, but seems doomed to sit on the back row of life among women who are old enough to be her mother or her grandmother.'

'But she does have to act as Jane's mother, as you will allow, seeing that her true mother is a permanent invalid.' Lydia paused, then, against her better judgement, pursued the matter.

'Why are you troubling yourself about her, Brandon?

She is hardly the sort of person in whom you normally take an interest. You have already caused a little comment by publicly arguing with your cousin Desmond over her. I have also had occasion to remind you not to make servant girls unhappy by your attentions. How much more distressing it would be if you gave the poor woman incorrent notions about your intentions towards her.'

'I have no intentions towards her!' he exclaimed, a trifle stiffly. 'But she is a guest here, and I would like her to be happy. Perhaps you could send a footman to ask if she is quite well, if she needs anything.'

Lydia's expression of astonishment grew. 'Well, really, Brandon. . .' And then, 'No need to trouble yourself. I see that she has just entered the room and is talking to Lady Letcombe. There! I hope that sets your mind at rest.'

'Only trying to be a good host, Lydia. If I ask her for a dance, you will not think that I am about to seduce her, I trust.'

'No,' Lydia shot back. 'Only that I find you unfathomable. You will be losing Jane to young George Alden. He might not have your fortune, but he will inherit his father's title one day, and he is nearer to her in age than you are.'

Brandon muttered something under his breath which fortunately Lydia did not hear, and bowed to Lady Letcombe who, with Nan in her wake, was crossing the room. Nan, he noticed, as did his sister and Sam Stone, to say nothing of Desmond, was looking more *comme il faut* than she had previously done at Gillyflower Hall. Her duenna's cap was not quite so extinguishing as usual, and her dress of cream silk, although more suited to a dowager, enhanced her complexion rather than diminished it as most of her other clothes did.

They all bowed to one another. Formality was more

treasured in the country than the town, Brandon was discovering. Lady Letcombe monopolised Lydia, to leave Nan and Brandon together, much to Lydia's annoyance.

Nan tried not to let Brandon dazzle her overmuch with his splendour. Evening black became him so well. The touch of silver in his black hair, his broad shoulders, narrow waist and long legs were all enhanced by the fashionable clothing which fitted him so snugly. As usual his cravat was a valet's dream of heaven, and tonight he wore round his neck a quizzing-glass which depended from a black cord. He lifted it to examine her, remarking coolly, Lydia's reprimand still sounding in his ears, 'You look well tonight, Miss Fielding. That colour becomes you.'

Well, he could hardly praise anything else about my turn-out, was Nan's irreverent thought, but nevertheless her cheeks glowed with pleasure at the small compliment, and when he finished by saying, 'And you will take a turn on the floor with me, I hope. I promise to behave myself tonight,' she felt almost dizzy with delight.

The smile she gave him transformed her face. So much so that Brandon decided at once that he ought to provoke it more often.

'Lydia told me that the next dance is a waltz. Will you waltz with me, Miss Fielding?'

And he put out his strong and shapely hand, so that for good manners' sake Nan was compelled to take it, saying breathlessly, 'But I have never waltzed in public before.'

He held on to her hand to lead her on to the floor almost against her will. 'And if not in public when did you waltz, Miss Fielding? You intrigue me.'

'Oh,' she told him, aware that many eyes were on them, including Jane's furious ones. 'When I taught my sisters in the Rectory parlour before they had their season in town. But I always took the man's part—so I fear that if you insist on dancing with me you may find that I will lead rather than follow.'

To her secret delight Brandon gave her his dazzling smile, the smile which made the silver eyes crinkle, which affected his whole face and was no mere slight movement of his lips. 'Oh, now you intrigue me even further—to have a lady who leads! But,' he could not resist adding, 'I think that you have led twice in our encounters already.'

Nan's blush was all-enveloping. For some reason being reminded in such a public place as a ballroom floor of what had passed between them in the pantry and in the woods seemed tremendously exciting, almost wicked. Before she could make any reply—and what reply could she make?—the music had started, she was in Brandon's arms and was being whirled around the floor.

And she was certainly not leading. Brandon was most definitely doing that, and she could think of nothing more delightful. She knew now why Lord Byron, of all people, had condemned the waltz for being immoral, for surely it must be immoral for her to be feeling such extraordinary pleasure in Brandon's arms. She was tall enough for him to need to bend his head only a little to look into her eyes, and when he did so the strange dissolving feeling which being with him in the pantry and the woods had caused was upon her again.

It lightened her footsteps, as well as her heart, so that Brandon felt that never before had he waltzed with a partner who seemed almost to be his other self, so exquisitely did she follow him and the music. Lead, indeed! No, far from that, she was following him perfectly, and the delicate scent of lavender, mixed with warm and living Nan, which rose from her was strong in his nostrils, and was seduction itself. Lydia was quite wrong. He was not seducing Nan. She was seducing him, merely by being her own sweetly modest self.

And this is heaven, and I am in it, and I wish the music would go on forever, was Nan's thought. It will come to an end all too soon, but I shall have this memory to take away from Gillyflower Hall, to hold to me in the endless dark winter nights. Not since the long-ago days when Randal and I roamed the woods together in Hampshire have I felt such pleasure.

She was unaware of the many jealous and critical eyes on her; among them, Desmond's and Jane's were hard and angry, Lydia's and Sam's rueful. I might as well have saved my breath, was Lydia's reaction. What can he be thinking of? For I know him too well; he can't be serious. Her eyes met Sam's and they exchanged a wordless message. How do we save her from misery and disillusionment?

It was over. The dancers and the spectators were all clapping. Brandon was bowing to Nan, and she was bowing back. He took her hand to lead her off the floor, saying into her ear, 'You need no lessons on following, Miss Fielding. You could give lessons yourself, so sweetly do you obey your partner's lightest touch.'

'You are pleased to say so, Mr Tolliver.'

'No.' They had reached the edge of the floor. Brandon turned towards her, having released her hand. 'No, Brandon, I beg of you. We are friends at last, I hope. And in return I may call you Nan. Or would you prefer Anne?'

Anne was the name which Randal had known her by, and it was sacred to him. It told of a past time when she had been young, happy and hopeful.

'So long as you promise to continue to behave

yourself, then you shall be Brandon, and in return I must be Nan. That is my name in Broomhall.'

If Brandon thought this answer a trifle odd he did not say so. He lifted her hand and kissed it. 'Now enjoy yourself, Nan. I think that Mr Stone is waiting for you, and I must play the part of mine host until the tower clock tells me that the dance is over.'

Yes, but her pleasure had ended with the music. He was leading her to a chair, not at the back, but next to Sam, who was looking at her with his kind eyes. Nan felt that she was floating on air. Sam thought that Nan looked transfigured—which was perhaps only a different way of saying the same thing.

'You are enjoying yourself?' he asked her.

Her reply, she thought later, was fit for Jane. 'Oh, famously!' she began enthusiastically, before catching herself and slowing down into normal staid Miss Fielding again. 'And I thought I would not, this afternoon. But Brandon—Mr Tolliver—sent word to me by a footman that the poor woman we rescued is sleeping and the baby has been fed and is sleeping too.'

Sam made appropriate noises, even though his heart was heavy. Like Lydia, he thought that Mr Brandon Tolliver was being a mere heartless seducer, who, even if he did not intend to ruin Nan, would at least make her very unhappy by causing her to entertain false hopes.

A quadrille followed, and Sam duly led her on to the floor, just cutting out Desmond who had been slow to cross the room to them. Desmond, however, made quite sure that he was all present and correct, as the saying had it, when her dance with Sam was over, in order to ask Nan to partner him in the country dance which followed.

While they were waiting for the music to begin he asked her if she would take a turn with him in the adjoining drawing-room, 'Where,' he announced, 'it is cooler and not so oppressive.'

By his expression he was about to read the Riot Act to her again, and so it proved when they finally found themselves in the big empty room with no one to interrupt them. Nan made a straight line for a wall of coloured prints by Gillray and Rowlandson satirising the follies and foibles of society. But Desmond was not to be diverted by such simple means.

'I wonder at you, Anne,' he began again, so that Nan irreverently pondered on whether or not to suggest to him that some slight variant on this mode of address to her might be no bad thing if he wished her to take him seriously.

'What have I done this time?' she asked him patiently as he paused to make the seriousness of what he was saying apparent to her.

'You must know, being so *au fait* with what should and should not be done by unmarried laides, that you ought not to have waltzed with such a philanderer as I have already informed you that my cousin is reputed to be. What kind of example, one wonders, do you think that you are setting poor young Jane? It is not surprising that the freedom with which she speaks and acts is already being commented on. I feel that my duty to you and to your family demands that I make you a formal offer of marriage so that I may be able to protect you both from those who would exploit and deceive you.'

For a moment Nan hardly knew what to think, let alone what to say.

'Am I,' she asked him, quite dazed, 'to infer from what you have just said that you are proposing marriage to me, Desmond? And after such a strange fashion, too.'

His expression was so wounded when this came out that it was almost comical.

'My dear Anne, I thought that I had made myself sufficiently plain. I fail to see how anything which I have just said could conceivably be construed as "strange" in any way.' And the inverted commas around 'strange' were heavy in his voice.

'Oh!' exclaimed Nan, almost ready to stamp her foot at him. 'Do you never listen to what you say to me, Desmond? You cast doubts on my judgement, on my chastity, on Jane's behaviour, which differs not at all from that of any other high-spirited young girl, and then you offer to marry me—not because you love or care for me, but because you wish to act as a kind of moral arbiter to me and my family. The only person you left out of the equation was Chaz. Do you propose to be his guide, philosopher and friend as well?'

'I thought, after all the years which we have known one another, my dear Anne, that you could take the love and the care for granted. And of course I should be willing to assist *Charles*——' and he trod heavily on the formal name '—to learn to moderate his present rash behaviour, although that task ought properly to be left to his father. I do grasp, however, that your father is so spiritually inclined that the assistance of someone who is a trifle more knowledgeable about worldly affairs——'

As this pompous sermon showed no signs of drawing to a close, Nan could not contain herself. 'Pray stop,' she exploded. 'Just because Chaz does not greatly care for you is no reason for you to go on so, and as for poor Papa. . .'

At this point she ran down, partly because she realised that were she to continue she would say something unforgivable, and partly because she suddenly understood that Desmond was so armoured in righteousness that nothing she could say would make any impression on the carapace of certitude in his own judgement which he carried around with him.

'I thought,' she resumed lamely, before he could begin on another lecture to her, 'that you had decided that you were not rich enough to afford a wife and so were unable to propose to me.'

This statement, Nan immediately realised, was an unfortunate one. It merely served to start him off once more on another self-serving diatribe.

'I conceive it to be my duty——' he began grandly, so that Nan interrupted him again, first putting her hands over her ears.

'No, Desmond, please stop. If I hear the word duty again I think I shall scream. It is only fair to tell you that despite the great honour you have done me in asking me, with all my imperfections on my head, to marry you, I must refuse your kind offer. Do not ask me again, I beg of you, for my answer will always remain the same.'

She saw the thunderstruck expression on his face. 'My dear girl,' he said heavily, 'I do not understand you. Are you sure that that is the answer which you wish to give me? I had always assumed that were I to offer marriage to you you would be only too happy to accept me. After all, you are getting on in years, are not likely to marry unless you do accept me, and this is your last chance to achieve an establishment of your own. Common sense alone would dictate. . .'

'No!' Nan almost screamed at him. 'Pray do not speak to me of common sense at all. I am sick of exercising common sense. Please leave me. You have your answer. I wish to remain your friend, Desmond. . . I want to be alone. Please!'

Whether it was the frantic way in which she spoke, or whether he finally understood that she meant her refusal, Nan was never to know. He dithered for a moment, opening and shutting his mouth like an agitated goldfish trapped in a bowl, before he finally grumbled at her, 'Oh, very well, but I warn you, I shall not ask you again. So if this is mere girlish megrims. . .'

The face that Nan rewarded him with after this unkind remark had him muttering again, 'Oh, very well. . .' before he turned and left the room.

Nan had scarcely drawn a thankful breath at his going when he opened the door again to fire his final arrow at her. 'And if you think that my unprincipled cousin will propose to you, Anne, you are very much mistaken. He will want someone young and pretty with a good dowry. I doubt that even Jane will satisfy him.'

He closed the door. Nan flung a cushion from the sofa at him as he opened it again—to fire another broadside at her, presumably.

But instead the cushion hit Brandon amidships as he came in.

'Now what have I done?' he asked her, pulling a comical face as he neatly fielded it, and tossed it on to a nearby armchair.

Nan burst into tears.

Brandon was across the room at once, to sit by her and take her in his arms. 'No, you are not to cry. I won't have it. He isn't worth it. What on earth did that pompous ass, my cousin, have to say to you which could distress you so?'

'He proposed to me,' Nan sobbed at him, wetting his beautiful cravat.

'And that is a cause for tears? Most women would be pleased.'

'Not by the manner in which he proposed to me.' The tears which she had held back for so long, had suppressed since the terrible day on which she had learned of Randal's death, flowed even more rapidly.

Brandon said nothing for a few moments, and then,

in a confidential tone, came out with, 'I shouldn't repeat gossip, I know, but it might cheer you a little to learn that Desmond has proposed to three young heiresses during the past year, and they have all turned him down!'

Nan offered him a watery smile. 'I suppose that was why he decided that he might as well settle down with me!' She could not prevent a loud sob from punctuating the end of the sentence.

'Come, come.' Brandon's voice was mock-severe. 'I am not a flowerbed to be watered, and it is not like you to be less than brave.'

'Brave!' Nan raised her head and stared at him fiercely through her tears. 'What do you, or any man for that matter, know about being brave? Oh, I don't mean brute courage as on the battlefield or in a duel. No, I mean the enduring of the unending littleness of daily life which is most women's lot.'

There was no answer Brandon could make to that. His own life had been wide-ranging and adventurous. He had no notion, he knew, of what life might be like for a spinster in her late twenties in a quiet country village. What he did know was that he was becoming aware that he should not be holding Nan to him so lovingly. If it was temptation merely to see her, then what was having her in his arms likely to do to him?

As though she had caught his thoughts, Nan murmured into his chest, 'You have left your guests again in order to speak to me, Brandon. You will be missed as I will be. This is most unwise; we shall occasion even more gossip.'

'No one will miss either of us yet,' he assured her, unwilling to leave her before necessity compelled him to do so. 'The whole party, even Lydia, who is being squired by your papa, is on the floor performing a country dance. Desmond, who might be permitted some suspicion of what we are up to, was, by the direction he took, on his way to his room. We are safe for a few more minutes yet.'

Safe for what? was Nan's sleepy thought. Tears over, she was caught in the languor of strong emotion's aftermath, and this, plus being held against a man's rapidly beating heart, was so comforting that she would willingly have remained there until he chose to move. . . Yes, all that she wanted was to be held. . .by him. . . She closed her eyes and relaxed against the strength of him, his heartbeat lulling her to sleep. . .

Brandon Tolliver did not consider himself to be the most sensitive of men, but he was sensitive enough to be aware that the last thing which Nan needed in her present state of mind was to be made love to. What she really wanted was to be cherished. What he wanted was quite another thing, but that could wait.

The very thought of making real passionate love to Nan, seeing that he was holding her so closely to him, was rousing him. Which had him moving a little away from her, unwilling to distress an innocent maiden lady. Besides, he really ought not to be pursuing her, putting temptation in her way unless he was quite sure in his own mind why he was doing so.

For, after all, had he not decided that what he really wanted for a wife was a pretty, reasonable biddable young girl, who would be an ornament on his arm when he went into the great world, who would grace his home, give him children, and make few demands on him—a trophy, in fact, to confirm his success in life? Someone to whom he need make no real commitment. Someone with whom he would have the kind of relationship which would enable him to take a lover when he pleased. Someone, in short, like Jane Fielding. He would make exactly the sort of marriage, indeed, which most of his contemporaries engaged in.

He had never once contemplated marrying a clever and strong-minded woman of mature years who would demand commitment from him, for that was Nan's nature; she would want him to surrender something of himself to her. He had always been, as Lydia had once told him, 'the cat that walked by itself', arranging his life to suit himself and no one else. He had no intention of changing that, either by marriage or by any other sort of tie.

The kindest thing which he could do for Nan Fielding was to walk away from her—as his sister had suggested—speaking to her only when politeness demanded, and not be putting her in the way of developing a hopeless *tendre* for him. That would be of all things the most unkind, would it not?

Wryly, he was also aware that these sane and honourable notions seemed feasible only when he was not with her. And now madam was going to sleep against him. By its cadences, the music floating in from the ballroom was drawing to its close, and they must not be found here together—and alone. He must leave her, having behaved nearly as badly as his sister had feared. Perhaps, after all, he ought to have encouraged Nan to think again. . .to reconsider. . .to accept his cousin's proposal.

More than his dislike of seeing her promised to another strangled that thought at its birth. Anyone but Desmond, perhaps even that old attorney who so visibly mooned after her, would be better. . . No, not him either.

'Nan,' he murmured gently in her ear, dropping the lightest of butterfly kisses on to her tawny hair. Her duenna's cap had slipped away, and her usually restrained curls were springing loose.

'I must go,' he whispered. 'For both our sakes. It would not do for us to be discovered here alone.'

'Oh!' Nan sat up, suddenly wide awake. 'Whatever am I doing? You have let me go to sleep,' she informed him accusingly.

She saw his long mouth twitch, the silver eyes flash. 'So I have,' he agreed gravely. 'You seemed to be in need of it. Let me prescribe for you.' He put on a solemn owlish face, looked at her over imaginary half-frame spectacles. 'For many years, I suspect, you have devoted yourself to working and caring for your family without respite. I give you, therefore, permission to retire to your room and rest—if that is what you wish. You may make your excuses prettily to my sister, while I reappear in the ballroom through the far door—like a genie in a pantomime—ready to look after all my other guests.'

He had a silver tongue, Nan thought—and so informed him.

His reply, she thought, was a little bitter. 'So I have often been told.'

He had disengaged himself, and was rising from the sofa. Her magical moment with him was in the past. He was sorry for the poor old maid, she thought, and now he would be off to be kind to someone else. . . She had no doubt, though, that if he wished he could be cruel or stern. . .anything he pleased.

Well, he had chosen to be kind to her for a short time, and that must be enough. She must not, dared not, hope for more. So after a little while, when her tears had dried and the scarlet they had provoked in her face had died down, she did as Brandon had suggested—made her adieus to Lydia and prepared to mount the stairs to her bedroom.

But the evening was not yet over for her.

CHAPTER NINE

NAN had a foot on the stairs when Jane shot out of the door to the ballroom.

'Wait, Nan.' Her voice was harsh and peremptory, so much so that the look Nan turned on her was an astonished one. Jane's face was scarlet and angry. She advanced on Nan as though she were going into battle.

'Why are you doing this to me, Nan?'

Nan's reply was not entirely truthful. She said, as innocently as she could, 'I don't understand you, Jane. Doing what?'

'Oh, don't pretend. You know perfectly well what I mean! You knew how taken I was with Brandon and he with me, but you have done nothing but make eyes at him since you first met, and now you have danced the waltz with him. That is almost a declaration of something or other, is it not? He should have asked me to waltz, not you. What did you say to him to persuade him to do so?'

Now she could be truthful. 'Nothing, Jane, nothing, I assure you. And you must know, as well as I do, that it would be quite improper for you, as a young girl, only just out, to waltz with a man of Brandon's age. Your reputation would suffer if you did so, whereas I. . .'

'Whereas you, being elderly, and past her last prayers, I suppose, could hardly be considered to have a reputation worth keeping or losing,' Jane flashed spitefully at her.

This was really too much, even from a sister who rarely considered her feelings. Nan clenched her fists and said as coolly as she could, 'I do not make the rules by which we live, Jane, but like you I have to abide by them.'

'Then leave Brandon alone, and cease making sheep's eyes at him. I saw him first, before you did.' This came out as childishly as though they were arguing over the possession of a doll. 'Why don't you make us all happy and agree to marry Desmond?'

'I don't intend to marry anyone, and for your benefit I have just refused to marry Desmond. Now I wish to go to bed. I am very tired.'

She saw Jane's lower lip protrude as it often did when she was being particularly selfish, whether the selfishness was concerned with a man or the ownership of a box of bon-bons. Nan's words flew out of her, of their own accord, almost as though she had not willed them, as words had done when she had been a lively young girl, younger even than Jane was now.

'One thing, my dear. If you wish to keep a man, or inspire him to marry you, let me give you a piece of advice. Do not pout and groan at him overmuch. Men like pretty, biddable young things, not scowling, ill-tempered ones.'

'Oh!' Jane almost shrieked. 'I'll have you know I have no intention of taking any notice of what an elderly prude, long past her last prayers, who has never managed to marry a man, says to me. I don't believe that Desmond ever offered for you. If he had I'm sure that you would have jumped all over him, and the wedding would be arranged for next week—or sooner.' She tossed her pretty head in the air, and shot back through the door by which she had come, determined not to miss any more of the evening's fun.

Any desire to sleep which Nan had possessed flew away after Jane had left her. Was it true? Had she been making sheep's eyes at Brandon? Had anyone seen, or was it that Jane had noticed something which no one else had? The eye of jealousy was as keen as the eye of love.

Nan did not think that Jane loved Brandon. She was at an age, and of a disposition, not to love anyone other than herself. She had seen and attracted Brandon before anyone else in the neighbourhood had met him, and he had constantly behaved towards her in a '*most particular*' way, as she had said, to give her the impression that he was interested in her. Jane did not persevere with men, young or old, who seemed to be immune to her charms.

And, if so, it must be especially galling for her to see Brandon taking a sudden interest in the despised elder sister for whose way of life she had always shown such contempt, not knowing that it was Nan, as the author of *Sophia*, who had made her own, and the Rectory's, comfortable life possible. It was absolutely necessary, then, for Jane's sake, that she should discourage Brandon, and cause him to stop his strange pursuit of her. Once again Nan asked herself in the small hours as she tossed and turned, sleep coming and going, What does he really want with me?

Brandon didn't know what he wanted with Nan Fielding. He had never been in such a pother over a woman before. Nothing in his sensible arrangement with Emma Milborne, or the other accommodations he had come to with various other young and willing women, had prepared him to deal with Nan Fielding. What on earth had led him to start the whole business off by wandering into the Rectory's pantry? It was enough to teach him not to go adventuring—that was to be left for his business, not his social life.

And, more, why had he not passed by on the other side when he had found her again, up a tree? And what on earth had the commonsensical and proper Miss Fielding been doing up a tree, freeing her brother's kite? Why couldn't she have walked back to the Rectory and found an underservant to do it for her, and have thus spared him temptation? Jove, what legs she had. . . He dragged his fevered mind away from mental contemplation of them—and of the rest of her.

And why could he not sleep for thinking of her, when it was Jane who should have been occupying his thoughts? And what was the business she had with the ageing attorney which should so preoccupy her? For Brandon's intuition told him that there was more to their association than Sam Stone's desire to make her his wife. There was something odd going on at the Rectory, and the oddity centred on the mysterious Miss Fielding—who would not let him sleep, damn her!

Like Nan he tossed and turned, before exhaustion claimed him in the small hours, his last thought being, I must be going mad to let a woman trouble me so, for, like most men, he agreed with the poet Byron. 'Man's love is of man's life a thing apart, 'Tis woman's whole existence.' So what was he doing to allow the business of Nan Fielding to take such a large part of his life?

He and Nan were not the only ones to be thus troubled. Jane, too, and George Alden, to say nothing of Desmond Tolliver and Sam Stone, were beset by love's cross-currents, and perhaps only Parson Fielding and young Chaz, dreaming of kites and plum tarts, were free from the attention of the little god of love. Plenty of time for Chaz in the future, though, however serene his present!

Nan expected the last day of the house party at Gillyflower Hall to be as fraught as the first two, but no such thing. The guests all straggled down to breakfast one by one, the last arriving just as a cold collation was served in the big dining-room. A wind had risen during the night, strong enough to make eating luncheon out of doors troublesome.

Even Desmond seemed to have recovered his spirits and went out of his way to be pleasant to her. Brandon, on the other hand, seemed to be going out of his way to avoid her. She told herself that this was an eventuality much to be desired—a piece of pomposity which gave her no comfort at all, even if Jane was happy to have her admirer back again.

Her pretty laughter rang out more than once. She was much admired by the older gentlemen of the party, although Desmond's one scowl that day was directed towards her enthusiastic enjoyment of his cousin's attention.

Sam Stone left towards noon. A messenger had come from his office to say that he was required there urgently—an important communication had come from London. He feared by what was said that Mr Murray was badgering him again about the identity of the author of *Sophia*. He had been much alarmed at breakfast-time, and happy that Nan had not yet come down for it, when Lady Letcombe, reading letters which had been forwarded to her from Letcombe's Landing, had given vent to a loud cry.

'Only think!' she exclaimed, putting down a much crossed piece of writing paper from a correspondent whose handwriting seemed to be distinguished mostly by its large and excitable scrawl. 'It is the *on dit* all around town that Mr Murray has said that he may soon be able to announce the true identity of the author of *Sophia*! Even more exciting, he says that she—he is sure that it is a she—lives somewhere in South Nottinghamshire, near to the borders of Leicestershire. Only fancy if that be true! Why, Sophia might even be one of us! What a thing!'

An excited buzz from the ladies drowned all male conversation. Nan, who had arrived just as Lady Letcombe had finished speaking, showed Sam a white, scared face. He shook his head imperceptibly, to reassure her that he had not given her away.

Brandon, seated next to Jane, drawled in his most teasing fashion, 'I suppose that Murray is setting this rumour on its way to increase the sales of the author's next novel. I have seen the advertisements for it in the public prints. He is making sure that when it arrives in the bookshops there will be queues down the street in case something in it will betray her identity.'

Sam nodded, and even Nan acknowledged the truth of what Brandon was saying. But she was also forced hard up against the fact that what Sam had told her recently was true: she would not be able to keep her secret much longer.

She sat quiet. Lady Alden, next door to her, anxious that Nan should not be left out of the conversation, remarked to her, 'Whoever she is, she knows country society as well as town. She has a pretty wit on her, and in my opinion must be well on in years to be able to see all our foibles and portray them so accurately. I have been trying to think who I know who might be the author, but I confess that I am at a loss. My guess is that she may be a he after all. What do you think, Miss Fielding?'

She was always kinder to Nan than Lady Letcombe, whose private judgement of her, made to the other women the night before, after Nan had retired, was, 'She is such a bore, my dears, so strait-laced, so proper. The only thing which seems to occupy her mind is the ordering of affairs at the Rectory and in the parish!'

Lady Alden's reply to that had been incontrovertible. 'Well, dear Lady Letcombe, knowing how matters stand at the Rectory, with a mother who has retired from the world and a father who was never in it, if she does not order affairs, who will?'

Lady Letcombe's answer had been a dismissive snort, and after it Lady Alden had determined to be kind to the poor thing, seeing that no one else would be.

Nan said slowly, 'I have really no opinion on the matter. I would have thought a lady more likely, but a sensitive gentleman might perhaps be able to talk so knowledgeably on matters usually discussed by the female sex.'

'Ah, Miss Fielding,' Brandon put in as he walked back from the sideboard with a large plateful of cold sliced ham. 'You think it possible for gentlemen to be sensitive, then?'

'Some men. . .' Nan was reflective '. . .seeing that men are more usually than women the poets and philosophers who make informed pronouncements on matters of the heart, although I believe that that may be because women are supposed to be quiet on such topics, whereas men are encouraged to speak their thoughts aloud.'

'Bravely spoken,' said Brandon as he prepared to demolish his breakfast. 'So, you are suggesting, Miss Fielding, that we must look suspiciously at everyone if we wish to determine who the author of *Sophia* is, not just the fair sex?'

Sam could almost feel Nan's agony as the discussion continued. She had already raised several eyebrows by her remark on the difference of what was expected from men and women. To bring matters to a close, he stood up and announced briskly, 'Well, seeing that Murray has chosen to break his silence, it is possible that we may all soon know the truth. Uninformed speculation is invariably useless.'

'True,' remarked Brandon, who was beginning to draw some astute conclusions about the possible

relationship between Sam Stone and an author who was
supposed to live in the district, although the real truth
as to Nan's involvement was still far from his mind.
'And all we have at present is the knowledge that
whoever it is knows more about our souls and the well-
springs of our behaviour than is comfortable.'

He gave a mock-shiver, said something half under his
breath to Jane, who laughed appreciatively at it, and
the subject of the author of *Sophia* was temporarily
abandoned.

Later, before he left for Broomhall, Sam spoke to
Nan, who was sitting on the lawn in the shade of a
stand of cedars, enjoying the unusual sensation of being
completely idle, with no task awaiting her, and no shrill
reminders from the rest of her family about what she
ought to be doing for them.

'My letter is from Murray,' he began without preamble. 'He is trying to put pressure on me to give the
author of *Sophia* away. I do not know how long I can
hold him off. He requires an instant answer, a reassur-
ance that I have done my best to persuade Sophia to
reveal herself. He threatens to send his man here to
talk to me, to put further pressure on me—and play
Paul Pry around the neighbourhood, no doubt.'

Nan sat up, her beautiful peace disturbed. 'You will
not give me away?'

'Indeed not. Although I fear that your secret may
soon be no secret. You ought to consider what your
course of conduct will be then.'

Nan sat bolt upright, all colour draining from her
face. Brandon, engaged in a game of cat's cradle with
Jane, was also surreptitiously watching Nan, and wondering what Sam Stone could be saying to her to affect
her so.

She shook her head, recollected that she was doubtless being observed, and tried to smile before saying,

stiff-lipped, 'I never thought that I should be so successful, although God knows I am glad of it, seeing how
much money it has brought in.'

'And will bring more in,' Sam told her quietly, also
trying to look as though their conversation was innocuous, 'after you are unmasked. Think of the uproar
when Scott was discovered.'

Nan closed her eyes. 'Oh, but I do not want that, you
know I don't. . .but what will be will be, I suppose.
Papa would say that we are all in the hand of God,
although I sometimes wonder how much God really
cares about any of us.'

This was a strange remark from a parson's daughter,
but Sam made no gloss on it. His own religious belief
was shaky these days, and he frequently wished that he
had Caleb Fielding's childlike belief in a benevolent
deity. Looking round the world as it had been wagging
for the last thirty years or so, with the emphasis on war,
revolution, poverty and distress, Sam had strong doubts
about that. But he never voiced them, and sat each
Sunday in his family pew at Broomhall, enjoyed singing
the familiar hymns—and wished that he still had the
unquestioning faith of his youth.

'We have to follow the path laid out for us without
complaint,' he told Nan gently, 'and you know that I
would marry you as soon as I could acquire a special
licence if only you would accept my proposal.'

Nan might have been tempted by this renewed offer
if she had not met Brandon Tolliver. All that she could
murmur was, 'You flatter me, but it would not do.' She
did not say, Find someone nearer to your own age who
will make you happy, not a woman young and flighty
enough to hanker after the impossible dream of finding
her true love who will sweep her off her feet and carry
her into realms unknown to kind, prosaic Sam.

'I am not worthy of you,' she told him earnestly, and meant it.

In the end, because her talk with Sam had ended with his renewed pledges of help to her and her expressions of gratitude to him, the happiness of her day was not diminished. Even though Brandon never came near her, turning his attention on Jane again, Nan was aware that he was always conscious of her presence, as she was of his. It was as though some unseen chain stretched from him to her and back again, finer than gossamer, stronger than any spider's web, so that each knew without looking that the other was there, and both were communicating without speaking.

Nan knew without being told, in the same way that she knew the innermost thoughts of her characters about matters which she had never experienced, that Brandon desired her—and that she desired him. But only in the world of fancy, she told herself firmly, can we ever consummate our love. We are kept apart by barriers as fine and firm as the thin cord which unites us, and which, sooner or later, for my own peace of mind, I am bound to sever. He cannot be for me. I lost the right to have him for a husband long ago.

Because she had found Brandon, even if only to lose him, seated that evening in the big drawing-room, listening to Mozart, Haydn and Handel, beautifully played by the musicians from Leicester, Nan also discovered something in the music which she had never found before: an affirmation of the heights and depths to which the human spirit could rise and fall. That night she slept peacefully and dreamlessly as she had not slept since the day on which she had met Brandon in the pantry.

Renunciation might bring its pains, but it also brought its pleasures too, even if these were bittersweet and known to few.

* * *

'Damn,' said Brandon violently. 'Damn everything!'

He, who usually knew why he did and said everything, did not know why he was cursing. He only knew by her manner, by the expression on her face, by the very tone of her leave-taking, that he had lost Nan.

There was a new serenity about her, and he knew what it was. He almost knew the moment when she had withdrawn herself from him—when he had felt suddenly and shockingly alone, even though he had been fooling with Jane and the others at the time.

He had known by then that he could never marry Jane, and bitterly regretted that he had ever put her in the way of thinking that he might offer for her. What he had said and done with her before he met Nan had bound him, had kept him from being able to be honest with Nan—that, and the nature of their first encounters.

How could he have ever thought that he could spend the rest of his life tied to such a pretty little emptyheaded charmer with no thought beyond her appearance and her immediate pleasure? He must have been mad. Yet he had arrived at Gillyflower Hall fully determined to offer for her as soon as possible.

Now he no longer wished to marry her, and the woman he did wish to marry had decided on renunciation. The calmness of Nan's gaze, the coolness of her voice as she had thanked him for her three happy days, the way in which she had spoken to Lydia, all told him that she was about to sacrifice herself again for the family which hung around her neck like a millstone.

Only when all his guests had gone on the following morning could he give vent to his feelings, raging and prowling around his study, cursing the misfortune that had made him meet the one sister before the other.

Finally he tried to acknowledge Byron's dictum and resume the public life whose demands made plain the differences between the lives of men and women. He

GET FOUR
BOOKS AND A
MYSTERY GIFT

Return this card, and we'll send you four specially selected
Legacy of Love novels absolutely FREE! We'll even pay the postage
and packing for you!

We're making this offer to introduce you to the benefits of Reader
Service: FREE home delivery of brand-new romances at least a month
before they're available in the shops, a FREE gift and a monthly
Newsletter packed with information.

Accepting these FREE books places you under no obligation to buy,
you may cancel at any time simply by writing to us — even after
receiving just your free shipment.

Yes, please send me four free Legacy of Love novels and a
mystery gift. I understand that unless you hear from me, I will
receive four superb new titles every month for just £2.50* each
postage and packing free. I am under no obligation to purchase
any books and I may cancel or suspend my subscription at any
time, but the free books and gifts will be mine to keep in any
case. (I am over 18 years of age).

11A5M

Ms/Mrs/Miss/Mr _____

Address _____

_____

_____ Postcode _____

↑ TEAR OFF AND POST THIS CARD TODAY ↑

*Prices subject to change without notice.

Get four books and a mystery gift FREE!

SEE OVER FOR DETAILS

POST THIS CARD TODAY

Mills & Boon Reader Service
FREEPOST
Croydon
Surrey
CR9 3WZ

No stamp needed

Offer closes 31st May 1996. We reserve the right to refuse an application. *Prices and terms subject to change without notice. Offer valid in U.K. and Ireland only and is not available to current subscribers of this series. Overseas readers please write for details. Southern Africa write to: IBS Private Bag X3010, Randburg 2125.

You may be mailed with offers from other reputable companies as a result of this application. If you would prefer not to share in this opportunity, please tick box. ☐

rang for Carteret, his secretary, a middle-aged man with a weary, cynical face, and told him to send for Thorpe, the ex-Bow Street Runner who carried out his investigations for him, and whose discoveries had helped to keep him on his way to creating a large fortune which was founded on a secure base. Not for him the doubts which his rivals faced when they contemplated courses of action. Thorpe—and others like him—was there to discover and reveal to him the secrets which he was not supposed to know.

Thorpe arrived a week later. He entered Brandon's study with his usual strong air of being engaged in a conspiracy with someone or something. He refused the seat which Brandon offered him.

'I allus prefer to stand. Think better that way. Well, what is it this time?'

Such surly independence, a refusal to see him in any way as his master, usually amused Brandon. Today he was beyond being amused.

'More than one thing,' he said curtly. 'Several things. All of equal importance.'

Thorpe's heavy brows rose. 'Difficult, that,' he muttered. 'I likes some sort of order.'

'Well, I'm sorry.' Brandon's tone was untypically nasty. 'I usually like obliging those whom I pay heavily to carry out my orders, but today I can't.'

Or won't, thought Thorpe, who knew his man, and that behind Brandon Tolliver's airy charm lurked a quite different sort of man—stern and hard. But something was rattling him today. His usual control was missing. Thorpe's feral eyes gleamed. Nice to see m'lord not at ease for once. He wondered who and what was responsible.

Brandon saw the gleam, and damned himself internally at the same time that he changed his manner to his normal one.

'I think that someone is trying to kill me,' he began, bluntly for him, 'and I want you to find out who and why.' He briefly outlined the two attempts, the failed shot and the cut girth, Thorpe nodding as he spoke.

'Now, no one knows of the cut girth except the two grooms who discovered it. I mentioned the failed shot to a party of local gentry and they all dismissed it as some disgruntled Luddite trying to kill, maim or frighten a local landowner. . .'

'But you don't think so,' finished Thorpe. 'Especially after the second attempt. Anyone else want to do for you? Benefit by doing for you?'

'No, I don't think either try was accidental. As for those who might benefit. . .' He hesitated. 'I've a cousin who thought he was inheriting the whole of his and my cousin's estate until the day the will was read, when he found that I had inherited it. But. . .he's a poor thing. . . I can't quite see him. . .'

He hesitated again. 'On the other hand, look what he lost and I gained, and he knows that I was already richer by far than the value of the estate he lost. . . And then there's the possibility—a slim one, I admit— that it might be a failed business rival getting back at me. . .'

'So's you want me to look into it—and him—and Luddites—disgruntled grooms. . .and anythin' else.'

Brandon nodded. 'That's it. Now, I've another task for you—or tasks. I want you to find out everything you can about the affairs of Caleb Fielding and his family. He's the Rector of Broomhall, and when I say family I mean family. I paid the lawyer Stone to tell me all about the Fieldings and the rest of the local gentry before I settled here, but I'm not satisfied that he was completely frank with me, which is why I sent for you. And, connected with that, I want you to ferret out all you can about Stone himself.'

He paused. 'There's something odd going on involving the Fieldings and Stone, and I've a mind to know what it is.'

Some expression on Thorpe's face disturbed him. 'What is it, man? What have I said that has you looking at me as though I'm a shilling lacking a penny?'

Thorpe's mouth twitched. 'Only that one reason why I didn't mind taking on this job for you in this God-forsaken part of the world is because as how I've been hired to do another here, and I thought I could combine the two. What I didn't know was that the two jobs might be related.'

Brandon knew that Thorpe thought that all places outside London were God-forsaken, but the news that someone else was interested in Broomhall's affairs was something of a surprise.

'Could you be more specific?'

His tone was acid, deadly—the tone of a man who had made a fortune before he was thirty.

'Confidentiality is what I allus promise. . .but what you know might help me with the first job—kill two birds with one stone—and what I know might help you with yours. So. . .'

'So. . .?' echoed Brandon as Thorpe paused tantalisingly.

'So, my other man wants Stone investigated because Stone is involved with some man or woman who writes novels under an anonymous name, and my man wants to know who the writer is. Stone knows and won't tell. My man needs to know for financial reasons, he says. What do you know, Mr Brandon Tolliver, sir? About Stone. Or is it all gin and moonbeams with you?'

Brandon took no offence. Thorpe was doing him a favour by telling him of his other assignment. 'I suspect that Stone is involved with the writer. I also suspect that there *is* some kind of a mystery involving Stone and the Fieldings, but I've only my bones to tell me so. That's why I'm hiring you—to find out if my bones have begun to let me down. They have never done so before. I don't think that the attempts on my life have anything to do with Stone or the Fieldings—they are a separate issue. That's all.'

'And damned small that "all" is. It'll cost you, is all I can say.'

'Anything, so long as you are discreet.'

'I'll use Miller as well; proper yokel-seeming Miller can be—you remember him, I'm sure. Cost a bit to keep him drinking in the local, but you won't mind that. Get him some work in the parson's household, perhaps—or, better still, have him ferret around Stone. I'll put a word in for him as a groom, or a gardener. Gentry often need gardeners. At the worst, take him on yourself. He can complain about your high-handed goings-on and tempt other people to tell him what they wouldn't if they thought that he was loyal. . .'

'Anything,' Brandon said. 'Anything, but keep away from here unless I send for you. Arrange a pick-up for your reports with Carteret. Remember, I want answers to my questions as soon as possible. I have another strong feeling that a further attempt will be made on me, and I don't want it to succeed.'

'That you don't,' agreed Thorpe. 'You shouldn't be so bloody rich, sir. Annoys people. Not me,' he added.

'Carteret will see that you leave here without being seen—as you arrived here. Here's some guineas as a retainer.' And he passed over a small purse.

Later, when Lydia came into the study, he sat with his booted feet up on a small occasional table, a ledger thrown to one side. He was stifling a yawn, and looked the picture of indolent boredom, not at all like a man who had just paid a discredited Bow Street Runner to spy on all his neighbours and relations because someone was trying to kill him, and the others were hugging secrets which he felt that he ought to know.

He particularly wanted to know Miss Fielding's secrets. Being a man who had a few himself, he was always aware when others had them.

But for the life of him he couldn't imagine what they were, and for the first time when he had sent one of his agents on his way he wondered whether he was doing a wise thing. . . .

CHAPTER TEN

'IT MIGHT be conjectured that if a handsome man of good birth and great fortune were to offer for a moderately good-looking young woman with a paltry dower she would accept his offer on the instant. No such thing: Nan's response to Brandon's proposal was to reject it outright. . .'

Oh, Satan, Belial, Beelzebub and Mephistopheles, she had done it again! She had written her own name and Brandon's instead of that of Louisa Gascoigne, her heroine, and Henry D'Eyncourt, her hero! Now she would have to rewrite the whole page, and this was the third time she had done such a thing since she had started work on her novel once the whole Rectory was safely in its bed and sleeping.

And Henry was not in the least like Brandon, being stern, upright, full of honour, and he would never, under any circumstances, kiss a servant girl in the pantry. Nor was Louisa like herself; she was a kinder, cleverer version of Jane. She must be going mad, and she had no time to go mad. Her fourth novel was about to be published, and she had promised, through Sam, that the next would not be long in following it.

So it was imperative that *Dearly Beloved*, as she had already named it, should be taking shape, not wandering about because her mind was on her own affairs and not those of her imaginary beings.

Come to think of it, would she refuse Brandon if he offered for her? She would be compelled to, would she not? There were, after all, very good reasons why she could never marry anyone, even if there had been occasions when she had thought that she might take Sam Stone's offer seriously.

The spoiled sheet of paper carefully torn up and consigned to the waste-paper basket, Nan began again, making sure this time that it was Henry and Louisa whom she was fetching from the back of her mind, not Nan and Brandon. She must concentrate on the task before her, but for once the activities of her hero and heroine were less riveting than those of the men and women among whom she lived.

She and Jane and their father had been home for some days before her mother had referred to what Jane had told her of their visit to Gillyflower Hall. They had been in her mother's little drawing-room which opened off her bedchamber, and from which she could look down the village street and watch the passing show.

Nan had been reading to her from *Amelia's Secret*, which Jane had recommended to her mother, and which Nan, who knew it off by heart and was heartily sick of both Amelia and her secret, was doomed to go on reading until all three volumes had been disposed of. It had been late afternoon, almost time for dinner to be served, when Mrs Fielding had sighed, closed her eyes, lain back in her armchair, and announced, 'That will do, my dear. A most interesting tale, and you read it well. I think that I could manage a roll and a little soup now.'

Nan had put down her book and stood up. She had barely done so when her mother had opened her eyes again and said, 'Before you go downstairs, I think that there is something I ought to say to you. Pray sit down, my dear. I dislike it when you tower over me so.'

Nothing, thought Nan, that I ever do pleases my mother. I wonder what it is that I have done wrong this time?

She was soon to find out.

Mrs Fielding made herself comfortable again. She was still a handsome woman, and despite claiming constant ill health had a rosy complexion and glossy blonde hair. Jane greatly resembled her as she had been in youth, if the little miniature of her by Cosway was any guide. She had not left her upstairs rooms these eleven years or more. She rose daily from her bed to walk into her drawing-room, to gaze out of the window, and to admire the view, before saying, 'I don't think that I will venture downstairs today,' to whoever happened to be with her at the time.

She was quite happy to allow Nan to run the household and carry out all the parish duties of a parson's wife, including regular visits to the sick and poor, but she always made it quite plain that she would manage everything so much better than Nan did—if only her wretched health would allow her to do so.

'Jane has been telling me of your visit to Gillyflower Hall,' she began, 'and I was a trifle disturbed by what she told me. It seems that although you knew that she had formed a *tendre* for Mr Brandon Tolliver and he for her you constantly put yourself forward when with him, to a degree which occasioned gossip on more than one occasion. Wait. . .' she commanded as Nan, her fine control broken for once, opened her mouth to deny what her mother was saying.

'Pray allow me to finish, Anne. She also told me that it was common gossip that Desmond Tolliver had offered for you, and that Sam Stone was showing a distinct interest in your company—again to the point of unkind comment.

'Now, that is most unlike you, and I have no hesitation in asking you to resume your more usual modest conduct. You know that it is important that Jane should marry, and marry well. Mr Brandon Tolliver would make her a most suitable husband. You also know, without me telling you, that it is not possible for you to marry anyone. We agreed on that long ago. I hope I do not have to remind you again that it is your duty to undertake those duties from which I am debarred and never to put yourself forward in any way.'

She closed her eyes, then opened them again, to say, in the most patient and long-suffering voice which she could achieve, 'I do hope that I shall not have to remind you again, Anne, what your place in the world must be.' Without changing her tone, she added, 'Pray tell Cook to be sparing of the pepper when she prepares my soup for me; she rather overdid the seasoning on the last occasion on which she served it. You really must learn to control the servants a little more, otherwise they will always take advantage of you.'

This time, before she closed her eyes again, she waved Nan away, as though she too were one of the servants about whom she was complaining.

Remembering this conversation brought the tears to Nan's eyes again. To be reprimanded so harshly, yet so casually, between two peremptory orders about her mother's dinner, had almost been enough to overset her. She brushed the tears away with an impatient hand, picked up her quill pen again, and began to write about Henry and Louisa's love-affair as rapidly as she could, in order to try to forget her own stunted life. Her mother was. . .what she was, and nothing now would change her.

At Gillyflower Hall, Lydia Bligh, who had suffered from insomnia since her late husband's death, had walked to the windows of her bedroom from which she could see the back of the Rectory. She glanced at her little fob watch to check the time. Two-thirty on a fine night, with the stars out, and, yes, there was a light in the back bedroom of the Rectory again.

This small mystery had occupied her since the first time that she had noticed it—not long after she had arrived at Gillyflower Hall. Someone at the Rectory was frequently awake far into the night. For her own part she rarely lit a candle, preferring to lie in the dark after drinking a little water, and reciting to herself some passages from Pope, an author whom, though now out of fashion, she greatly admired.

So intrigued was Lydia by what she had seen that the next morning she idly asked her maid, Nellie Forde, whether she knew who it was who worked far into the night at the Rectory. The servants, she shrewdly thought, would be sure to know the answer. For some reason she did not think that it could be the Rector— his unworldliness did not lie in working beyond the midnight watches.

Sure enough, Nellie told her, as she was arranging her hair, 'They say in the Rectory kitchens that Miss Fielding works late at night, ma'am. They know because of the number of candles she uses. They think that she is making a fair copy of her father's book.'

Greatly daring, she added, 'Jackson, their butler and man of all work, thinks that she probably writes much of it for him. They know that he gives her the notes for his sermons and she finishes them off for him!'

Does she, indeed? was Lydia's inward thought. Poor thing, to work both day and night as she does to keep the Fieldings afloat. I wonder that her mother allows it. And then she thought of the impression which both the Fielding parents had made on her when she had visited the Rectory: that the Rector's unworldliness lay in letting his eldest daughter do much of his parish work for him, and his wife's pleasant and charming selfishness, her easy life, was also accomplished by exploiting that same daughter.

All the more reason, then, for Brandon not to exploit her, and so she told him that afternoon at dinner.

He was looking particularly well. He had spent the day in the open air with his agent, and had worked up, he said, a healthy appetite. He, at least, unlike Mrs Fielding, was not eager to complain about his victuals. 'Commend the cook about the roasting of the rib of beef,' he informed Lydia as he poured himself another glass of good red wine, 'and tell me whatever it is that you are bursting to impart.'

Lydia thought, not for the first time, how shrewd her brother was behind his charming mask. 'I was about to inform you of some news concerning Nan Fielding which ought to make you think twice before you exploit her in any way, seeing how much she is exploited already.' And she told him about the light in the bedroom and what Nellie Forde had discovered about Nan's midnight work.

'Writing into the small hours, copying out that damned pedantic rubbish for her father! When does unworldliness become rank selfishness, tell me that? And the mother. You have met her as I may not, she being permanently upstairs in her suite of rooms. What do you make of her?'

Lydia was a little guarded. 'Not very much. She looks well enough. The doctor goes twice a week, I understand, and is perfectly happy to allow her to live a sedentary life. If you asked me my honest opinion. . .'

'Oh——' Brandon was sardonic '—by all means tell me your honest opinion. I rarely have the good fortune to hear many of those from anyone!'

Lydia made no comment on this piece of cynicism. 'Well, then, Brandon, I think that nothing much can be amiss with her. She has been living after this strange fashion for eleven years, since her son was born, and so far as I can tell has not deteriorated in health since.'

Brandon threw his napkin down quite violently. 'And all on the back of one poor daughter, as I see it. Jane never appears to have any duties and I gather the two other sisters were chaperoned by Nan and made good marriages. They appear to have lived like ladies also, never raising a finger, or so one infers from what Jane says. It is quite intolerable.'

'But it is not our business, Brandon—except that you must not do anything to make her hard life harder.'

'No, indeed; nor may I do anything to make it easier.'

'The thing I wonder at,' pursued Lydia, 'is that she does not accept either of the offers which your cousin Desmond and Sam Stone have made to her. To marry either of them would relieve her from servitude, and both offers are from most suitable men.'

For some reason Brandon did not like to hear that Nan Fielding had received offers from most suitable men. Still less, he knew, did he wish to hear that she had accepted either of them. Oh, yes, he was being a real dog in the manger, was he not? He was making no offer to her himself, but was wishing that others might not!

He became aware that Lydia was waiting for an answer, and said, as casually as he could, 'You could do something to ease Nan's lot by inviting her over to Gillyflower Hall—to take tea, or to talk of those matters which women value but which men do not.'

Lydia nodded and said no more. Best to keep silent from now on about the Rectory affairs, since anything which she might wish to say to Brandon *vis-à-vis* Nan Fielding was sure to be taken ill, and she was not used to quarrelling with him. Their relationship had always been harmonious—a pity to spoil it by allowing the Rector's daughter to come between them.

* * *

For the next few weeks Lydia kept to this good resolution. She did not invite Nan over to the Hall, although Jane was in and out with Caroline and Charlotte, but she did send her a short letter telling her that Mrs Blagg and the baby were doing well, that Mrs Blagg was proving to be a good sempstress and had been taken on to the permanent staff at the Hall. She stifled her bad conscience over leaving Nan to her fate by telling herself that she was doing her a favour in not encouraging her relationship with Brandon.

As Brandon said nothing more of Nan, she began to hope that he had forgotten her, but she could not have made a graver mistake. He could not remove her from his memories, the principal one being the sight of her holding Mrs Blagg's baby with an expression of such tender joy on her face. His own serious pursuit of Jane had been halted by her relative indifference to the fate of both mother and child by contrast with Nan's compassion.

He was seated at breakfast one morning when Cartaret brought in the first letter from Thorpe. It was short and to the point. He had discovered nothing yet about 'the main business', as they had agreed to call the attacks on Brandon.

As for Mr Sam Stone, he deals only with local people. His main client, who sees him more often than any, is Miss Fielding from the Rectory—which I thought that you might like to know, being interested in their doings. By the by, the Rev earns very little from his writing, a cully of mine from London informs me, so the Fieldings' income does not come from that.

Thorpe added a PS.

As Mr S never sees anyone out of the way, if he is running the author of *Sophia*, then he, or she, must be someone local. He goes to Highborough once a week, but only to Paget's Bank, or to his Gentleman's Club, next to the Assembly Rooms.

Brandon tossed the letter to one side. It told him nothing that he did not already know. . .but something niggled even as he dismissed it. . .

He had already suspected that Parson Fielding's theological tomes sold poorly. . .but. . .if his only income was the miserly stipend from Broomhall Parish, and nothing came from his rich relatives, then how was it that the Fieldings lived so well, had a houseful of servants and were able to afford a London season to launch Jane on the world?

Something Lady Letcombe had said quite idly in his presence recently, when watching Jane and Caroline romp together, had, without his knowing it, stuck in his mind. 'I remember when the Fieldings first came to Broomhall they had hardly two halfpennies to rub together. It was quite distressing—so much more pleasing to us all to see them so comfortable these days.'

So what had made them comfortable?

Brandon picked up the letter and read it again.

'His main client, who sees him more often than any, is Miss Fielding from the Rectory. . .'

He began to attack the problem of the Fieldings with the remorseless cold-blooded logic, intermingled with intuition, which had made him a rich man even before he had inherited his cousin's property.

Item: the Fieldings are comfortable, who were poor.

Item: this is not through Caleb Fielding's writings, nor his stipend, nor through any income from his rich relatives.

Item: Sam Stone is almost certainly acting for the author of *Sophia*, who is a local personage.

Item: his most constant client is Nan Fielding. All Broomhall believes that this is so because she manages her father's business, mostly his profits from his theological writings—but as he has none this belief must be mistaken.

Item: Miss Nan Fielding is an uncommonly clever, well-read and observant young woman.

Item: Miss Nan Fielding works far into the night—as Lydia has discovered and as I have recently confirmed for myself—by spying on the Rectory through the kitchen window at Gillyflower Hall at three a.m.

Item: Miss Nan Fielding, therefore, must be the author of *Sophia*, is earning considerable sums of money, and is deceiving everyone, including the sophistical parson whose unworldliness is a cloak for his blind selfishness.

Item: Nan Fielding, therefore, is the prop and mainstay of the parsonage in every way—including the financial one.

Brandon stood up, cursing steadily. Could he conceivably be correct in his suppositions? Was he imagining things? Put it to the test, he informed himself coldly. Would you gamble good money on this supposition? And if the answer is yes, then it is likely that you are correct.

He had read and been entertained by *Sophia* and the author's other novels, but he had not examined them to look for clues as to their true author. Before he finally made up his mind he would read her latest to see if he could find echoes of Nan's voice in it.

Noise and conversation outside told him that Lydia was finally up. He strode over to the double doors, flung them open, and hurled at her as though she were one of his clerks, 'Lydia! Pray listen to me. You have a copy of that woman's latest novel, have you not?'

His sister stared at him. 'Do you mean the author of *Sophia*, Brandon? Of course; why do you ask?'

'Because I want to read the damned thing, that's why! And as soon as possible, too.'

All his usual careful charm was missing. What bee could possibly be buzzing in his bonnet that he wanted to read a novel at nine in the morning on a fine summer's day?

The sight of his sister's outraged and puzzled expression restored Brandon to his senses as she said coolly, 'You will find *Amelia's Secret* on the desk in the library. It is quite her best.'

Good humour suddenly restored, Brandon kissed her on the way to collect it. 'Blessings on you, my dear. You are always so charmingly helpful.'

What was even more surprising than his sudden desire to read a novel at such an hour was that he went through *Amelia's Secret* with the same speed and intensity which he usually brought to his financial papers. His brow furrowed, and giving the occasional snort of laughter, he did what he had never done before: read every word instead of dipping in and lightly browsing. He had spoken to Nan as though he had previously given to the author of *Sophia*'s novels the kind of attention which he was at present devoting to *Amelia's Secret*, but he had only been uttering a half-truth.

At the end of the morning he put the book down. He had already recognised several of the characters in it. Parson Fielding was there, gently mocked, and Jane, her sister. Oh, it was an idealised portrait of her, it was true, but Jane was the undoubted inspirer of the heroine, Amelia. And the older woman, her friend and adviser, the epitome of common sense, was Nan herself.

But Lancelot Beaumains, her hero, who the devil was he? That handsome, upright, brave creature, once a soldier and now a landowner of liberal tendencies, caring for his tenants? No one like that frequented the fields, woods and drawing-rooms around Broomhall and Highborough, that was for sure.

But the country in the book was that which lay around them, and Bridgeford, the little town by the River Rill, was Highborough, near to the Soar, no doubt of that either.

He ate his luncheon savagely, hardly knowing what he put into his mouth. How was it that no one had seen what he had seen? But then, they had not been looking for it, as he had been. And Sophia's voice was Nan's, with an added acerbity which must be hers in secret, for the face which she showed the world was, if he was correct in his suppositions, not quite the true face of Nan Fielding. As, he acknowledged to himself, the face which he showed the world was not his true face—so who was he to criticise Nan?

No, he didn't wish to criticise her, he wished to admire her all the more for her gallantry, as well as her ability to write clearly and wittily.

He picked up his stick from the little cloakroom off the hall and set off to walk through the woods and ponder on the enigma which he thought that he had uncovered.

Unaware that Brandon had pierced to the heart of one of her mysteries, Nan was in the drawing-room patiently copying the Rector's latest chapter out in her finest hand, hoping that this time he would not suddenly determine to revise it again—for the fifth time—so that all her careful labour would go for naught.

Upstairs, in his study, her father was teaching Chaz. Jane was over at the Letcombes' and Kelsey was in the kitchens, superintending more jam-making, so the house was quiet for once.

Until a door banged and there was the noise of feet as Chaz thundered downstairs, his father, voice raised for once, shouting after him, 'Boy! Come back immediately.'

The drawing-room door was flung open and Chaz stood there, shaking, his face scarlet, his eyes full of tears.

'Oh, Nan, Nan, what am I to do? He never listens to me, never. I don't want to be a parson, but it is all that he can say to me—that I must be one. And today, because I construed everything correctly, and my Greek exercise was completed without a fault, he ranted on and on about what a great scholar I should make when I went up to Cambridge as he had done.'

Nan stood up, just as Chaz flung himself into her arms, saying, 'But why has that occasioned such a storm?' for she could hear her father walking agitatedly about overhead. He would not demean himself, she knew, by coming after Chaz, but would expect her to send him back upstairs again to be punished.

'Oh, Nan, you're the only one who ever listens to me,' Chaz wept into her chest. 'I told him that I had no intention of going to Cambridge, of being a parson, but that I wanted to be a soldier. I know that I find all book learning easy, but I would die if I stayed indoors all the time, and could not be in the open with the horses and the dogs. I would rather sign on as a humble trooper than be a curate—yes, I would. And he told me that he would thrash me daily if I ever said that I wanted to be a soldier again.'

Nan stood transfixed, hearing another boy saying similar things to her—that he too wanted to be a soldier, not to sit tamely at home waiting to inherit his father's estate, or waste his time going to university.

Were all boys the same? Did they all wish to wear a brave scarlet coat, regardless of the fact that war meant death and destruction more than it meant fine clothes and marching bands? Randal had died so soon after he had entered the Army, after his father had been persuaded to grant him his wish and buy him a commission.

'Papa could not afford to buy you into the Army,' she told the sobbing boy, 'so it is foolish of you to provoke him for nothing.'

This prosaic piece of advice was unlikely to afford Chaz any comfort, or any hope that his future might change—but she was unable to offer him anything better. Time was making it painfully obvious that he was temperamentally unfitted to follow in Caleb Fielding's footsteps—yet what else could a poor young man with a good brain do but enter the Church and hope for preferment? Even if she earned enough money to buy Chaz a commission, her father would never allow it, and that was that.

He gradually stopped sobbing as she stroked his dark head. Finally he broke away from her, dashed his hand across his tear-stained face, and said slowly, 'I suppose you're right, Nan—you always are. I had better go upstairs to apologise to him.'

'Better so,' Nan told him gently, resisting the urge to kiss his soft cheek. He must learn, and learn soon, that men must put a brave face on things, that tears were for women, and that what couldn't be cured must be endured.

Which was exactly her own case, after all. To make matters even more difficult, Desmond chose to call and be admitted into the hall just as Chaz shot upstairs again, the marks of his distress plain on his face, his greeting to Desmond perfunctory, to say the least.

His comment to Nan on Chaz was typically critical. 'The sooner that boy is sent away to school, the better for him. He needs strong discipline, and your father is too kindly to see that he gets it, I fear.'

'Whereas you would,' Nan retorted, Chaz's hopeless misery still with her.

Desmond never heard criticism of himself. 'Indeed,' he said complacently, 'and one of the benefits of your marrying me would be that I could see that Chaz was set on the right course.'

This unfortunate remark did not improve his chances with Nan at all. She wondered why he had come—to lecture them all, presumably.

But she did him a little injustice there. He had brought with him from his gardens a couple of baskets of early plums and several great bunches of flowers— surplus to his own requirements, he told her—somewhat ungraciously, she thought. He had the unhappy knack of making even his kind actions sound grudging.

Such generosity made Nan feel compelled to ask him to stay a little; in any case, he showed no sign of wanting to leave. She accordingly rang for the tea board—they had eaten a late luncheon, as had Desmond—and invited him to take supper with them later.

With the best will in the world Nan had no real wish to entertain him; she had far too much to do. Her father would expect the chapter to be rewritten before the morrow, which would mean that she would have to neglect Henry and Louisa, and she would much rather have been attending to them than to her father's clotted prose.

Chaz clattered by the window, proudly carrying his kite, on his way to the open country beyond the woods; small Jem, squat George and tall Roger were in attendance. Well, at least *he* was happy again, having placated his father.

Jane arrived with the tea board, Caroline Letcombe

in tow, and they began to drink tea, eat Bosworth Jumbles, and drive Desmond slowly mad. He had been hoping for a few sober words with Nan, and hung on in the hope that Jane and Caroline might retire to Jane's room to giggle and laugh together about life, hairstyles and clothes.

Her afternoon's work was definitely lost. Nan resigned herself to that, and consented to listen to Desmond prose on about the coming trial of the Luddites who had wrecked Harvey's Mill at Highborough; he showed no pity for the poor wretches who had lost their livelihood to the new machines.

Not that Nan condoned machine-breaking, but she had only to think of the men's poor wives and little children to realise that, hard though her own life might be, it was as nothing to the sufferings of the very poor.

After that Desmond complained gently about the changes Brandon was making to Gillyflower Hall, changes which Nan privately thought long overdue, and had the advantage that extra work was being brought to the district, for all the changes meant that more hands would be needed, both temporarily and permanently. He droned on remorselessly until Nan was hard put to it to stifle a yawn. Constant working far into the night was beginning to take its toll.

Desmond had just begun what she hoped was his final peroration when Chaz, his face on fire, shot by the window, hallooing. She saw Jackson come from the kitchens, and one of the grooms from the mews. By their expressions something was up.

'Goodness,' yawned Jane. 'Whatever is the matter with Chaz *now*?'

But her indifference was soon to disappear when Chaz flung open the door for the second time that afternoon, exclaiming breathlessly, as Jackson and the others made for the woods, 'Only think, Nan! When we were on our way home we came upon Mr Tolliver in the woods. He was being attacked by some rough men who took to their heels when we arrived. We don't think that he is badly hurt, but Roger and George stayed with him while we came for help. . .'

Jane's response was to throw up her hands like a heroine in a play, and exclaim, 'Oh, how very dreadful!' in a die-away voice.

Nan's response was to do something totally unexpected and untoward, quite out of character. She turned as white as any sheet, as Chaz said later, and fell forward in a faint. Exasperation with life and Desmond, extreme exhaustion and the news that Brandon had been hurt all combined to overset her quite.

CHAPTER ELEVEN

'WHAT a pother about nothing,' Brandon said, but the voice in which he said it was faint, his colour was poor, and he sat half propped up on the big sofa in the Rectory's downstairs drawing-room.

Mr Hampton, the local doctor-cum-surgeon, had been sent for—he had assumed, when Chaz had come panting to his door with the news that he was wanted at the Rectory, that Mrs Fielding had had another of her mysterious turns which no care of his, or any nostrum he might prescribe, seemed to be able to cure, they came and went so erratically.

'Mr Brandon Tolliver attacked and hurt!' he had exclaimed when Chaz had finally gasped out the true nature of his errand. 'Luddites, no doubt! Whatever is the world coming to?' A question to which he required no answer since to his mind the world had been going to the dogs since the French Revolution of 1789, when he had first arrived in Broomhall.

'You are wrong, sir, quite wrong,' he told Brandon now, pushing him back against the cushions as he tried to rise. 'You have suffered a heavy beating, your left wrist is damaged, and it is a wonder that nothing has been broken. You will be one vast bruise tomorrow, I fear. Today you must remain here and rest, no going home until the morning, and then only if I give you permission. You were fortunate that your attackers were interrupted, or Mother Linley would have been laying you out in your coffin!'

'But she isn't,' grumbled Brandon, even though he was happy to lie down again, for his head showed a disturbing tendency to swim whenever he tried to do anything vigorous. A bruise was purpling his cheek and one of the blows had damaged the top of his left shoulder, but his attackers had been disturbed before they could do him any mortal harm.

He had consented to having his wrist bandaged and to his arm being placed in a sling made from one of Parson Fielding's black silk scarves. Desmond and the Rector himself, who had deigned to come down from his study, stood about looking concerned, and making suitably sympathetic remarks. Kelsey, holding a bowl of warm water, assisted the doctor in his ministrations, and it was to her that the doctor gave orders as to how the patient was to be treated. Nan, who would normally have been taking charge of affairs, had been banished from the room when she had recovered from her faint, as had Jane, who, having seen Nan drop like a stone, had decided to do the same herself.

'Much liquid, a low diet, and rest,' the doctor finally ordered. 'Some port—but not too much, mind—will be beneficial.'

'You cannot really mean that I am to remain here until tomorrow,' Brandon protested, his voice strengthening as he began to recover a little from the shock of the sudden attack on him, so near to the Rectory. 'I cannot allow Mr Fielding's household to be so burdened.'

'No burden at all, my dear fellow,' Caleb reassured him. 'It is my Christian duty to play the Good Samaritan. You may stay here as long as the doctor deems necessary. Miss Fielding will prepare a room for you.'

So what Brandon had privately feared would come true was already doing so: any playing of the Good Samaritan in practical terms would fall on the already overburdened Nan—and where was she this afternoon?

He was enlightened a few moments later when
Parson Fielding asked the doctor to be good enough to
examine his daughters, who had retired to their rooms.

'They both fainted on hearing the dreadful news of
the attack upon Mr Tolliver, I am told.' He hesitated a
little, looking puzzled. 'I can understand Jane's fainting, she is such a sensitive creature, but Nan, now, that
is a surprise. She is usually of a much tougher fibre. It
was, I gather, her collapse which precipitated Jane's.'

He frowned. 'I trust it is only a passing malaise. My
wife has come to depend so much on Nan's good sense
about the house—and she is busy copying out my latest
work as well. I should be sorry if anything happened to
render her unable to carry out her duties.'

Shaky though he felt, Brandon might have come out
with something unforgivable as this piece of crass
insensitivity was poured over his aching head, had not
the door opened and the subject of her father's selfish
fears entered.

Nan's pallor was pronounced, but when she spoke
she was as composed as ever. 'So stupid of me to be so
childish as to forget myself, and make myself unable to
be of use,' she announced. 'I trust, Mr Tolliver, that
you are not greatly hurt?'

She could hardly look at Brandon, she was so worried
for him. She had sat in her room, in a stew of misery,
twisting her hands together, and the moment her legs
had become steady enough to take her downstairs she
had made her way to the drawing-room.

'It was most fortunate,' Brandon told her, 'that your
brother and his companions arrived just as the ruffians
were about to finish me off. It is kind of you to ask, but
should you be downstairs? You look as though you
need the rest which the doctor has prescribed for me
more than I do.'

It was as much as he dared to say before her father

and his cousin Desmond. Desmond indeed, frowned heavily, and added as soon as Brandon had finished, 'Just what I was about to remark myself, cousin. Nan must not overtire herself. She has a heavy load to bear.'

Another selfish swine willing to see her exploited, and not to say or do anything to assist her, was Brandon's internal reaction to that. He could not help continuing, as though Desmond had not spoken, 'One reason why I should like to be conveyed home is that I do not want to add to Miss Fielding's burdens.'

'Oh, no burden, no burden at all,' Nan cried hastily. Nothing, no, nothing should deprive her of the most delightful burden of all—looking after Brandon Tolliver. The mere idea was so exciting that colour returned to her cheeks, her whole body vibrated, and she felt as though she could do anything, anything at all, if that anything had to do with *him*. Brandon saw the change in her, and registered again that Miss Nan Fielding, when roused beyond her usual state of passive endurance, looked twice as handsome as she normally did.

'You are sure?' he asked her gently.

'Oh, quite sure. Think nothing of it. It is my Christian duty to look after those in need of succour,' she explained, consciously echoing what her father had often said, in case anyone should think that there was more to her eagerness than was proper.

Brandon didn't think nothing of it—he knew the extra sacrifices she would be called upon to make—but said no more. He could almost feel Desmond's irritation at his speaking to Nan after so personal a fashion. He was not surprised when his cousin said, as though the idea had just occurred to him, 'If the burden is intolerable, and it worries you, cousin, then I will take the liberty of driving you home. I shall be most careful not to jolt or distress you in any way by driving too fast.'

But the doctor, who had just returned from examining Jane, who was lying in her bed looking interesting, and who had announced that she too might rise and, like Brandon, partake of a low diet only, was having none of this.

'By no means,' he said bluntly, 'and I would ask that Mr Tolliver be put to bed as soon as one is prepared for him. I shall call early tomorrow,' he added severely, 'and I want no loose talk of him being driven around the country before he is well enough to be moved again.'

Desmond gave way with an ill grace, while Brandon, anxious to be rid of him, placed a hand across his eyes and murmured in a low voice which immediately had Nan looking worried, 'If you are intent on being of assistance, cousin, you could perhaps go over to Gillyflower Hall and inform Jenkins, my valet, that I need nightwear and a change of clothes. I wish you may also inform my sister of what has happened to me, and that I am safe, if a trifle damaged. She will be growing worried by now, seeing that I should have returned from my walk some time ago.'

'And I will see that the constable is informed of the attack on you,' said Caleb Fielding, showing a little practical sense for once. 'Although I think that the miscreants may be long gone. Luddites and Jacobins, one suspects.'

Privately Brandon doubted any such thing. He had done nothing to either Luddites or Jacobins to provoke three attacks on his person, and he was beginning to harbour quite different suspicions. They could wait until he saw Thorpe again. He must ask Carteret to set up a meeting through the system of private post which he and Thorpe had arranged.

In the meantime he wanted to enjoy the delightful ministrations of Miss Nan Fielding, who was hovering about him, her fine eyes anxious, her father's book and her own novel alike forgotten. To be of use to the man whom she now knew that she had come to love—what could be better?

Only his knowledge of the extra duties which he was creating for her by his presence at the Rectory spoiled Brandon's pleasure in being the subject of Nan's care and attention. A room was prepared for him, and Jackson was called on to help him up to bed where he was promptly served his supper.

His cousin had grudgingly visited Gillyflower Hall and had returned with Brandon's valet, who was found temporary quarters in one of the rooms above the mews—not exactly the kind of accommodation he was used to, but needs must, he told himself.

Nan watched with sad amusement as Jane invaded the drawing-room where Brandon lay on the sofa while his room was being made ready for him and offered to read to him. 'Something light, or something improving?' she prettily begged him.

He cried off, announced that his head would not allow him to concentrate on anything more serious than his next meal, and a comfortable long sleep after it, so Jane was unable to play her role as a ministering angel to the injured. Nan busied herself with organising the kitchen for two extra guests at supper—Desmond and his cousin—and spent some little time explaining to her mother what all the commotion downstairs had been about.

'How splendidly convenient!' Mrs Fielding announced, as though poor Brandon's attack had been kindly arranged by God to be of service to her family. 'Now that he will be here for a few days he will have time to get to know dear Jane better. Being with her daily, and seeing her in the bosom of her family, will surely convince him that he need look no further for a bride.

'I do trust, Nan, that you will make yourself scarce when they are together—let Kelsey act as chaperon. There can be no question that he might turn his attentions to *her*! In any case you will have quite enough to do in the way of extra duties without dancing attendance on him. Jane can perform any little errands about the house which he may require.'

Nan said nothing, being too busy wondering what these duties might be which Jane could perform, she being singularly unable to do anything other than beautify or entertain herself—neither of which talents could be seen as being of any real benefit to Brandon— other than that of pleasing his eye, that was.

All in all, by the time that she climbed the two flights of stairs to her room she was feeling that poor Henry and Louisa had grown very far-away and distant. The effort of reviving them both, and ending the scene which they had begun at such outs with each other that she could hardly imagine how she could ever make them be at ins again, seemed beyond her. All that she really wished to do was sleep.

Nevertheless, after she had undressed, not troubling to ring for the maid whom she shared with Jane, washed herself at the big wash-stand, had slipped into her sensible flannel nightgown with its large collar trimmed with a little cheap lace, undone her long tawny hair and brushed it until it shone and glowed, she felt refreshed enough to sit at her desk and begin to work again.

Unaware that in the distance at Gillyflower Hall an insomniac Lydia Bligh had registered that Miss Fielding must be at her work again, Nan wrote steadily along for some three quarters of an hour. She paused once, to laugh briefly as she thought up an amusing ploy which would have her hero and heroine incensed with one another just as it seemed that they were on the verge of reconciliation.

She also noted, a little drily, that in her mind's eye, on the stage on which he performed, Henry was growing to resemble Brandon Tolliver more and more. She was just reminding herself that she had given him blue eyes, not silver ones, when she heard a noise outside on the landing. She shook her head; she must be imagining things. The only other bedroom on the top floor besides her own was barely furnished and unoccupied: the servants slept either in the mews or in the atticks above Jane's bedroom.

There it was again—a sound as though someone had stumbled. Perhaps someone had entered the house for nefarious purposes, although why they should then mount to the top floor Nan could not imagine. She rose, picked up the candle by which she was working, crossed the room and carefully opened the door on to the corridor which led to the small landing at the turn of the stairs. . .

Brandon Tolliver slept almost immediately after he had eaten the light meal which Kelsey had taken up to him. After that his valet helped him out of his clothes and into his fine lawn nightshirt. He was more shaken than he cared to admit, although he also thought that the doctor's insistence that he should stay at the Rectory was rather nonsensical. He was not so overset that he would not have been able to manage the drive back to Gillyflower Hall.

On the other hand it was perhaps no bad thing for him to be made even more aware that Jane was not for him, and that Nan was even more exploited than he had imagined. Perhaps while he was here he could make up his mind what he ought to do about her, and his almost certain knowledge that she was the author of *Sophia*.

He fell into an uneasy sleep while thinking of her, and when he awoke in the small hours she was the first thing which came to his mind. The devil! What was wrong with him that he was mooning after a young woman past her first prayers—or for that matter any young woman at all? He would not have mooned after Jane if he had decided to marry her, that was for sure.

Now wide awake, and not likely to sleep, he lit his candle and looked about him for a book. Alas, all that was to be found in the way of reading matter was a copy of Parson Fielding's turgid masterpiece, and some aged numbers of *The Gentleman's Magazine*, hardly the most exciting reading even at the best of times, and this was most definitely not that. Not when all that occupied his errant fancy was the thought that Nan Fielding was sleeping directly overhead, with her hair down and all her clothes gone except for a nightgown. . .

Damnation! Simply to think about her was enough to rouse him—in God's name, he had not been as excitable as this about a woman since he had been a green boy! Perhaps it was simply the unorthodox manner in which he had met her—but no, there was more to it than that.

He tossed and turned. His shoulder and his wrist ached, his cheek throbbed. . .and somewhere else ached too, and was even more unassuagable than the rest of him.

The watch on his night-stand told him that it was two o'clock. Was she awake, writing, or had she finally blown out her candle?

Brandon sat up. Her room was above his. His room was opposite to the stairs which led to the upper floor. It would be the work of a moment for a man used to moving about without drawing attention to himself to mount the stairs and to check whether there was a light under her door. Why should he not do so? Risky, no doubt, but he had taken such risks before and got away with them—and he had nothing better to do with himself.

Between his varying aches and pains, further sleep was unlikely for the moment. Besides, the rest of the family slept in the far wing, the rooms on the floor he was occupying being dedicated to the Rector's study and a now unused nursery.

He crept cautiously out of his bed, picked up the candle, opened the bedroom door and began to mount the stairs. He reached the landing in time to see that, yes, there was a light under what must surely be Nan's door. A light, but no sound. It told him very little—other than to confirm that the light he had seen from Gillyflower Hall *did* come from her room as his sister had said.

Time to return—for how could he explain his wandering in the dark on the upper floor of the Rectory if anyone should discover him? Brandon turned towards the stairs. But his injuries had made him clumsy; he stumbled, recovered, and stumbled again, falling against the wall of Nan's room.

He swore to himself and stood still for a moment. There was no sound of movement from her room and perhaps she had heard nothing, or, if she had, had discounted it. But he was wrong, for even as he was reassuring himself the door to Nan's room opened, and she stood there, her beautiful turquoise eyes huge, her tawny hair unbound, candle held high, staring at his guilty self as though he were Mephistopheles in person, come to tempt her. . . .

For a long moment neither of them said anything. Brandon wondered for one glorious and impudent instant whether he ought to claim that he was delirious, and in his raging fever had wandered—he knew not where. He could stagger a little, fling his hand across his brow and moan at her, but no, he would not cheat her thus—and, what was more to the point, he didn't want her to react in such a way as to bring the servants along on the run. He shuddered at the inferences which might be drawn if they were discovered alone, in their nightwear. . .

'I could not sleep. I thought I heard something, feared a burglar, and came to inspect. I do apologise for disturbing you.'

Nan roused herself from the paralysis brought on by seeing a large and handsome gentleman clad only in his nightshirt. She was aware that his silver eyes were hard on her, mostly because of the charming spectacle she presented with her glowing hair hanging down to her delightfully rounded bottom. What would it be like, he mused, while she gathered her wits to answer him, if he stripped off her ugly gown, removed his own, and pulled her glorious tresses around them both. . .?

'As you see,' Nan finally managed, astonished by her own coolness, 'there is no one here but myself.' She paused, and said, a little naughtily, 'You were perhaps fevered, imagined what was not there. I think that you ought to return to your bed as soon as possible. You might take a chill, and that would never do.'

Her eyes were steady on him. Yes, he would pretend to be feeling weak, stagger a little, dammit. He wanted to enjoy the sight of her so informally clad for more than the few minutes she was offering him.

So Brandon did clutch his brow after all, muttering hoarsely, 'Yes, a fever. . .' adding something indistinct in the way of mumbling explanation, since invention told him that to be too specific about what might ail him would be unwise. He leaned forward against the

wall, his candle wavering dangerously about as he did
so.

'Oh. . .' Nan, prepared to dismiss Brandon briskly,
found herself holding him up instead. Through the
nightshirt she could feel his hard, warm body as, leaning
against her, he could feel her soft curves. The excuse of
not dropping his candle had him staggering backwards
into her room to sink into an armchair, at the same
time that he gave a surreptitious look about him. . .

Nan was too preoccupied to notice Brandon's deceitful goings-on. She took the candlestick from his
unsteady hand and placed it beside hers on her desk,
before going to the jug on the wash-stand to pour him
a glass of water.

His drinking it with avidity was not all deceit, for
Brandon found to his astonishment that he really did
feel decidedly shaky. Small wonder, what with a battered torso, a damaged wrist and shoulder, wandering
about a strange house in the small hours, and avidly
desiring an accessible female with whom he was now
alone.

Mixed with Nan's feelings that she really ought not
to be tête-à-tête in her own bedroom with Mr Brandon
Tolliver in the small hours was the very real temptation
to her common sense that he presented. Half of her
wanted him gone as soon as possible, but the other
half, the half which no one but Nan knew that she
possessed, wanted him to remain with her come what
may. . . Like Brandon—and some of her characters—
she was beginning to think in exclamation marks and
little dots. The sane part of her, which was rapidly
sinking beneath the waves of passion, told her that she
was doing so in order not to think of what they stood in
place of—the vision of herself in Brandon's arms.

'You are feeling a little better?' she ventured as she
saw colour begin to return to his ashen cheeks.

He was not lying when he told her that he was. His recovery was enabling him to look over to her desk where he could see two small piles of paper, an inkstand and a quill pen. Nan, who was being as deceitful in her way as Brandon was in his, felt compelled to explain why she was still up and about in the middle of the night.

'I was copying Papa's book,' she told him earnestly. 'I had no time to work on it today, and time, you understand, is of the essence.'

Which was, she thought, about the biggest thundering lie she had ever come out with, seeing that the book and a half which her father had written had taken most of his fifty-five years to accomplish; indeed, the first one had only been finished at all because of Nan's devoted secretaryship. But the explanation would have to do.

Brandon did not believe a word of what she was saying. He was more than ever sure that it was the warm hand of the author of *Sophia* which was holding his slightly fevered brow. To her horror Nan found herself stroking him gently and to touch him was temptation indeed. In another effort to excuse her forward behaviour she said gently, taking the naughty hand away, 'You really ought to return to your room as soon as possible. You should not be out of bed.'

'Nor should I be in your room.' Brandon stirred himself at last. The temptation which Nan was presenting to him had become so great that what he wanted more than anything in the world was to hurl himself into a tub of cold water to stifle desire. If he remained much longer in her company he was in danger of falling on her and throwing her on to the bed. How could she be so damnably cool? That alone was enough to excite any normal red-blooded man.

Nan was not cool at all. She wanted him gone. The devil was whispering in her ear, and Nan knew all about the devil and his works and did not want to encounter him, or them, again.

She watched Brandon rise reluctantly and make his way to the door. Before he left he turned to take one last look at her. The candle behind her on her little desk created an aureole of golden fire around her tawny head and body, adding to the enchantment of the night. For Nan the light it cast on him enhanced the strength of his face and the power of his body, barely concealed by his thin nightshirt. Her shiver was the result of passion, not of cold.

They stood staring at one another, until Brandon gave a muffled groan and, before she could stop him, strode towards her and caught her to him. He tipped her head back so that her hair fell like a shining waterfall down her back, his two hands cradling her skull. His mouth came down on hers with such magnetic force that Nan's shudder of desire in response to it consumed her whole body. She felt his hard arousal through his thin nightshirt—and felt her own knees weaken in an instant response to his urgency. She was on the verge of offering herself to him without reserve.

No, something shrieked inside her, no. He must have come here to seduce me, as he would have seduced the servant he took me for when we first met. I will not be his whore—for what would be the end of that but shame and misery in exchange for a few moments of passionate fulfilment?

With as much strength as she could muster she wrenched herself away from him, whispering fiercely, 'No, Brandon, no,' and lifted her swimming head to stare him full in the face.

His eyes, she saw, were blind. Desire had him in its thrall. So she repeated her refusal as loudly as she dared, fearful that she might wake the house, and if she did, what then? What then?

Still he resisted her, reaching for her mouth again, his hands beginning to roam her body, arousing sensation of such sweet delight in her that it took all Nan's moral as well as physical strength to place her hands on his chest and thrust him away from her.

Brandon blinked.

His eyes changed; he saw her again. Sanity returned. He said hoarsely, stepping away from her, his face full of passion shot with remorse, 'I'm sorry, Nan. Oh, I'm sorry; I shouldn't have done that, but the good God alone knows how much I was tempted. . .how much merely to see you undoes all my good resolutions.'

Nan shook her head at him, and said as coldly and severely as she could, for he was not for her, 'No, Brandon, you shouldn't. And as for temptation, you brought that on yourself when you came to my room uninvited. Recollect it is Jane to whom you have been paying your attentions.'

But he took no note of what she was saying. Jane meant nothing to him, and Nan meant—what?

Someone whom he should not violate. Someone whom he must respect. Someone with whom he must not be found in the dead of night.

Brandon took her hand, kissed it, and started down the stairs. On reaching his room he fell shuddering on the bed. He was not a man who had needed to practise much self-denial in life or in love. He had always taken what he wanted, when he wanted it. He had never forced a woman, or been wanton or cruel, only, as he was now coming to recognise, he had always been selfish in his attitude towards them. For the first time he was having to take heed of the needs of another in a wholly selfless fashion, and the experience was not only new, it was disturbing. He was sailing in an uncharted sea, without a chart or a pilot, and his destination was unknown to him.

CHAPTER TWELVE

'Now, Jane, leave the poor man alone, do,' commanded Kelsey briskly. 'He needs to rest and you are moithering him.'

Jane rattled the backgammon dice angrily, and pouted across at Brandon who was reclining on the sofa and had been playing a losing game against her, partly because his conscience, that new-born baby creature, had been troubling him over Nan, and would not let him concentrate.

'I am keeping him amused, not troubling him,' she riposted angrily, waiting for Brandon to support her, but he had only been playing the game to keep her happy, and to stop himself from thinking about her sister. He didn't know which hurt him the more, his head or his heart.

'He doesn't look particularly amused,' remarked Kelsey acidly. 'Have you no duties to follow? Nan might welcome a little help today. I know that she is troubled because she is falling behind in her copying of your papa's book.'

'Nan has gone out this morning. She said that she needed to visit Mr Stone's office, so she cannot be too exercised about falling behind!'

Kelsey's answer to this was to lift the backgammon cup from the table and remove it, so that the game came to an abrupt stop. Jane's intention to protest again was stifled when, after a knock on the door, the little maid came in to say, 'Mrs Bligh has called, Miss Jane, and has asked if she may be allowed to speak to her brother—if he feels sufficiently recovered, that is.'

Jane's petulance was immediately dispelled by Lydia's arrival. Mrs Bligh was reassured to discover that Brandon had not been as badly injured as she might have feared. She thanked Jane, Kelsey and the absent Nan for their care of him, and handed over fruit and flowers from the newly restored Gillyflower Hall hothouses.

Jane, who was finding that having Brandon at the Rectory was proving less satisfactory than she might have imagined, preened herself a little, and sent Kelsey into the kitchen with the flowers and fruit so that she might have Brandon and Lydia to herself.

For some reason of which she was not entirely sure, Brandon was slipping away from her. When he had first arrived at Broomhall she had been certain that a proposal from him was only a matter of time. But his extreme attentiveness had slowly leached away, had turned into polite indifference, and she was sure that, of all unlikely things, it was Nan who was interesting him rather than herself!

Now how could that be possible? She had boasted to Caroline and Charlotte that she would be Mrs Brandon Tolliver before the summer was out, and it was the loss of face which Brandon's defection would cause her which troubled her more than the loss of his love, or of hers for him. What was worse was that she had discouraged George Alden, who had more than once been on the point of proposing to her, because he seemed so much less exciting as a possible husband than Brandon did with his charm, his maturity, and the slight air of mystery which had caused George to remark disapprovingly to her that his father thought him 'not quite the gentleman' for all his old name.

Kelsey brought in the tea board during the mid-afternoon—a country habit, since it more commonly followed dinner in fashionable circles. Chaz had come in, and between large helpings of sandwiches and pound cake was quizzing Brandon about his life in London. The whole party had become uncommonly merry when the door opened and Nan arrived, looking rosy.

Jane was just handing Brandon his cup of tea when he saw Nan come in. He looked up over it, and for a moment he forgot everything except that she was back with him. It hit him with the blinding force of a revelation that, whatever else, he loved her, would always love her, and had never known before what true love was. His whole expression changed before he recollected where he was—and that he was a man who never gave his true feelings away if he could possibly help it.

Jane saw.

Nan saw.

Oh, not Jane's stricken face, but Brandon's, with its momentary expression of revelation before it resumed its usual cheerful impassivity. For a brief moment her own face reflected his.

Jane saw Nan's face too.

In that moment Jane grew up. Jealousy roared through her. She knew at once that she had lost Brandon, that he would never now propose to her. She did not even want him to. She would die rather than have a man who preferred her plain elder sister to her own beautiful self. But if she was not to have him she would make sure that Nan never would. How she did not know. But she would. . .she would. . .do anything. . .anything. . .to thwart the treacherous lovers.

A few moments before she would have pouted, been petulant, shown her anger with the pair of them, even if they were not aware of why she was showing it. But her new maturity told her to bide her time, to pretend that nothing had happened while she waited for her revenge.

She was, indeed, very lively, very much the girl who would do anything—yes, anything—to ease Brandon's malaise and to help Nan. She even offered to go to the kitchen to order extra tea when Lady Alden and George arrived. Lord Alden was over at the Assizes and sent his compliments and best wishes to Mr Tolliver, and the hope that he would soon recover. As Jane bounced busily out of the room on her unaccustomed errand Nan wondered whatever could be the matter with her usually idle sister!

But she had no time to worry about that or anything else; the necessary work of the house engaged her. Later the Aldens were offered supper, which they declined—much to Brandon's relief; he was beginning to feel tired. She left Jane to play the gracious hostess, and once the arrangements for supper were in train, and she had discovered that her mother was willing to let Kelsey read to her for once, she retreated to her room to think over not Brandon and her love for him— that would have to wait—but what Sam had told her when she had seen him earlier.

'Murray is determined to have you unmasked,' he had said, bluntly for him. 'He sees more profit in that than in carrying on the excitement about your anonymity. That is beginning to die down, he says.'

'My unmasking would die down too,' Nan offered robustly. 'Particularly when it became plain to him and everyone else that a dull clergyman's daughter is the author of *Sophia*.'

'I suspect he is willing to take that risk. Besides, you may be sure that he will think up some other ploy to keep your public entertained.

'But it is not only that of which I wish to speak. You must take care, my dear. This attack upon Mr Tolliver may signal that none of us is safe. I have become aware that not one man but two are roaming the neighbourhood of Broomhall, enquiring not only who the author of *Sophia* might be, but also wanting details about your own family and Mr Tolliver's cousin, Desmond. I cannot think what else they can conceivably hope to discover.

'Anyway, one man has been discreet, the other clumsy. The clumsy one offered my clerk, Knowles, money. He knows nothing, and therefore was able to tell the man nothing, and handed him his guinea back. Even had he known he would have said nothing, he tells me.'

'Asking around the neighbourhood about our family as well,' echoed Nan thoughtfully. She seized on this point because it was the one which troubled her even more than any questions about her novel-writing. Please God, the past would remain safely dead! She shuddered.

Sam saw the shudder and misread it. He thought it was her authorship which troubled her, and said tentatively, 'Would it be so very terrible for you if the truth were known, my dear? It would free you from the burden of work you carry and would surely not distress your father overmuch.'

'Oh, you do not know him,' sighed Nan wearily. 'He has such a sense of honour. . .' She could not use the true phrase to describe her father's character, because had she done so she would have said 'sense of self-importance', and that would never have done. She could not confess to Sam that she had long ago judged her father and mother with the clear eye which she wished that she did not possess, but which made her such a powerful writer. So she concluded, 'It would trouble him greatly.'

Sam shrugged at that and said, 'You know best, my dear,' in a doubtful voice and did not pursue the matter further. . .

She heard the visitors leave, heard Jane come upstairs and go to her mother's room, and wondered a little that Jane had not chosen to remain with Brandon. On her way downstairs she met Kelsey in the hall carrying a silver salver with a glass of port on it.

'Your papa left word before he rode to the Letcombes' to dine with them this afternoon that I was to see that Mr Tolliver was kept supplied with this.' And she indicated the port. 'Would you help me by seeing that he gets it? Cook is in a fantod about supper. Jane has said that she cannot endure the thought of salmon this evening, and salmon is all she has! I need to smooth her down.'

The last thing which Nan wanted after her stressful afternoon was to have anything to do with the equally stress-inducing Mr Brandon Tolliver, but since Kelsey often tried to make Nan's hard life a little easy she felt she must try to help Kelsey whenever she could.

She found Brandon not reclining on the sofa but seated in the big armchair which faced the window and the back garden with its lawns and shrubbery. He seemed withdrawn and a little pale, but rose at her entrance. She carried the salver over to a small occasional table standing by his chair, and made to withdraw without speaking. Since the sure and certain knowledge that she both loved and desired him had struck her down last night, she wished to have as little as possible to do with him. Safer so.

It was not to be. He put out his hand and caught her by the wrist.

'Why are you avoiding me?'

His voice was as hard and blunt as though he were speaking to a recalcitrant clerk. He was showing her the face of the man of power which he truly was and which, so far, Highborough and its neighbourhood had never seen. He could hardly have looked or sounded less lover-like but, like Nan, in order to try to fight off desire he needed to control himself, and the effort of doing so was having its effect on him as well as on her.

Nan stood quite still. She looked away from him, for to look at him, feeling as she did for him, was more than she could bear.

'You know perfectly well why I am avoiding you. And now please release my hand. I have work to do.'

He gave a violent exclamation and tightened his grip. 'Damn your work, Nan. Look at me! No, do not turn away; I won't have it; look at me. Look me in the eye and say that again; I dare you.'

Nan looked him in the eye as he commanded, then dropped her own, and repeated in as colourless a voice as she could summon up, 'You know perfectly well why I am avoiding you.'

His face hardened still further; his grip grew almost cruel.

'No, I do not.' He was doing his damnedest, he knew, to make her confess her true feelings for him. He knew also that he was being cruel, but he could not help himself.

It was Nan's turn to look stern, to say, 'You must know, Brandon, that when you met my sister Jane you were so particular in your addresses to her that everyone assumed that at some stage in the near future an offer for her hand would shortly follow; you cannot pretend otherwise.

'Not only did she tell me so, but your sister, as well as all Jane's friends and acquaintances around Highborough, thought the same. Until she met you it seemed inevitable that she would marry her childhood playmate George Alden—a most suitable match.'

Brandon slackened his grip on her hand and said, his voice stifled, 'I had not met you then. I was not to know that——'

Nan interrupted him. 'To know what, Brandon? That you were so flighty in your attitude towards the female sex that you could be off with the one and on with the other, when you had allowed the whole of the county to assume that you were dead set on marrying Jane? For you were, were you not?'

'I can be accused of many things, but flighty is not one of them,' was his stiff response to that. 'And I made Jane no offer, no offer at all. . .'

'And that is no matter either. If you were not flighty, then you must admit that you behaved unscrupulously towards a young girl with little experience of life, and your withdrawal after being so particular will be as badly seen as though you had jilted her. You know as well as I do what that will involve for her future prospects. You see, I don't think you understand how different country morals and standards are from those of the town, of London. You were so conspicuous in your attentions to her that you might just as well have proposed.'

He was still holding her hand.

'Every word you say is a dart which pierces me to the core. Would you really have me propose to a female I do not love, when the one whom I prefer to her is standing before me?'

She must be brave. He must understand that even if he did not propose to Jane she could not allow herself to have anything further to do with the man who had been so treacherous towards her sister. If only they could have met before he had so much as seen Jane. . . But no, even that would not have done. She could not marry him; she could not marry anyone.

'I think that you did not love Jane when you made yourself so particular to her, nor when you thought of proposing to her, as I am sure you once did. But in any case it is for you to decide what you intend to do. . .'

So far, Nan thought, he has said no direct word of marriage to me, although he has said much of admiration, of preference—and of desire. Is it simply lust he feels for me, and I for him? If so I *must* refuse to have anything more to do with him, for it will not last.

Brandon lifted the hand which he held and kissed it tenderly. 'Nan. . .' he began.

The door burst open and there was Jane, staring at them, at Brandon holding Nan's hand, which he gently released at the sight of her sister, his sentence left unfinished.

'Oh, there you are, Nan. Kelsey was asking if Brandon had finished his port. I see that he has not.'

The prosaic words, flung into the storm of passion which, despite the coolness of their speech, had been consuming Nan and Brandon, had the effect of quenching it. Brandon sighed, snatched up his glass of port and drank it in one giant swallow before replacing the glass on the salver. Nan picked up the salver and moved away to leave Brandon alone with Jane, the last person on earth with whom he wished to be tête-à-tête.

No need to worry, though. Jane was almost as cool towards him as her sister had been. Looking at her, at her charming unspoilt beauty, her little air of command, he could understand why he had been so attracted to her when they had first met, but oh, how he wished that it had been Nan whom he had met at Sampford Lacy and then he would not be caught up in this damned confounded tangle.

He tried to be pleasant to her, ate his supper at table—the first meal at the Rectory which he had not taken as an invalid—and announced firmly that come what may he would return to Gillyflower Hall in the morning, for among the letters and papers which had been brought over to him earlier were some which demanded his instant attendance in London.

He did not also tell his kind hosts that among them was a report from his spy, Thorpe, concerning the Fielding family which had made him begin to think most furiously. Thorpe had written:

I have to inform you that Parson Fielding and his family left their previous living in Hampshire rather abruptly around the time of his son's birth. As I understand them, the circumstances were vague, and I would prefer not to confide the details of the matter to paper. I will report to you on your return to Gillyflower Hall.

Now, what the devil could that be all about? Brandon wondered. Was Thorpe manufacturing mysteries to justify his pay, or had he uncovered another secret? Useless to speculate; he would know more on the morrow, or the day after. Meantime he must go carefully. It had been his intention to challenge Nan over the question of her authorship, but living at the Rectory and seeing how vulnerable she was had changed his mind over that.

Whatever else, he must not hurt her more than he had already done—or Jane either. Who in the world would ever have guessed that, having seen and been mildly attracted by the younger sister's youthful and heedless charm, he would then fall headlong for her elder sister's character and gallantry? And, yes, for Nan's mature beauty, which was not of the common kind, enchanting when first seen, but was more like a difficult strain of music, which after a time, once mastered, was more attractive than the melody easily understood at the first hearing.

He shook his head again, astonished at his thoughts. He had never been an introspective man, but knowing Nan was beginning to change him, for she challenged all that he knew, or thought that he knew, about women. And he was beginning to understand that she was hedged about by secrets. One of them, he was sure, concerned her mother, the woman who was so seldom seen, the woman who lived in her suite of rooms upstairs, and whom few had ever seen or spoken to.

Lydia had been graciously allowed to visit her once, and had told him that she was well-informed, spoke trenchantly about the affairs of the day, and of the books she had read. He wondered whether Nan resembled her at all, and what had led to her life of retreat—which depended on Nan's utter selflessness. . . All thoughts led to Nan these days—and that was another new thing for him.

Both he and Nan went to bed that night not to sleep, but to think about the other. 'Star-crossed lovers', Shakespeare had called Romeo and Juliet, and each thought ruefully that his description applied to them both.

'Well, one of the Rectory's secrets is on the verge of being revealed,' Thorpe told his employer two days later as they sat in Brandon's study at Gillyflower Hall.

'You are about to inform me,' Brandon could not resist saying, 'that you have discovered that Miss Fielding, the Rector's eldest daughter, is the author of *Sophia*.'

Thorpe, who had accepted the chair which Brandon had offered him, and a large helping of good sherry, raised his glass to him in mock-salute and offered Brandon his congratulations. 'No need to have employed me. You have teased it out for yourself—while you were over at the Rectory, I dare say.'

'Before that.' Brandon was brief. 'Being more with the lady simply confirmed my suspicions.'

'And those of others.' Thorpe was equable. 'There was another spy in the neighbourhood—Murray's, the publisher's man, no doubt. He has been making his enquiries, and I don't think that Miss Fielding's secret will remain one much longer. I bribed the clerk at Paget's Bank in Highborough, who told me that Sam Stone personally pays into Parson Fielding's account the bank drafts which come from Murray. I don't doubt but that he took a guinea or two from Murray's man as well.'

'No secret can be kept forever,' was Brandon's comment to that, 'however careful one is. Which leads me to your other enquiries—I am not so forward in discovering the answer to those, I do confess.'

He was amused by the wryly cynical expression on Thorpe's face. 'Oh, no,' his man said simply. 'I am sure that you know the answer to one of them. Your cousin, Mr Desmond Tolliver, is certainly, as I believe that you suspected, behind the rather clumsy attempts on you, including the last one.'

Thorpe looked at Brandon's bandaged left wrist. 'I understand that Master Charles Fielding and his friends came upon his latest nasty effort. I have found the villain whom he hired, wormed Master Desmond's involvement out of him when he was getting drunk upon his hirer's payment, and frightened him away from undertaking any further villainy by pretending that I am still the Bow Street Runner which I once was. He gave me the name of another rogue who was his accomplice. What do you want me to do? Put the frighteners on Master Desmond? Or do you want to do that yourself?'

'God knows what I want! I want this not to have happened. Think of the scandal if it were revealed! And it would rebound on me, as you well know. I am the stranger, the interloper—"Not quite the gentleman",' he added, mimicking Lord Alden's measured and stately tones. 'If I had not existed,' he went on, 'then Desmond would have inherited and all would have been well. As it is. . .' He shrugged.

Raised eyebrows told him that Thorpe was waiting for him to finish. He went on, 'As it is I want you to watch him, act as *agent provocateur* even. I believe that you did that when you were with the Runners. Keep me informed of all that passes. He might prefer to hire a more subtle villain like yourself, rather than the incompetent simpletons he has been lumbered with so far.'

A nod told him of Thorpe's agreement. 'And then you deal with him—as you have dealt with others.'

Brandon nodded. 'Draw his teeth, quietly, when I have the evidence of his villainy. I want no man hanged on my account, and, damn him, he is my cousin.'

'True. Now, as to the other matter to do with the Fieldings. They came here from Hampshire, from Frensham Major, a small town with a richer living than this one—which you will allow was a strange move for a poor man. . .'

'The parson's patron there was one Sir Frankfort Scott. Scott's eldest son, Randal, and your Miss Fielding were childhood playmates. When she reached sixteen Sir F gave orders that the friendship was to end: they had turned into sweethearts. He intended his son to marry wealth, a rich heiress, not a penniless parson's daughter. The son, Randal, was desperate to be a soldier, and as a reward for giving up the girl his father bought him a commission in the Army. He was sent to the West Indies, and died there, of the yellow fever.

'At the same time Mrs Fielding was with child with Master Charles, and Miss Fielding suffered a long illness after Randal Scott left to be a soldier. The doctor ordered the two women into the country, for their health, it was said. Miss Kelsey looked after the parson, and the other three girls, while he threw up his living and came north to this one, found for him by his cousin Sir Charlton, as soon as his missis had given birth to Master Charles and was fit to travel.

'Mrs Fielding became an invalid permanently when she reached Broomhall, saying that bearing Master Charles had ruined her health. Miss Fielding, by now recovered, and being the oldest of the children, took over the burden of looking after the family with Miss Kelsey's help.

'So you see, first Miss Fielding lost her sweetheart, and then became the family drudge, by all accounts.' He stopped.

'And that's it?'

'All that I could discover, yes. The only odd thing is, as I said earlier, that of Parson Fielding giving up his good living for a poor one, but I gather Sir F went a trifle mad when he realised that his son and the parson's daughter were serious, like. Social living between the big house and the parsonage a bit difficult after that, one supposes.'

'Hmm.' Brandon rested his chin on his hands and thought of poor Nan, sweetheart lost, her mother withdrawn, devoting herself to a life of sacrifice—and all from the age of seventeen. Somehow something seemed to be missing from the story.

But it did account for her attitude to him, and to men in general, if for nothing else. He remembered the middle-aged autocrat Carrington Beaumains, Lancelot Beaumains' father, in her novel *Amelia's Secret*, who had tried to ruin poor Amelia's life for her. No doubt who *he* was modelled on, if Thorpe's story was true. Which, of course, it was.

He pulled open a drawer in his desk, took out a purse full of guineas, and tossed it over to Thorpe, who took it without counting it.

'More of that,' Brandon told him, 'when we have

settled my cousin Desmond's hash for him without the whole neighbourhood being thrown into an unseemly pother. The less pother, the more guineas for you, you understand?'

'Understood.' Thorpe rose. 'You don't want me to pursue the Fielding business any further?'

'Nothing further to discover.' No need to tell Thorpe that he was off to London for a time, would visit Frensham while he was at it, and try to find out anything he could. He had a merchant friend who knew the Scotts: Sir Frankfort had been a successful plunger in the stock market, and he was sure he could think up some useful excuse for visiting him.

He was not sure why he was going to such lengths, but in his business dealings it had been his usual habit to quarter his ground like a general before battle, and it had always paid off. Social life was no different, and the vultures hovered above its unsuccessful participants as well as the gods bearing wreaths for those who succeeded.

Brandon had every intention of succeeding, in love as well as in business life. It was for that reason that the next day, while his valet finished the packing of his bags, and while his post-chaise was being readied for him, he sat at his desk composing a letter which he had never thought he would write. He had, indeed, delayed writing it until the morning, for in a way he was surrendering the independent life which he had lived since he was sixteen. But he had slept badly and the reason, he knew, was that he wished that he had written the letter earlier, or had made the effort to offer for Nan in person.

It was, of course, to Miss Nan Fielding, and it contained not only a proposal of marriage, but a declaration of love from a man who had always laughed at the notion that love existed. He had expected to find the writing of it difficult, but as he began he discovered that the words flowed from him in a steady stream of passionate expectancy. It was as though he had found harbour at last, and having done so he was freed from all the constraints which he had bound around himself from the day he had been sent out into the world to make his way in it. He wrote:

My dearest Nan,

You will forgive me, I know, for writing to you when you have not given me permission to do so, but I must inform you that I have found in you the woman whom I never hoped to meet, the woman to whom I could give not only my love, but my unbounded respect and admiration. My respect is for the selfless manner in which you look after your family, and my admiration is for the cheerfulness with which you have performed, and continue to perform, your unending duties.

This being so, I humbly ask you to consent to marry me, as soon as the ceremony may be arranged after I have approached your father and asked him for your hand in proper form. Do not fear that our marriage will leave your family financially unprotected. It will be my duty, as well as my pleasure, to care for them and ensure that they are not financially harmed.

Whatever your decision is, I shall respect it, as I love and respect you, but I can only hope that it will go in my favour. I have loved you from the moment that you fell into my arms in the Rectory's pantry, and I hope that you will allow me to finish in marriage what we began then.

So far Brandon had written in the careful script which he used in his business letters, but now he finished in an impassioned scrawl.

Oh, my darling, my dearest love, do say yes, and make both of us as happy as I know we can be. Your loving and humble servant, Brandon Tolliver.

He sanded the paper, folded it, sealed it with the seal which he had inherited from his cousin Bart, and carefully wrote Nan's name on the front. He rang for Leeson, his most trusted servant, and told him to deliver it to Miss Fielding at the Rectory. 'I ask you most particularly,' he said, 'to make sure that if you are unable to deliver it into her hands, then you will give it either to Miss Kelsey, the housekeeper, or to Jackson, the Fielding's man of all work.'

Leeson assured him that he would, and set off on his errand. All Brandon's servants were particularly eager to see that his orders were promptly and punctually carried out, for they found him a hard but fair master, who rewarded well those who served him well.

Brandon, on his way to his chaise, watched him go. Surely Nan could not refuse such an offer, made from the heart as it was? He would live in hope until he returned from London. It was annoying that his presence was required there at this juncture, but he had learned to live with expectation, and he thought that Nan would find it difficult to refuse someone with whom she was so obviously passionately taken.

Leeson walked briskly to the Rectory, to discover that Miss Fielding was not in. She was making parish calls to the poor, Jackson said, in company with Miss Kelsey, for whom Leeson asked when told that Miss Fielding was not available. But Mr Tolliver had told him to give the letter to Jackson, failing anyone else, and so he did.

The letter was duly placed on the silver salver which reposed on a small side-table in the Rectory's entrance hall for Miss Fielding to pick up when she returned from her errand of mercy. It rested there for the best part of an hour until Jane reached home after a ride with Caroline Letcombe. She recognised Brandon's hand and stared at the name of the addressee. Jealousy rode on her shoulders. Jackson saw her pick it up and remarked, 'Mr Tolliver's man Leeson left that for Miss Fielding.'

'Oh, indeed.' Jane waved the letter in the air. Whatever could Brandon be writing to Nan about? She made for the stairs, throwing at Jackson over her shoulder, 'I will put it in my sister's room for her to read when she returns.'

Jackson thought nothing of that, if he thought at all. The Fieldings were given to such small and helpful acts, particularly Miss Fielding. It was perhaps a blessing that Miss Jane was being a little more thoughtful than she had been of late.

Jane's thoughtfulness actually took her into Nan's room. She was about to place the letter on Nan's desk when jealousy and curiosity both overcame her.

Why ever should Brandon be writing to Nan? What could he have to say to her that was so urgent that he should send a letter to her on the day that he left for London? The small hesitancy which had the letter hovering in Jane's hand over Nan's desk stretched on and on. . .

And, almost as though her hands belonged to someone else, Jane found them opening Nan's letter, carefully preserving the seal so that she might refasten it— to read it feverishly, listening for any sound from downstairs which might herald her sister's return.

He was proposing to Nan! She was his darling! His dearest love! Oh, the devil, how dared he? It was she, Jane, to whom he had been '*most* particular'! And then the villain had transferred his attentions to Nan! And what had he been doing in the Rectory pantry with Nan—and when? At the very thought of Nan in

Brandon's arms, Jane's hands—without her consciously willing them to—crumpled the letter, breaking the seal into pieces, so that she would be unable to reseal it.

She stared down in horror at the crumpled paper—and the full enormity of what she had done struck home, so that she stood trembling. She would not now be able to give Nan the letter without letting her know that she had opened it and read it. . .

Even as she thought this the devil prompted Jane. Why should she not keep the letter? Why give it to Nan at all? Brandon did not deserve her; he didn't deserve anyone—and nor did Nan if she had been pursuing an intrigue with him behind everyone's back. If Brandon received no answer he would assume that Nan had turned his offer down. Besides, wasn't it likely that Nan would turn the offer down? He obviously half thought that she would—and what could he mean by all the work that Nan was doing to keep the family going? The maunderings of someone besotted, no doubt.

All the time that she was thinking these distressing and unpleasant thoughts Jane had been walking out of Nan's room, along the landing, down the stairs—the letter pushed into her hanging pocket—and up the other stairs to her own room, where she took the letter out of her pocket and pushed it out of sight to the back of the drawer in her little dressing-table, beneath a small pile of pocket handkerchiefs. She could neither bring herself to destroy the letter nor to hand it back to Nan with an apology for having opened it.

Putting it into the drawer made it almost as though it had never been delivered. She would pretend that it had not, and, doing this, she tried to persuade herself that she had not meant to injure Nan when she had intercepted and opened it. She heartily wished that she had never seen it.

But the damage had been done.

CHAPTER THIRTEEN

UNAWARE that Brandon had sent her a love letter proposing marriage, Nan returned from her afternoon of charity, to learn from her mother, who had watched Brandon's small procession make its way through Broomhall, that he had left for London—'or so Jane says'.

Left for London! Unexpectedly Nan found that to think of Brandon not being near by at Gillyflower Hall carried more than a hint of desolation. Which was stupid, she reproached herself. She had lived for nearly twenty-eight years without Brandon, and must most probably resign herself to living many more without him.

The long littlenesses of Rectory life surrounded her. Jane, for some reason, was being uncommonly irritable. She snapped at Nan when Nan asked after George Alden who had visited Letcombe's Landing while Jane was there. Jane's irritability grew worse as the evening wore on, for the sense of guilt which she felt over Nan's letter grew stronger, rather than weaker, with time. Always before, when Jane had done something naughty, she had been able to shrug it off, but this time the enormity of her sin began to overwhelm her as the days passed by.

She could hardly bear to speak to Nan, repeatedly snapped at her, and was even cross with her devoted admirer George Alden, who sadly put it down to the absence of that cad Brandon Tolliver. Jane herself could hardly bear to think about Brandon—she was beginning to wonder why she had thought him attractive at all if he had been able to make her do anything so wicked as steal his letter to Nan.

Of the three most involved, Nan was, for the moment, the only happy one. Jane was living in a hell of her own making, and Brandon was wild to return to Broomhall to discover what answer Nan had sent to his letter. He was as conscientious as ever in his dealings with the Rothschild brothers whose letters to him had drawn him back to London. He and they were satisfied with one another, and his business with them was completed much sooner than he had expected, so that he made his way to the Fieldings' old home in Hampshire two days earlier than he had hoped.

Frensham Major was a small and pretty town, visibly rich, which made Parson Fielding's translation to the poorer living at Broomhall even more mysterious. Sir Frankfort had expressed his willingness to entertain Mr Tolliver at his home, and had even asked him to stay for several nights if he so wished.

He was, Brandon discovered with some amusement, a pompous man, exactly like Carrington Beaumains in Nan's novel. He had obviously been handsome in youth, and had worn quite well, although he was now heavy; his wife was another matter altogether. She was a duke's daughter, and proud of it, and Brandon had no doubt, after taking dinner with them on a late and sunny afternoon, that she was the one who had resisted Nan as a possible bride for her oldest son.

He met the heir, Hervey Scott, who resembled his mother in being large and blond, unlike his father who was large and dark. He was sluggish, too, and Brandon found it difficult to believe that he resembled poor dead Randal, his elder brother and Nan's lost love. Nan could never have loved such a stolid lump as Hervey Scott was.

'Broomhall?' drawled Lady Scott at dinner, over a

delicious rack of lamb—she kept a good table, which accounted for the family's size. 'Isn't that where the Fieldings went, Frankfort, my love?'

She knew perfectly well that it was, was Brandon's sardonic reaction, but he allowed Sir Frankfort to confirm his wife's belief before Brandon remarked that the Fieldings were still at Broomhall.

'And the eldest daughter, Nan? Is she still unmarried?' Lady Scott asked. 'She and my poor dead Randal had a tiresome romance, a rather ridiculous *tendre*, you understand. The girl was a perfect hoyden. Not at all suitable to be a wife for a Scott, as I think Randal realised before he went to the wars. We should never have let him have his way and become a soldier.'

She raised a handkerchief to tearless eyes, rather because she was expected to than because she was genuinely moved. Hervey stolidly ate his dinner. He could hardly be expected to mourn his brother's death, seeing that he had inherited as a result of it. Brandon deplored the cynicism which the Scotts were inducing in him, and he could only be grateful that Nan had been spared marriage into such a tasteless *galère*.

But a hoyden when she was young? Yes, he could believe that of the woman who had fallen into his arms in the pantry and whom he had found up a tree, rescuing her brother's kite. Lively young Nan Fielding still existed beneath the armour of propriety which she wore as the Reverend Caleb Fielding's eldest and responsible daughter.

It was difficult to know how to answer her. He decided to be bland. 'Oh, no, Miss Fielding has not married, although two of her younger sisters have already made good matches, and the youngest, Jane, is expected to do so.'

'Too clever for most men, one supposes,' offered Sir Frankfort, in a remark which was slightly vicious, or rather shrewd, whichever way you wanted to take it. Both, probably, was Brandon's somewhat uncharitable thought, seeing that Sir Frankfort's keen eye for a bargain or a deal was causing him to double the considerable fortune which his father had left him.

Later Brandon drank tea in a magnificent drawing-room filled with Chippendale chairs, a sideboard by Hepplewhite, and some superb china set out on shelves around walls hung with a marbled paper of great beauty and equally great expense. His eye was caught by a small portrait of a tall dark young man wearing hunting clothes and carrying a sporting gun. Behind him was a groom flying a kite.

Lady Scott saw the direction in which he was looking. 'My poor son Randal. One of Thomas Phillips' better efforts. Worth a second look, I always think.'

Indeed it was, was Brandon's reaction, but perhaps not for the reason which Lady Scott assumed.

'You will allow?' he asked, and walked over to inspect the portrait more closely.

Lady Scott chattered on behind him, but Brandon ignored her, parts of the puzzle which the Fieldings presented falling slowly into place as he carefully examined Randal Scott's boyishly handsome face.

'I hear that Mrs Fielding is now an invalid,' Lady Scott volunteered to his back. 'I understand that she has been so since before the birth of her last child and only son. Charles, is he not? She had to go deep into the country away from the bustle of the town when she became enceinte with Charles.'

'Yes.' Brandon sat down at last. There was a rather strange look on his face, and his dislike of the self-satisfied company he was in grew with each moment. The poor Fieldings, to have found themselves involved with such a graceless and selfish crew! Sir Frankfort was particularly appalling, because Brandon's own clear-sighted self-assessment informed him that were he to continue living a life in which he only cared for himself, his pleasures and making money he would probably end up like him.

Politeness kept him anchored in Frensham for two nights. Before he left he promised to pay Sir Frankfort and Lady Scott's respects to the Fieldings—'they were, after all, of good family, if a trifle eccentric', was Lady Scott's epitaph on them. He thought grimly that if Lady Scott knew the whole truth about the Fieldings, which he now thought that he did, she might feel constrained to reach a different verdict.

All in all he was happy to be on his way back to Gillyflower Hall, and Nan, again. Visiting Frensham had had the effect of making him love her more than ever—and had also filled him with a fierce desire not only to get into bed with her, but to shelter her from the world's despite.

Nan was too busy trying to cope with her family to spare Brandon much thought. Only at night when she was alone did she permit herself the luxury of remembering her times alone with him.

It was bad enough that her father had revised the last two chapters of his book again, that her mother was having a fit of the restless megrims which made her send for Nan every hour or so, usually on some imaginary pretext connected with her health, but as a kind of rancid icing on a singularly dry cake Jane was driving everyone mad by her temper, her tantrums, and her frequent unexplained fits of sobbing.

Questioned by Nan and by Kelsey as to what was wrong with her and should the doctor be sent for, she threw them off, exclaiming pettishly, 'I have a fit of the megrims these days; my head hurts and my nose is sore!'

'That is because of all the crying you have been doing,' remarked Kelsey bluntly. 'Really, child, you have been making the most unseemly fuss over Chaz's not being as respectful to you as you think he ought to be.'

This was because her latest crying fit had been caused by a quarrel with Chaz which had ended with him informing her what a poor thing she was compared with Nan. 'Now, *she* knows how to talk to a fellow, and you don't. You've never once helped me to fly my kite.'

For some reason—oh, but she *did* know what the reason was—these days the mere mention of Nan's name was enough to send Jane into a fit. It reminded her too much of Brandon's letter, which, although it lay physically upstairs in her dressing-table drawer, also lay heavily on her conscience, and she could find no way of ridding herself of her unwanted burden. She felt like the unfortunate man in the fairy-tale who was doomed to carry a heavy load with him everywhere he went, and who saw no prospect of ever being rid of it.

Nan said, exasperated, 'I thought that you had arranged to visit the Letcombes today, Jane. For goodness' sake, go upstairs, ready yourself, and tell Jackson to bring the carriage round for you. You will feel better after a good gossip with Caroline.'

Such kindness from the sister whom she had betrayed was almost the last straw. Jane's eyes filled with tears. For a moment she almost gave way, told Nan what she had done, gave her the letter and begged forgiveness.

And then she thought of Kelsey's reproaches, of what Nan would think of her—and Brandon. . .and she allowed herself to be persuaded to visit the Letcombes, to try for a little time to forget the pains and penalties which followed sin and plagued the sinner. Nan watched her carriage go down the drive, her face puzzled—for her sister's behaviour was most uncharacteristic. Then she shook her head, and forgot Jane's megrims while she performed the endless and busy tasks of her day.

Late in the afternoon Kelsey came in and told her that Brandon had returned from London. He would be present, or so his man had said, at Sam Stone's soirée the following evening, when half of Broomhall and district—or rather the gentry portion of it—would turn up for the ladies to take tea and coffee and eat cake, and the men to drink his good port in his splendid gardens. The news had Nan singing under her breath as she helped Kelsey to make jam of the first of the summer's plums.

I shall see him tomorrow, she thought, and talk to him, and that alone will be bliss—like playing gold harps in heaven and singing with the archangels! A flight of fancy which had her laughing at herself.

Brandon was not so happy.

There was no letter from Nan waiting for him. He had made straight for his study and the small pile of correspondence put on one side for his return, sure that her letter would be there. But no. She had not answered him.

Oh, but she had! By her silence, she meant refusal. He swore nervously to himself, his brow black. By God, he would neither repine nor surrender! He would carry the attack to her. She should not so lightly escape him. He knew that she loved him. It was written on her face and on every line of her body when they met, so what nonsense, what piece of piff-paff, what quirk of imaginary morality, could be keeping her from him?

He would convert her! No missionary to a savage island would be as sincere as he would be in his campaign to make Anne Fielding his wife. He would not have her devoting her life to her selfish family. No, indeed, she must devote it to selfish Brandon Tolliver instead!

Like Nan he laughed at himself a little. He would not descend on her immediately—that would be boorish—but he would be seeing her at Sam Stone's. He would find a secluded part of Sam's splendid gardens, and he would begin his campaign there. And if he could not make Sam Stone's soirée Nan Fielding's Waterloo, then he would find a better site where he would bring her to surrender at last.

Just as though he were one of the Scots Greys going to that last great battle, Brandon dressed himself as splendidly as he could. The day was hot, so he wore a light short jacket, a cravat which was not too confining, but whose understated and well-bred elegance was yet another tribute to his valet. His hair was brushed into a modified Brutus cut, and he would have been blind not to be aware that he was a man who would always attract a second glance. Not only his clothes but his height, his shapely body, honed to muscular perfection by the hard work of his early youth, were always sure to draw admiration. The Tollivers had been famous for their looks, and he was no exception.

Nor was his cousin Desmond, even if his clothing was of a more sombre cast. He was the first man Brandon greeted when he made his way through the glass doors of Sam's drawing-room into the gardens, a glass of port in his hand. He was looking for Nan, but seeing Desmond was always a bonus. By Thorpe's latest report, read that morning, his agent had almost drawn Desmond into the snare where Brandon could confront him with his villainy and—if he was lucky—draw his teeth.

But today he was joviality itself to his cousin, even if his eyes quartered Sam's garden for a sight of Nan.

And there she was!

Oh, damn the clothes she was wearing! He would see, when they were married, that she was dressed to show off the perfect body, the creamy complexion, the great turquoise eyes and the splendid tawny hair. Mrs Tolliver would be the envy of all, and no mistake!

Today she was the envy of no one, but Brandon did not love or desire her the less. She was the pearl of great price, hidden away from the multitude, if not in the gutter, then in the drab drawing-room of a thankless father. He would pick up the pearl, polish it, and put it in a perfect setting, so that all should envy him. . . .

Why, he thought in wonder, I am like to run mad, I want her so, and I want the world to see what a treasure they have passed over.

Who would have thought it? Lydia, watching him, suppressed a sigh, for she read him truly, and hoped that the brother whom she loved would find haven with a woman whom he loved and who loved him.

'Miss Fielding,' he said, and bowed to her punctiliously. Jane was by her side, but he did not see her. He saw only Nan in her drab dark grey gown with its Quaker-like white linen collar and its three-quarter-length sleeves. He wanted to tear it off, not only to make joyful love to her, but to replace it with something more suitable.

Before the others they made small talk. Not only Lydia, however, was aware of how much of a blind that was. Poor suffering Jane, and Sam Stone, also watched and endured. Lydia saw Sam's eyes on the lovers, and, moved by the anguish she saw there, felt constrained to say something to him to relieve it.

'They are meant for each other,' she told him gently, and though she uttered neither name he knew of whom she spoke. 'She will soften him, and he will make sure that she does not constantly sacrifice herself for others—if he persuades her to marry him, that is.'

Sam said, through stiff lips, 'I want her to be happy, whomsoever she chooses. And your brother is nearer to her in age than I am.'

Lydia nodded, put her gloved hand on his arm, and murmured, 'Come, let us leave them together. It is easy, I know, to say what can't be cured must be endured, but it is a motto of whose truth I have painfully come to be aware.'

They moved away. Sam gave up his dream of a life with Nan, but, almost without knowing it, another life was opening up before him as he escorted Lydia Bligh to a table where a light summer punch stood. Serving Lydia with a cup of it, he began, for the first time, to forget Nan a little.

Brandon could not forget Nan, nor Nan Brandon. With a light touch on her arm he led her away from the rest of the company, down a long alleyway to a corner of the garden where a stone Cupid stood behind a bed of roses. For a moment Jane made to follow them, but, seeing George with a group of friends, gave up the notion and instead joined them, and tried not to worry over whether Nan and Brandon would discover, either at once, or later, that Brandon's letter had gone astray.

Without knowing it, luck was with her. Near to his love, Brandon could see that there was almost a transparent look about her. For the first time she betrayed a fragility which troubled him, and which was owing, he knew, to the double life she was living. Working both during the day and the night was taking its toll of her. Whatever he said, he must not distress her.

Nan felt that she must say something, and that something must be innocuous. 'You are back earlier than you expected, I believe?' There! Surely that was banal enough for anything?

Apparently so. His silver eyes glinted. He said, gravely, 'Indeed. For once the Rothschilds moved quickly—I am usually a little too impatient for them, but this time their impatience matched mine. We agreed, and the business was done.'

'That is a whole world of which I know nothing,' Nan told him.

'As I know little or nothing about being a member of a parson's family,' was his riposte to that.

'That is little enough to know,' Nan sighed back at him.

Just to be with him was enough. He had taken her hand in his, and was swinging it gently as Randal had done when they were children. But she was not a child now, and nor was Brandon. He was very much a man. Even at the end, before he had left for the last time, Randal had still been a youth, with his man's strength yet to come.

'You have made your choice, then,' Brandon said, his eyes hard on her now, 'and it is to stay with your family. You will not regret what you have done, or reconsider?'

Nan found this a little ambiguous. She concluded that he meant the choice she had made when she had agreed to act as the family's mother and guardian, once her mother had retired from life. So she answered him with a little sigh. 'A hard choice, I know. But what is left to me? One's duty has to be done, and a parson's daughter is the person most likely not only to know that truth but to obey it.'

Brandon would have preferred there to be a little regret in her voice, some acknowledgement of what they must both be suffering as a result of her decision to refuse his offer. Not answering him had apparently been her way of refusing him. Was it a kinder way? He thought not.

Having her so near, and being alone with her, was causing him to forget all the good resolutions he had made to go slowly with her, not to disturb her, or attack her with his love.

'Nan!' he exclaimed hoarsely, taking her by the shoulders and swinging her around to face him. 'I beg you to reconsider, Nan, I love you, worship you. You can have little doubt of that now.'

Holding her was compounding his distress. He bent down, kissed her on her tender mouth, murmuring, 'To see you is enough to make me want to break each of the ten commandments. Slowly, one by one. Surely, as a parson's daughter, you will relieve me of that temptation? You already know that I am willing to offer you everything which is mine. My name, my fortune—and, dare I say it to you, my body. Think carefully, my darling, before you refuse me.'

His kisses grew stronger, his hands more urgent. Nan replied in kind, her senses swooning to the degree that she saw nothing odd in what Brandon was saying to her—for when had he made her such promises before? Only—and she did not know this—in the letter which she had not received.

For a second they were 'The world forgetting, by the world forgot,' but even as their passion mounted the consciousness that they might be disturbed at any moment moved them both. Both stood back together, the warning bell of prudence having sounded for them both at the same moment. In this, as in everything else, they lived and thought as one.

'No!' The word exploded from both of them.

Nan said, almost shyly, hanging her head, as she stepped back from his embrace, 'You told me that I must know how deeply you feel for me, Brandon. Now how should I know that, seeing that so far we have said much of mutual attraction, of desire even, but nothing more than that?'

Even in the throes of thwarted passion, for Brandon's

body had responded as strongly to having Nan in his arms as a virile man's might have been expected to, he had enough rationality left in him to understand the true sense of what she was saying.

She was telling him quite plainly that he had given her no indication that his feelings for her were more than those of passing desire, of lust. But he had written to her much more than that, had he not? Oh, but he had; he had bared his inmost soul to her in his letter, had he not? And asked her to marry him. Something which he had never done before. And she had rejected it, and him, had she not?

But had she? The look she gave him was limpid, filled with truth. Nan would not flirt or palter with him. If she had read his letter she could have no doubt of his love, or his intentions.

Like a trapped animal trying to escape from the pit into which it had fallen Brandon's mind twisted and turned as he contemplated this unexpected puzzle.

What if?

What if?

What if she had not received his letter?

Was that possible?

He had given Leeson the letter to deliver and he had said that he had handed it to Jackson—so she must have received it.

But, by every word she had uttered, she had not.

So it had gone astray. She had never received his proposal, the letter which he had written with so much love, and, much though he now longed to propose to her again on the instant, he could not do so until the mystery of the letter had been solved. He wanted nothing to mar his offer when at last he made it, solemnly and in proper form. To rant about lost letters would be desecration. More, he did not wish to propose here in Sam Stone's garden where they might be interrupted at any moment.

Thought was rapid but, even so, Brandon's silence lasted longer than he supposed. Her eyes suddenly filling with tears, Nan assumed that perhaps, after all, he had been toying with her.

'You would wish to return to the others,' she ventured, not wanting to look at the stone Cupid, the little god of love who seemed to have been playing games with her.

'Not quite yet,' he said, his voice hoarse again, with desire, mixed with anger, for he thought that he knew who might have been playing tricks with Nan's letter. 'Not before I have told you how much I love and honour you. So much so that I will not treat with you here. What lies between us must be, and shall be, done in proper form. I shall not assail you again, and here is my word on it.' And he went down on one knee before her, taking her work-worn little hand in his to kiss it reverently.

'Bear with me for a time, my love. Trust me and all shall be well.'

'No, Brandon,' she told him. 'Wait. I cannot be for you.'

'No,' he said, in his turn. 'Make no decisions now, my love. When the time comes you will, I know, accept me. Think only that I love and honour you. Hold that to you in the dark watches of your long nights. For the moment let us return to the others.'

Nan was silent. There was something compelling about him, almost as though he was willing events to go in the way in which Brandon Tolliver wished them to go—had ordered that they go. For once she would be will-less, she decided, and she walked away from the stone Cupid, down the glorious flower-bordered alley. Never in her life had she felt as she did now, Brandon by her side: that every nerve in her body thrilled at his presence, as though he were a master musician, plucking at his violin.

Of all those present there were three who had noticed their absence, and watched them return. They were Jane, Desmond Tolliver and Sam. Although he had surrendered all hope of making Nan his wife, Sam still felt that it was his duty to care for and to protect her since no one else would. He needed to speak to her, and when Brandon had departed to take Desmond to one side and talk lightly with him as though he had no idea that it was his cousin behind the murderous assaults on him Sam made his way to her.

Like Brandon he thought that she looked frail, and like Brandon knew the true reason why. He handed her a glass of lemonade and offered her a plate of his cook's best biscuits before he said, 'You must bear with me for what I have to say, Nan. Murray's spy has discovered your identity. He has written to me and asked me to so inform you. He intends to make the news public any day now, and you must be ready for the excitement it will inevitably cause. There is nothing more that I can do to protect you. And, you know, we were always aware that in the end discovery was inevitable.'

Nan nodded, feeling numb. It was simply one more blow to fall on her hapless head.

She had turned so white on hearing this unwanted news that Sam put his hand out to steady her. 'Come, my dear, sit down, I beg of you.' He led her away from the crowd into a seat by a gap in a small hedge which separated them from the big lawn, where the majority of his guests were gathered.

Once there he began to speak again, to try to reassure her. 'One good thing about your identity being revealed is that you will not need to work at dead of night, and I shall persuade your father that your burden must be lightened. There is no reason why Jane should not spend some of her time copying your father's book. I am fearful that carrying out all your many other duties on top of your writing will result in your falling into a decline.'

Nan smiled shakily. 'You are kind to say so, Sam. But I am sturdier than that. Allow me to sit and think a little of what I must say and do when everyone learns that I am the author of *Sophia*. I must confess that were it not for the money which has helped to make all our lives easier I would wish that I had never started writing, never sent *Sophia* to Mr Murray.'

Sam hesitated. There was something else which he needed to say to her. Yes, he would say it.

'My dear,' he began, as gently as he could, 'I am of the opinion that we have not deceived everyone.' He paused, and in that pause Nan spoke, her breathing growing a little rapid.

'Why, Sam, why do you think that? And who could have guessed?'

'Perhaps I should not have said anything, my dear, but you are intelligent enough to be aware that in such a profession as mine one picks up hints and clues not only from what people say, or don't say, but from the very manner in which they say it.

'Last week Mr Brandon Tolliver came to see me. He was speaking generally of parish matters. . .of your father—of whom, by the way, he is not an admirer. Something he said stuck in my mind. He indicated that your father did not deserve your devotion to him and the parish, which was, he hinted, in addition to all the other work which you did and which helped to sustain your family's style of living. He told me that he was worried about your health, and sought my assurance that I would try to influence your father to lighten at least that part of your labours—of which he knew.

'There was something strange, a little guarded in his manner. Looking back, I am sure that somehow he knows that you are the author of *Sophia*. He has said nothing to you on that score?'

Nan felt as though she had taken a hard blow in the stomach. She faltered, 'O—only of how much he admires her writing. He has repeatedly told me that. . .' And she stopped. 'I fear you may be right. But he has said nothing to me—nothing direct, that is.'

Could it be true? Had Brandon somehow guessed? Had he even used his formidable wealth to hire a spy of his own to check what he thought to be true? And should she be distressed if he had? Was that why he so constantly spoke to her of her many labours? Had he guessed that night when he had come to her room? And had he come to find out whether his supposition was true, as well as to take the opportunity to make love to her? And what did his knowledge, and his silence about it, tell her of him, and of the love which he now said that he had for her?

These were puzzles more important and more serious than any puzzle which she had invented for her novels.

Memory gave her the final clue which told her that, yes, he did know. He had spoken to her so often of all that she did for her family, and almost his last words to her had been to tell her of his love, and he had added, 'Hold that to you in the dark watches of your long nights.' Yes, he knew. And delicacy—yes, she was sure now that it was delicacy—had prevented him from saying anything to her—even if it had not been very delicate of him to pry into her secret life!

Another person to exercise delicacy was Sam. He saw the changing expression on Nan's face, and guessed that she wished to be alone. 'I have not troubled you?' he asked.

'No,' was her reply. 'On the contrary.'

Sam left her shortly after that, leaving her seated well away from the hubbub of the rest of the party—to which she could see Brandon contributing in his usual cheerful manner, and she thought once again how much more complex a man he was than his social behaviour would lead anyone to understand.

But she was not to remain alone for long. Desmond came through the gap in the hedge by which she sat and said a trifle reproachfully, 'Why do you insist on hiding yourself away this evening? First you disappear altogether, and then you tie yourself up with that dry stick old enough to be your grandfather.'

'Oh, come.' Nan's laughter was genuine. 'Even to call Sam my father would be an exaggeration, Desmond. And I wish to be alone; I feel a trifle weary tonight.'

'No wonder, with your family sticking to you like leeches, leaving you so little time for yourself.'

Well, at least he had noticed that, as Brandon had done, even if his language was a trifle coarser than his cousin's. He continued, 'I suppose it is useless for me to renew my offer to you, so I will not make it. But I must continue to warn you about my cousin. . .'

Nan shook her head at him, but he still grumbled on for a few moments before beginning again on his disapproval of Jane, ending with, 'She is flightier than ever tonight. I cannot think what has got into her.'

'Only her youth, I suspect.'

Nan was not being entirely truthful. She thought that there was something almost feverish in Jane's manner, something unnatural in the way in which she had been avoiding and cutting Brandon, who until this week had been the one person on whom her undivided attention had been centred.

'I wish that *he* had never come here, and not just because he inherited everything instead of me. Since he arrived everyone seems to have taken leave of their senses. It is Brandon this and Brandon that, until I am sick of the sound of his name. Nothing seems to be able to be done without him. . .'

'Perhaps because he is so able,' returned Nan equably, punning a little.

'He does not need you to champion him when he has everyone else,' barked Desmond.

'Not quite everyone,' Nan remarked quietly. 'As you know, he has been the subject of some nasty attacks. He was sorely hurt that time when he was on the way to the Rectory.'

She seemed to have said something right at last, for Desmond nodded and said stiffly, 'Ah, well, Nan, envy is present everywhere in these benighted times. I thought that things might reform when the war ended, but no, Jack is determined to believe that he is as good as his master, and often desires to kill his master in order to prove his point. Poor Brandon has undoubtedly been the target of Luddites. I always said that they should have hanged more than Cullen for frame-breaking and attempted murder. Cullen's associates were dealt with too lightly.'

Nan said nothing. Visiting the poor—and even prosperous Broomhall had its share of them—she daily saw the misery of those families where the wage-earner had lost his work because of the introduction of the new machines, and consequently she could not so lightly dismiss the sufferings of others.

She also thought that Brandon, who was not a textile manufacturer, unlike Linley whom Cullen had shot, was a strange target for Luddites, and said so.

'You are wrong there, my dear.' Desmond's voice was insufferably patronising. 'They see us all as enemies and my cousin is so rich that he is bound to have roused a great deal of hatred among Radicals and dissidents. He is too easy, as well, and therefore they think that he must be an easy target. He should be more careful of himself.'

Nan shuddered and turned the conversation into other, more cheerful avenues. She could hear Jane's feverish laughter as the group of which she was a part walked towards them. Desmond looked his disapproval of her, but said nothing. Nan seemed in a strange contradictory mood this afternoon and did not want to destroy completely what small rapport still lay between them.

Seeing Nan, Jane winced. She had George Alden in tow, and he was only too happy that she was ignoring Brandon and concentrating her attention on him. She was flirting outrageously with him, and he was enjoying every minute of it. The girls in her set were only too painfully aware that, having lost Brandon to her, they now appeared to be on the brink of losing George as well.

The only consolation they had was that Jane could not marry both George and Brandon—plus the indisputable fact that at the moment it did not appear that Brandon wished to marry any of them.

He had been sufficiently careful in his recent pursuit of Nan to protect her from any criticism that she was pursuing him, or that he was more than ordinarily interested in her. Once he had proposed and been accepted, for he was sure that in the end he would be, then there might be a little gossip behind their backs, but Mr Brandon Tolliver was such an important local personage now that no one would dare to be at open outs with him for long over anything, least of all his choice of a wife.

Unaware of the direction in which Brandon's thoughts were going, for like everyone else in Broomhall and district she could not imagine that he would ever seriously contemplate marrying Nan, Jane still hoped that somehow his interest in her might revive.

The summer lightning which split the clear blue sky above them, and seemed an omen to her of better things to come, had her exclaiming, 'Oh, look! What can it portend?' For everyone knew that such manifestations had a deeper meaning, and Jane could only hope that that meaning might centre round, and favour, her.

She was soon to discover whether or not her wish might come true—and in what fashion!

CHAPTER FOURTEEN

'NAN FIELDING is the author of *Sophia*! Now that I do not believe.' Lady Alden, who had been reading her correspondence while her family ate their breakfast, waved her letter about as though it were a flag which she was using to semaphore with.

'But my sister Belville assures me that it is so, and that the news is all round London that Mr Murray has announced that the author of *Sophia* is a country parson's daughter—that she is Miss Fielding of Broomhall in South Nottinghamshire, and that a new novel by her will be on sale in the bookshops before Christmas! I must say, Lord Alden, Charlotte, George, this beats all! What a sly creature she must be! I am sure that neither her papa nor her mama had the slightest notion that she was doing any such thing as writing novels.'

The entire breakfast-table at Alden Hall was staring at her. George Alden, who had always seen Nan Fielding as the plain and dull elder sister of the pretty girl whom he loved, was particularly disbelieving.

'Oh, surely, Mama, Lady Belville has grown light in the attic. When would Nan Fielding find time to write *Sophia* and the other novels? Her entire day is taken up with running the Rectory and the parish, looking after her mother and Charles, and chaperoning her sisters.'

His mother said with great amusement, 'Oh, pooh to that, George. Such a busy creature as she is would find time to do anything! Now I know why sister Belville said that that unpleasant snobbish creature in *Sophia* was just like Lady Letcombe. . .' Her voice died away as an unhappy thought struck her. 'I hope no one considers that I resemble any of the freaks in her novels.'

Charlotte Alden said wistfully, 'I should like to think that I resemble Sophia. But yes, Mama, what a sly thing she is. Sitting there listening to us, and then writing about us without saying a word—and looking as though butter wouldn't melt in her mouth.'

Lord Alden, who had been busy reading *The Times*, put the paper down before saying, also amusedly, 'And that, of course, explains why the Fieldings have been flush lately, after being as poor as church mice for so many years. I never did believe that Fielding's great theological work could possibly have sold so well as to put them in Threadneedle Street after they had been sailing up the River Tick for so long!'

This conversation was being repeated, with variations, all over Highborough and district, as well as in London. Nan's worst fears had come true. Mr Murray had broken his word, revealed all, and had gained—at the expense of Nan's peace of mind—an enormous number of extra subscribers. The only benefit to her was the increased money which this would bring in—but at what a personal cost. Money was being won and lost in London clubland, for bets as to the sex of the author of *Sophia* had become commonplace. Many had thought that only a man could write anything so trenchantly witty and downright.

Did her father and mother know? was the delicious question which everyone in Highborough and district asked themselves. Was it possible that they could not? But the rector was so unworldly and his wife so withdrawn from society that it was considered that the truth could lie either way.

Lady Alden, together with George and Charlotte,

descended on Gillyflower Hall straight away to pass on
the news and find out what Brandon and Lydia thought
about it. Disappointingly Brandon was out, paying calls
in Broomhall, but Lydia was, as usual, pleased to see
them and exclaimed in the most satisfying manner at
the exciting and scandalous news.

Like everyone else in South Nottinghamshire, her
first reaction was one of disbelief, and then she said in
her thoughtful, sensible way, 'Of course, one was
always aware that she was clever, and I know that
Brandon admires her mind, but not as clever as that!
You are sure that your information is correct, dear
Lady Alden?'

'Oh, my sister Belville is always up to the minute and
would never send me such a piece of news without
being sure of its truth. She writes that Mr Murray
himself made the announcement—so it is straight from
the horse's mouth, my dear.'

Delighted by Lydia's response, Lady Alden ordered
the carriage to be made ready again that afternoon, and
personally passed on the message to three more families, enjoying the sensation that she created. Life in
the country usually ambled along as though it were a
fat old horse, and such a splendid titbit as this was sure
to provide plenty of excitement until the next scandal
came along.

Brandon, who already knew Nan's secret, but not
that it had now been made public, had missed the
Aldens by about five minutes. He was on his way to the
Rectory, but not to discuss the author of *Sophia*. His
errand was quite a different one. He knew that Nan
always spent Thursday morning visiting Broomhall's
poor, Kelsey attending, so that when he reached the
Rectory and asked Jackson if Miss Fielding was in he
was not at all surprised to be told that she was not.

Saying that he would call again when she was, and

that Jackson need not see him to the door, he made to turn away, but then appeared to change his mind, and called back Jackson who was on his way to the kitchens.

'Oh, by the by, Jackson, you may remember that my man, Leeson, called about a fortnight ago with a letter from me to Miss Fielding, with express orders that you be sure to see that she received it as soon as possible. I take it that the letter was given to her?'

Jackson thought for a moment before replying, 'Oh, indeed, Mr Tolliver. She was out when Leeson called, so I put it on the salver for her to find when she returned. I distinctly remember Miss Jane picking it up and telling me that she would take it to Miss Fielding's room and place it on her desk so that she would be sure to have it immediately.'

The look which Brandon gave him was an enigmatic one. 'Thank you, Jackson. You have greatly relieved my mind. I had the notion that it might have gone astray.'

Now, what was all that about? was Jackson's reaction when Mr Tolliver had closed the door behind him. I wonder if the letter went astray somehow? I'd better have a word with Miss Fielding when she returns.

The deceitful, thieving bitch! Brandon was cursing Jane inwardly all the way down the path from the Rectory front door to the garden gate. He had no doubt now of what had happened. She had seen his writing on the letter, and had stolen it before Nan had had the chance to see it.

He was so lost in anger that he almost passed Jane without seeing her. She was returning from her walk, and was a trifle horrified at the sight of Brandon leaving the Rectory. There was no way in which she could avoid meeting him. For a moment she thought that either he had not seen her or was cutting her, and that she might be able to escape having to speak to him, but at the very last moment, even as he was passing her, he came out of his trance and saw her.

The mood of blind rage which had seized Brandon when he had realised that his worst fears were true and that Jane had stolen his letter to Nan ebbed a little. He saw how wan and dejected she appeared; her usual bright looks and airy charm were smudged. She had the air of one who was utterly wretched.

Conscience smote him hard—a new experience for him. For had he not created the situation which had lured Jane to commit her wanton act of jealousy by having sought her out and favoured her beyond all other women, to the degree that his partiality had been gossiped about and speculated on—as his sister had warned him?

And then what had he done but withdrawn from her? And even if he had done it gently that must also have been the subject of unkind gossip, and, unwittingly, without meaning to, he had diminished her in the eyes of her small world.

He checked the angry words which were almost on his lips, bowed, and said in his most gentle voice, 'Good morning, Jane; I trust I see you well?'

So weighed down was she by her sin, and her fear of him which had followed it, that Jane could scarcely look at him, let alone speak. She nodded mutely, tears springing into her eyes.

Shocked by her reaction, and by the fact that she was about to walk on without so much as a word to him, Brandon said urgently, 'Stay, Jane; there is something which I must say to you.'

'No!' Her voice was faint and fear distorted her pretty features. She seemed almost on the verge of fainting.

'Yes, Jane. I must talk to you, for both our sakes.'

And I must apologise to you, profoundly. Without meaning to I have caused you a great deal of misery.

'When we first met I was so enchanted by your charm——' and that was no less than the truth, he acknowledged '——that I committed an error of manners. I was too partial to you, exposed you to gossip, and that was unforgivable of me. You must put it down to my sad lack of knowledge of how to behave in good society. In the circles I frequented before I came to Broomhall no one would have thought twice that I was showing such pleasure in the company of a charming young lady.

'I know that you will find it difficult to forgive me, but I also know that, though you and I may be friends, we are not suited to each other in any other way. Like all of us, I find it difficult to confess a fault, but I trust that you will find it in you to forgive a sinner. We must all hope that our sins will be forgiven, as you, a parson's daughter, must surely know.' And he looked keenly at her.

He knew! Somehow he knew, was Jane's wild reaction to this. Astonishingly, however, he was not saying so. It was as though the weight of the letter, which was still hidden in her drawer upstairs, had been magnified a thousandfold and was pressing on her poor bruised heart.

She also knew something else, something important: that what he had said about them not being suited to each other was true.

She had never known him. She had been entranced by his difference from all the other men whom she knew, by the power of him, and by his fine body and good looks. But behind all that was the true Brandon, a clever and ruthless man of whom, little by little, if she had married him, she would have become afraid. He was complex and she was simple. He could, as he was

showing her, be compassionate, for she was sure that
he was sparing her, but she could never have lived in
comfort with a man who knew his fellow human beings
and their frailties so well.

Jane could never have articulated any of this. She
knew it instinctively—and, once she did, the lure of
him slowly disappeared, never to return. He might one
day be her friend again, but nothing more.

'There is very little for me to forgive, but confession
is said to be good for the soul,' she managed hoarsely
at last, for she must say something, and he was waiting
so patiently and, yes, so humbly for her to speak. 'Do
you find it so, Mr Tolliver?' And she used his full name
deliberately to show that she was severing any last
emotional tie which might once have bound them
together.

Brandon was surprised by her question, yet at the
same time he acknowledged that by putting it to him
she had touched on the truth. He *did* feel better now
that he had confessed the wrong which he had unwittingly done her.

'Yes,' he said, equally simply. 'As much all of us who
need to confess our wrongdoing.' So saying, he looked
steadily at Jane after a fashion which seemed to pen-
etrate her soul.

'I will remember what you have said,' she whispered,
dropping her head as the weight which she secretly
carried seemed to increase with each word that passed
between them.

Brandon amazed himself by saying, as she bowed
again and moved away, 'My good wishes go with you,
Jane. I know that you will always do the true and right
thing.'

Oh, yes, he had spared her; she knew that. But why
had he done so? He was obviously aware that she had
stolen his love letter to Nan.

And then, in her new maturity, the answer came. So that I may repair the wrong I did without knowledge of it going further to create scandal and distress. I, and no one else, must tell Nan what I have done, give her back her letter—for he must hope that I have not destroyed it—but even if I had he would want me to tell her the truth and beg her forgiveness.

Jane couldn't wait, for even as she made this decision the burden which she had carried since she had stolen the letter disappeared. She began to run down the path, away from him, to fetch the letter from its hiding place and wait for Nan's return.

'Nan.'

Kelsey was abrupt. They were standing in the hall, taking off their bonnets, and Nan had just announced that a pot of tea might be a good reward for their morning's work among Broomhall's poor, when Kelsey decided to speak to her of something which had been on her mind for some little time.

'Is there something wrong with Jane? Has she given you any indication that she might be feeling ill? Her manner is quite changed. She has had a fit of the sullens for the last two weeks or more, and when she is not sulking she is inclined to fits of unexplained sobbing. Yesterday, when I asked her if she was feeling unwell, she fled from the room crying even harder. I can get no sense out of her these days.'

Nan, too, had been worried about Jane. She was usually so high-spirited, so full of herself, that to have her walking about like a grey creepmouse seemed as unnatural as though the sun had decided to rise in the west instead of the east.

'She has said nothing to me about anything. In fact,' Nan continued slowly, for the thought did not please her, 'she has taken to avoiding me lately.'

The unwelcome notion that Jane's misery over Brandon's ceasing to be 'most particular' to her might have something to do with her patent unhappiness had been worrying Nan ever since her sister's manner had changed so dramatically. But she could hardly tell Kelsey so. Especially since she was only too well aware that Brandon had changed towards Jane after he had begun to be 'most particular' with her.

But he had now, it seemed, abandoned Nan herself. Despite the fact that he had spoken to her of love and marriage at Sam's, his manner to her had been most odd, and in consequence she was unable to trust him, leaving her to feel desolate and unhappy. Unlike Jane, however, she was keeping her misery to herself. It was one more secret which she could share with no one.

Further conversation with Kelsey brought no answer to the riddle which Jane, as well as Brandon, had become. Then another riddle was presented to her by Jackson. He had been hovering while she and Kelsey talked, and finally came forward, an odd look on his face, to ask her, somewhat diffidently, 'The letter which Mr Tolliver left for you on the day he travelled to London—you found it in your room, I trust?' He did not mention Jane's role in promising to deliver it—as general factotum he had learned never to say too much of what he knew.

'A letter for me, from Mr Tolliver?' Nan's surprise was patent. 'I have not received one. You are sure it was placed in my room?'

'That was my belief,' replied Jackson diplomatically.

'Perhaps it was mislaid on my bureau. It is never very tidy. I will look for it.' Nan sounded cool on the outside, but inside her mind was whirling. Brandon had sent her a letter on the day he had left for London!

Why? And why had she never received it? And was

that why her last conversation with him had been so. . . so. . .odd. . .?

All the way up to her room the mystery of the letter and the equal mystery of Jane's behaviour occupied her mind. She could only hope that Jane might soon come to terms with the fact that she could not have everything which she wanted from life. It was a lesson which Nan had been compelled to learn eleven years ago, and it was one which she would never forget.

To her surprise, there on the landing before her room, where once Brandon had stood in the dead of night, was Jane. She had been crying and her face, usually so carefully tended, was smudged with tears. On seeing Nan she hung her head, turning it away from her sister's gaze. The reality of what she was about to do smote her hard. But she must be brave, because only by being so could she purge herself.

'I want to talk to you, Nan. Could we go into your room?'

Nan was surprised by her sister's humility. Usually Jane was impatient with her, was only too happy to suggest that her elder sister was behind the times, scarcely worth wasting words on.

She opened the door, and waved Jane into her one armchair, the one in which Brandon had sat pretending that he felt ill. The memory of him caused her cheeks to flush, and for once it was Nan who was rosy and Jane who was pale.

Jane refused to sit down, and said with surprising dignity, for she felt that she was going to her execution and the only way in which she could endure it was to suffer it bravely, 'No, thank you, Nan; I prefer to stand.'

Perforce Nan was compelled to stand as well. She wondered what was coming, for Jane suddenly gave a great sob and, all bravery gone, blurted out, 'Oh, Nan,

I have done a terrible thing. I have committed a great
wrong, and I did it to you. Brandon sent you a letter
before he left for London. I stole it, and read it, and
hid it away—and I have never had a happy moment
since!'

Her sobs turned into a storm of weeping as she came
out with the truth at last. She flung herself into the
chair which she had just refused, buried her face in a
cushion, and, shoulders shaking, cried as though her
heart would break. The true enormity of what she had
done had struck home at last at the sight of Nan's
stricken face as she had come out with her confession.
For the first time in her short and selfish life she was
feeling for another, and it was almost like the pangs of
birth, so strong was the pain.

'Stole my letter?' echoed Nan. 'My letter? From
Brandon?' The letter which Jackson had just asked her
about? Jane's misery, added to her confession, temporarily bewildered her. And then she exclaimed, in a rare
spurt of anger, 'Look at me, Jane! What can you mean?
You stole a letter which was meant for me? I cannot
believe it—even of you.'

These last harsh words from a sister who had
patiently endured her petty bullying and small jeal-
ousies further undid Jane, but she had the courage to
lift her streaming face from the cushion, and stand up—
as cautiously and warily as though she had suddenly
grown old.

'This letter,' she said tremulously, and she took it
from her reticule. 'I found it on the salver the day
Brandon left for London, and I told Jackson I would
see that you received it, but I stole it and read it—and
I know, once you have read it, that you will never
forgive me. Never. I would never have forgiven you if
you had done such a terrible thing to me.'

She did not tell Nan that Brandon had discovered the

truth, and had worked on her to confess, for she knew—how did she know?—that he would not want her to do that. Instead, without more ado, she handed Brandon's battered letter to her sister who took it without a word, an expression on her face which Jane could not read.

Before she could speak Jane made for the door, crying as she reached it, 'I know that you will never forgive me, but I pray that you will try, although I know I don't deserve it.'

All her bright beauty had gone, all her pretty grown-up ways which charmed all those about her. She was once more the small girl who had stolen Nan's old doll and deliberately drowned it in the stream because she thought that Nan had been overly harsh to her.

But the letter was no doll, and, although Nan had forgiven her the drowning, once her sister had read Brandon's letter, Jane thought that there could be no forgiveness.

Nan made no attempt to read her recovered letter. She had devoted her whole life to her family, but she would have been the last to claim that that made her a saint. For a moment she was almost faint with rage and anger against the sister who had betrayed her. But the memory of the child that Jane had once been was strong within her.

She said slowly, 'I want to read my letter when I am alone, Jane. It will be difficult for me to forgive you, but I will try—because of the love we once had for one another. You are my sister, after all.'

There was something so patient and dignified about Nan as she stood there, so brave, that Jane had her second revelation of the afternoon. She suddenly understood how hard her sister's life was, how selflessly she had lived it.

She could not help herself; she flung herself on Nan

and, tearless now, hid her face on Nan's breast. 'I will try to be good in future,' she whispered. 'Being bad is so unpleasant. Try to forgive me.'

For a moment the sisters clung together, until Jane pulled away from the comfort of Nan's arms. She smiled a watery smile. 'I will go now and leave you to read what Brandon wrote to you. I hadn't the heart to destroy it, and it was like the burden on the back of the old man of the sea.'

Nan nodded. She knew all about such burdens. 'Go and bathe your face,' she told Jane practically and sensibly, 'and change your dress. You will feel better then.'

It was all that she could offer, and when Jane had gone Nan sat down in the armchair which Jane had cried all over, and read Brandon's letter, and knew why Jane had said that she would never forgive her, for it was a declaration of love such as she could never have hoped for.

And every word must have been a dagger in Jane's heart, as every word was like incense and balm to Nan. He loved her and wanted to marry her, and that was riches indeed, but she put her face in her hands and, like Jane, wept.

For, of course, she could never accept him.

Broomhall and district was in a ferment over the news that Nan Fielding was the author of *Sophia*. The only family which remained in ignorance of the news was that of the Fieldings themselves. No one quite knew how to broach it to them. The etiquette for such a situation did not exist. Sam sent Nan a note telling her that the news was out in Broomhall. She read it shortly after she had read Brandon's letter, and sat mute on her bed, trying to order her thoughts.

It was plain from her recent conversation with Jane

that she was still ignorant, for had she known she would
have been sure to mention it. So there were some small
mercies to be thankful for. What did distress her was
what her father and mother would say when they found
out what she had done. She knew that she must go
downstairs and confess that she was the author of
Sophia before the news reached them from other lips.

She had just determined to do so when there was a
knock on the door and Jane came in again. She had
taken Nan's advice and washed herself, re-dressed her
hair and changed into a pretty cream muslin dress
decorated with rosebuds. There was a new reserve in
her manner; she would never be so frank and free in
company again.

She was carrying a letter. 'Lady Alden has sent me
an invitation to spend some days with Charlotte,' she
told Nan, adding hesitantly, 'I may go, may I not? She
says that her sister will chaperon us, so that you are not
to worry that we shall run wild.'

She paused, and added something which she would
never have said before her confession of guilt. 'Do not
worry that I will say or do something stupid, and if you
think that I ought to stay and help you here I will send
a message back to say that it is not convenient. The boy
who brought the letter is waiting for my answer in the
kitchen.'

She was so humble that Nan hardly knew her. 'Of
course you may go,' she said gently. 'It will be a good
thing for you to be away from the Rectory for a few
days.'

And away from Brandon, thought Jane. I can face
Nan, but how can I face *him*? But she said nothing, and
both went to her room, Jane calling on Kelsey to help
her to pack, for Lady Alden was sending the carriage
round for her at two o'clock if it was convenient for her
to visit.

'Take Margaret with you for a lady's maid,' advised Nan, who thought that she might feel better if she did not have to face Jane for a few days, particularly if the storm over *Sophia* was about to break over her head.

Jane's arrangements made, Nan went downstairs to find her father and confess her sins, but, alas, he was not in. He had gone to a parish meeting, Kelsey said, and would not be back until dinner. 'Which, at the present rate,' she added meaningfully as she stowed Jane's clothes for her visit into a large hamper, 'might be rather late in being served.'

So that was that. The evil moment would have to be postponed.

Of all the great ones who lived in and near Broomhall, Lady Alden was by far the most frank in her manner, and the most free with her opinions, but Lady Letcombe ran her a close second. She was visiting Broomhall that afternoon and after a happy coze with several of her friends about the deceitful way in which the Fieldings had carried on over Nan's authorship, for they surely must have been in on the secret, she had the great good fortune to see Parson Fielding dawdling home after his parish meeting.

She stopped her carriage, an open one, by the simple expedient of ramming the coachman in the back with her parasol and commanding him loudly to stop immediately.

He duly obliged and she leaned over the side to beard her friend even as he was turning in at his own gate.

'My dear man,' she roared imperiously at him as he swept off his hat and made her a low bow, 'I vow that I shall never forgive you for keeping your daughter's secret from such an old friend as I am. You have not been neighbourly, sir, not neighbourly at all, and so I said to Letcombe when we heard the news. It would have been more proper to hear it from your lips than from someone who is merely an acquaintance of yours!'

A faint expression of alarm passed over the Reverend Caleb Fielding's placid face as one of his patronesses came out with such an oblique reprimand. His face showed its bewilderment. Lady Letcombe recognised that he was nonplussed, and, being no fool, at once grasped the reason for it.

'What?' And now her roar was as genial as that of a dragon which had found another source of treasure to add to its hoard of gold. 'Never tell me that the naughty gel has not informed you that *she* is the author of those witty books which have had all society agog! I wonder, given all that she accomplishes for you and the parish, that she has found the time to write them, but talent, I understand, will always find a way. No doubt, though, the knowledge that a parson's daughter is Sophia will sell even more of them, which is doubtless why Mr Murray has broadcast her identity to the world.'

Poor Caleb Fielding, feeling as though someone had fired a cannon before his garden gate, and that the ball had carried his head away, stammered nervously at the great lady who was so mercilessly quizzing him. 'Oh—oh, madam, forgive me; I am sure that you have been misinformed.'

'Fiddlesticks, my good sir! I'll have you know it is in all the public prints, and is going the rounds of society. Are you sure that you have not been aiding and abetting your daughter's saucy plot, sir?

'What a party of tricksters the Rectory has been sheltering! Letcombe and I wonder at you all; he is quite sure that such a quiet creature as your daughter could not have carried this off by herself. She must have had an accomplice, and who better than one who is already an author of note? You must bring her over to dinner, and the toast will be the author of *Sophia*.'

So speaking, Lady Letcombe rammed her unfortunate coachman in the middle of his bruised back again and was swept away in a cloud of self-satisfied patronage.

The dazed Rector stood stock-still, his head buzzing. A thousand questions were swirling through a mind which had originally been a sharp one before indolence and self-satisfaction had taken it over. His expression growing ever more baleful, he walked rapidly into the Rectory to find Nan immediately and ask her whether Lady Letcombe had been telling him the truth.

There was one important question to which he did not particularly desire an answer. Was it from Nan's writings that the money had come from, which had made the Fieldings' lives so easy in recent years, and not from his theological masterpiece? Such a notion did not bear thinking on. His *amour propre* and his intellect both rejected what must, he instinctively knew, be the true answer.

Rage and hurt pride battled within him and boded ill for Nan.

Nan, seated in her mother's room, overlooking the main road which ran through Broomhall, had seen Lady Letcombe accost her father, seen her gesticulations, and her father's distressed response to the great lady's hectoring.

She did not need to be told of what had passed between them. She knew only too well, by the unaccustomed speed with which her father was walking and by the expression on his face, that the arrogant busybody who was driving away so speedily had just informed him who the author of *Sophia* was. For a moment she contemplated flight. It was too much to bear on top of everything else which had fallen on her during this dreadful afternoon.

The strength of will, the courage, which informed everything Nan did prevented her from doing any such thing. She became aware that her mother was speaking to her. She was reclining on the sofa at the other end of her private drawing-room and was looking in singularly good health for a woman whose invalidity was a by-word.

Mrs Fielding's rosy face, her carefully dressed hair, her well-cut deep blue gown of the latest mode, all enhanced her appearance of happy and self-satisfied middle-aged charm. Beside her Nan, overwhelmed by the cares and revelations of the day, felt extinguished, and that in some way she had changed places with the mother who had battened on her for so long.

'What can you be staring at, Nan?' her mother remarked petulantly. 'Do begin to read. You know how much I want to find out what happens to poor Amelia.'

Nan picked up *Amelia's Secret* wishing that she had never written it, nor any of the others. Being poor and eating bad food might be better than comfort purchased at such a cost to her health and her peace of mind. She opened the book just as her mother remarked unkindly, 'Really, Nan, do you need to look so fly-away? Even your hair needs to have a brush and comb run through it. I can scarcely bear to look at you.'

Amelia's Secret was put down again as Nan stood up, trembling a little.

'You will forgive me, Mother,' she remarked as coolly as she could, the worm turning at last, 'if I leave you to read *Amelia's Secret* yourself. If you wish me to appear a little more *comme il faut* than I do, then you must give me time to be so. Between organising the parish, the household and the kitchen, transcribing and rewriting Papa's book, arranging for you to be properly dressed, organising Jane's affairs so that she looks her best in order to catch a wealthy husband, and seeing that Chaz behaves himself, I have scarcely the time to put my clothes on, let alone make the effort to transform myself into a fashion plate.

'But, since you wish it so much, I am sure that you will make the sacrifice of releasing me from my duty as reader in order to arrange myself more to your liking.'

She turned on her heel and walked steadily to the door, her mother calling angrily after her, 'Come back here, my girl, and do as I bid you!'

'No,' replied Nan, without turning her head. She heard her mother's angry indrawn breath, but put her hand on the doorknob all the same, just as the door was forcefully thrust open by her father.

She had seldom seen such an expression of rage and temper on his handsome face. He was usually almost bovinely placid, accepting his easy life as no more than his due, the Rectory revolving around him when it did not revolve around his wife and his youngest daughter.

He caught Nan by the wrist as she moved to pass him, ignoring his wife's imperious call of, 'You come pat, Mr Fielding, indeed you do. Nan needs reminding of what her duties are in this house, and so I trust you to inform her.'

'Anne, I require an explanation from you.' His tone to Nan was peremptory in the extreme, and he was calling her by her long-disused proper name. His wife tried to engage his attention, but he continued to ignore her, betraying the depth of his distress: he was a man who prided himself on his punctiliousness towards everyone around him.

He released Nan's wrist but continued to address her, both his colour and his voice high. 'It is you to whom I must speak, Anne, and I prefer to do so before I speak to your mother. I have a question to put to you to which I demand a truthful answer.'

The day of reckoning was upon her. Nan swung slowly round to face him. Her hands, clasped behind her back, were gripping each other tightly.

'Yes, Father,' she said, her head high, determined to meet her doom with courage. 'What is it that you wish to know?'

'Is it true, as Lady Letcombe has just informed me, that you are the author of this. . .novel. . .' he picked up *Amelia's Secret* from the table on which she had placed it '. . .and of all the others written by the author of *Sophia*?'

A gasp was wrenched from Mrs Fielding as he asked this question in a voice which she had never heard from her husband before, so harsh and bitter was it. Her eyes were trained on Nan again. She saw her daughter's face grow ashy pale, saw her sway a little, before she replied, her voice as steady as she could make it, 'Yes, Papa. That is the truth.'

Her father closed his eyes, then opened them to say in a grating voice, 'And I suppose that you did not inform me of what you were doing because you knew that I would not have allowed you to do such a thing. You, a single young woman, to write this.' And he held poor Amelia up by two fingers as though she were contaminated.

It was no less than the truth, as Nan acknowledged. 'Yes, I wrote it and sent it to Mr Murray, who liked it and published it. Yes, I knew that you would not approve of my either writing it or selling it. But I don't think that you and Mother quite understood me when I told you after we came to Broomhall that your stipend was barely enough to feed us, let alone clothe us. It was certainly not enough to keep Mother in comfortable idleness and give the girls a London season, and Chaz an education when the time came. And so I wrote *Sophia*——'

Before she could say any more in her defence her father put up a hand and interrupted her. For the first time in his life, thought Nan irreverently, he resembled the Old Testament prophets of whom he so often spoke in the pulpit. Only the long white beard was missing.

'Sin and defiance and lying are no less so,' he thundered at her, 'even if they result in the accumulation of earthly wealth and luxury. God must have wanted us to suffer in poverty; it was not for you to deny Him. Besides,' he added a trifle pathetically, 'there was the money from my book to help us.'

Nan closed her eyes. She must tell him the truth, whatever the cost. 'There was, and is, no money from your book, Papa. It did not sell. I found that out when we came to Broomhall and took over your accounts. Mr Stone told me what our true financial circumstances were. It had not mattered previously that your book had not sold; your stipend at Frensham Major was more than enough to keep us in comfort.'

'Ah, yes, Sam Stone.' The Rector's underworked intellect, now working again under great stress, had correctly informed him who must have helped his daughter to carry out her wicked plan. 'It was he, I suppose, who assisted you to deceive me and the world——'

Now it was Nan's turn to interrupt him as the devil took hold of her. 'And feed you all,' she proudly announced. 'Never forget that, Papa. Without Sam and *Sophia* we might have starved.'

'And I am to be mocked because of you and Sam and *Sophia*. Considering all that you have done in your short life, I can scarcely bear to look at you. You have humiliated me before, and this second slight which you have placed upon me is the last I intend to endure from you.'

It was the first time that he had admitted that he had

known exactly what had happened twelve years ago. Nan bowed her head, the tears springing to her eyes.

'I did not mean to hurt you, Papa, then or now. This time I meant to help you.'

But her appeal to him was unavailing. His pride had been powerfully injured. His book had been a failure, and Nan's books had been successful. He owed the very bread in his mouth, the clothes on his back to her, and he could not endure the knowledge. Only his belief that such a thing would mark him out as a savage was preventing him from threatening to thrash her for her sins.

Instead he held his face away from her and ground out, 'No matter. You shall not help us again. Whatever the cost you shall not stay here to be my permanent reproach. You will go to your room and remain there until you leave the Rectory for good. Kelsey will take over the running of the household.

'You, Mrs Fielding——' and he swung on his wife '—will resume your duties as mistress of this house, since your refusal to do so has led our daughter into sin and wickedness. You will come down to supper, and carry out all Anne's duties—including the copying of my latest book. As for Anne, she shall be sent to Aunt Smithson's to be her companion, and if we must retrench to make up for losing her earnings, then so be it.'

'No!' Nan cried violently. 'I do not deserve to be treated so harshly! Do not send me away where I may never see my family and Chaz again. I have worked faithfully and long to see that we all lived a happy and fulfilled life. I did not care what sacrifice I made to do so—the only one I was not prepared to make was the one which would have followed your forbidding me to do what I did. I am only sorry that I did not immediately tell you the truth when Sam informed me that Mr

Murray was about to reveal the author of *Sophia*'s identity to the world.'

But he had turned his back on her, and all she stood for, to cry at his wife as imperiously as Lady Letcombe had cried at him, 'Get up, woman, and go downstairs. You have been idle too long, and I have been wrong to allow it.'

The last thing Nan heard as she left the room was her mother's sobs. The Rector had reassumed the authority over his life and home which he had long abdicated. Nothing would ever be the same again.

CHAPTER FIFTEEN

REMARKABLY, on that evening, Brandon Tolliver was one of the few people who was not thinking or talking about Nan Fielding. The first reason for this was that he had decided to be patient after his conversation with Jane. He would let events take their course. Or, rather, he would wait for Nan to reply to his letter when Jane at last gave it to her, for he was sure from her manner that Jane had not destroyed it. She was, he had decided, weak, not wicked.

If in the next few days Nan did not reply to his letter, then he would visit her and make one last great push to win her. Since his visit to Frensham Major he was no longer puzzled by her insistence that she could not marry him. He knew why she thought so, and it was up to him to convince her that she was mistaken.

The second reason was that once he was back in his study Carteret handed him a note from Thorpe, asking to see him at their secret rendezvous. 'Matters are drawing to a conclusion,' his agent had written.

Brandon stared and sighed at the hastily scrawled words. He could have done with having to deal with this at another time, when his mind was not centred on Nan, but, on the other hand, he was also relieved that he might be on the point of drawing Desmond's teeth, thus enabling him to enjoy his quiet life at Broomhall.

Before he had arrived in South Nottinghamshire he had told himself that he would be bored, but he was beginning to acknowledge that the charms of a rural existence were stronger than he might have thought. He had spent his life in the bustle of the commercial world, in great cities, mostly living in the *demi-monde*, that world which was a kind of mezzanine floor between the respectable and the completely *déclassé*, and now he had discovered that he wanted more from life than excitement. He wanted stability, the respect of his social equals, a family of his own, and a settled home with the woman he loved in an area whose natural beauty appealed to him.

He was still pondering on this when at just about the time that Nan's father was condemning her to banishment and exile, he met his agent Thorpe, in an out-of-the-way little inn on the other side of Highborough. Like Thorpe he was dressed inconspicuously, nothing of the gentleman about him. He was young Brandon Tolliver again, rising in the dangerous world which he was on the point of conquering with the help of such tools as the man he was meeting.

'Well, what is it?' he demanded, nursing his tankard of ale.

'All and more than you wanted, sir,' responded Thorpe. 'Our man has grown tired of delay. He has hired me and some other villains to do his dirty work for him. He wishes us to attack and kill you, either by beating you or shooting you, from ambush. He intends to be present himself to see that the job is properly done on this occasion after his previous boss shots.

'He knows that most evenings you stroll away from the park at Gillyflower Hall into the scrub and wasteland outside it to take your ease after dinner, not far from the point where the earlier attack on you failed. He thinks that since you were attacked there once before you would conclude that lightning does not strike twice in the same place, and not be particularly wary.'

'He knows that,' replied Brandon lightly, 'because I continued the habit when I realised who was trying to kill me, and told him I was doing so because I thought that he would probably attempt that particular gambler's double bluff, and in the doing would trap himself.'

Thorpe nodded. 'With a little help from me, that was what he decided on. From tomorrow evening we shall be waiting for you in the clearing in the wood between Gillyflower Hall and the Rectory where the path turns sharp right. You know it?'

Brandon nodded. Of course he knew it. It was where he had seen Nan up the tree, rescuing Chaz's kite.

'We are supposed to attack you there. We shall begin to do so, and then, at a suitable point, when he is fully involved, my mates and I will take to our heels without warning, shouting that we are on the point of being discovered, leaving you alone with him. At least, that is what I suggest to you that we do. It may be that you have other ideas. You will, of course, be armed and ready for us whatever plan you adopt.'

The beer Brandon was drinking was poor—warm and sour; it matched his mood. He grimaced as he swallowed it and placed the pot down on the grimy table. 'As usual I was right to trust you to come up with a plan which seems feasible,' he said. 'Go ahead, and with luck no one will be injured.'

He had no wish to harm his cousin, only to defeat his murderous plans and frighten him so much that he would abandon them. He had not wanted anyone else to learn of Jane's treachery to Nan, and neither did he want Desmond's villainy made public. Best that it lay between the two of them so that it might be forgotten provided that Desmond would have the common sense to understand that the last thing which Brandon wanted was a scandal.

And so it was arranged. Brandon rode home to Gillyflower Hall hoping that this chapter in his life might soon be closed, without recriminations and without bloodshed. This over, he might be able to think of Nan again, not merely enjoy the memory of her in his dreams.

The Aldens could not help but notice how uncharacteristically quiet and subdued Jane was when she arrived in mid-afternoon. Only Lady Alden noticed the trace of recent tears, and chose to say nothing of them.

She had hoped, before Brandon Tolliver had arrived in the district, that Jane would make a suitable wife for George. She was not rich, she would bring no large dowry with her, but then, she need not, seeing how wealthy the Aldens were. Better for George to marry someone suitable, even if she had little money, than someone who would bring a fortune but who might make him unhappy.

True, the child was a little flighty, but she obviously appealed to George's protective instincts, and her family was good. Lady Alden knew all about Sir Charlton and the well-born Fieldings up north. If Parson Fielding could hold on he might yet be a rich landowner himself!

Well, if Jane chose to moon over Brandon Tolliver that was her privilege, but George would make her a better husband. . .

Organising dinner, chatting to some of her London cronies who had come to stay, she forgot Jane, who, again unusually, did not sparkle at the dinner-table.

Lady Alden was not the only one to notice Jane's changed manner. George, sitting by her, found that her usual liveliness was missing and regretted it. Once the gentlemen's after-dinner port-drinking was over, he walked through to the drawing-room to find her. Again, strangely, she was not part of the group of younger women enjoying themselves by playing at speculation while they waited for the men to appear.

He looked about him. His mother interpreted his glance correctly. 'Jane is in the little cabinet next to the library, I believe. She said that she had a slight headache, and might look at some of your father's new prints instead of joining in the game with the other girls.'

His mother was right. He found Jane, but she was not looking at prints. She was sitting on a small sofa, staring blindly at the opposite wall. Something, he knew, was wrong.

'I trust you are well, Jane? You seemed a little *distraite* at dinner.' Now this was daring of him—to make such a personal remark to a young girl—but Jane, staring blindly at him, took no note of it.

Her stare became less blind. She suddenly realised that George was, after all, quite a personable man. During her fascination with Brandon she had thought him young and callow, but now that that was over almost miraculously George had changed back into the beau whom she had been proud to acknowledge.

But did he want to acknowledge her? New maturity told her that recently she had been cruelly indifferent to him, and that she might as a consequence have lost his admiration—which had suddenly become precious to her.

She gave a great sob. Alarmed, George sat down beside her as he saw the tears threatening to fall. A large handkerchief of the latest fashion, edged with lace, depended from his pocket. He withdrew it and handed it to her, saying, 'Oh, do not cry, my darling girl. You will break my heart if you do.'

Jane's answer was to take his handkerchief, give another wailing sigh and hold it to her eyes. After she had wiped them she said, 'Oh, you must not be kind to me; I don't deserve it.'

She meant because of the way in which she had recently treated him, but George took no note of that. Her manner to him had changed completely; she had reverted to the Jane whom he had once known and loved, the girl whom he hoped to marry.

'Oh, no,' he replied swiftly. 'I don't believe that. You deserve all and more which the world has to give you, I am sure.'

Jane lowered the handkerchief to look at him over the top of it. All, apparently, was not yet lost.

'Do you really mean that?' she asked him tremulously.

'Of course.' His answer was gallant in the extreme and, fixing her with his earnest brown eyes, he said, almost humbly, 'I suppose I ought to ask your papa for permission first, but I can't wait. I must know my fate.' And, improbably, unromantic George slipped down on to one knee, took her hands in his—she had dropped his handkerchief in surprise at his sudden action—and kissed them.

'Dear Jane, I am asking you to be my wife—pending your papa's permission, of course. Oh, do say yes. I am sure that when we are married we shall be as happy as we were when we played our childish games together.'

A great surge of the deepest affection for him swept over Jane. He was not as handsome, clever or rich as Brandon. But he was kind George who loved his horse and his dogs and would love his wife with the same unthinking devotion.

Let Nan have Brandon; they could be clever together. And now that at last she had done her duty, as Nan had always urged her to do, and told the truth—purged her sin, as Papa would have said if he had known the terrible thing which she had done—she could accept George.

And, it would not be because he could make her Lady Alden and thus cause the other girls to envy her, or because it would extinguish the hurt of losing Brandon, but because she had discovered that she loved him and the simple life which he was offering her.

Brandon had been right. She and he were not suited, but she and George were. She looked up at George, tears forgotten, and said, as simply as a child, 'Of course, George. I shall be honoured to be your wife. I have always loved you.'

Which, she was about to discover, was no less than the truth. So much so that when, on George's arm, she met Brandon again, she could not understand why she had found him so attractive.

Alone, locked in her room, Nan contemplated the dismal future. Her father had already informed her that when she was sent to Aunt Smithson, that elderly tyrant, to be her companion her aunt was to make sure that she had no access to pen and paper. 'There will be no more novel-writing,' he had ordered.

Until the arrangements for the journey were made she was to remain in her room, and Broomhall was to be informed that she was suffering from one of the low fevers common in summer. Kelsey, and no one else, was to bring her meals.

During her first morning's imprisonment, after a sleepless night, she heard Chaz come running up the stairs, to beat on the door of her room, shouting in a despairing voice, 'You are not to go, Nan; don't let them send you away. I won't let them. You are the only friend I have. No one else is kind to me—not Papa, not Mama and not Jane. I want to go with you.'

His hammering redoubled when she said, trying not

to sound defeated, 'Oh, Chaz, you must do your duty and remain here.'

The noise he made when she told him that brought her father up the stairs to drag him away. A moment or so later, he came into Nan's room, saying, 'I will not have you encouraging Charles to mutiny against his parents, Anne.'

Nan looked steadily at him. 'You know perfectly well that I did not encourage him, Papa. I told him to do his duty.'

'As you must learn to do yours,' he told her brusquely, and left her.

The day dragged on interminably. She had run out of paper, so could not write. Sam had promised to bring her some that morning, and when Kelsey brought up her luncheon she asked if he had called.

Kelsey put the tray on Nan's small table which stood in the window. 'He called with a parcel for you. Your father gave orders that he was not to be admitted again, refused to accept the parcel and handed him a letter which told him that he was transferring his business to an attorney in Highborough.'

Nan swallowed. Her throat seemed to have closed and she could not eat the food which sat before her. Her whole world was falling about her ears, and she could not longer hope that her father might change his mind and relent sufficiently to allow her to remain in Broomhall.

From her window she watched the daily life of the household go on. She saw the undermaid feed the chickens, the gardener gather up vegetables for the evening meal and flowers for the house. Beyond the lane she could see the path which led to the scrub and small wood, and ultimately to Gillyflower Hall. Perhaps Brandon would come along it; perhaps. . . But it was foolish to think so. Her father would not admit him either, if he said that he wished to speak to her.

Shortly after luncheon she saw Brandon walking briskly along the path to the Rectory and through the paddock gate. She had no doubt that he was calling on them, even though from her room she could not hear the front-door knocker. But a few minutes later she saw him walk away down the path, back to his home. He had been turned away.

In mid-afternoon Kelsey brought her a cup of tea, and told her that Mr Tolliver had called and been informed that Jane was at the Letcombes' and that Miss Anne was ill and confined to her bed.

After Kelsey had gone Nan lay on her bed in a half-doze and let her mind roam. She was walking with Brandon in the woods; his hand was in hers. But was it his hand or Randal's? She looked up at her companion and it was Randal. For some time now she had found great difficulty in remembering what he really looked like; time was causing his image to fade ever more rapidly.

But in her dream he looked exactly as he had done on that last afternoon they had spent together. The sun was on his eager face, his eyes shone—and oh, he looked so desperately young, little more than a boy! He would always remain so, she knew, while she was the prisoner of time in another way, for each year took her further away from him. He remained forever young, while she. . .she slowly aged.

They looked at one another as they had done then. She tried to say his name, but the word would not come, and he began to fade, leaving her in her dream as he had left her in reality. As he finally disappeared both sleep and dream ended, and she was back on the bed, knowing that in some strange way she had finally said goodbye to him.

'To live and love again,' Nan said aloud as she awoke, and wondered why she did so. She rose from the bed, and for some reason—why she did not know—she tried her bedroom door. It was open. Either Kelsey had forgotten to lock it or had deliberately left it unlocked.

The orange light of late afternoon filled the room. Inside was prison, outside was freedom. Without thinking, almost in a trance, Nan picked up her light cream shawl and threw it around her shoulders. She had dressed herself, as an act of defiance, she thought afterwards, in her one good dress, which was also cream and fashionably cut.

She pushed the door open cautiously and, still cautious, walked downstairs. No one seemed to be about. Her mother would doubtless be napping—downstairs now, not in her own room—and Kelsey and the servants would be in the kitchen preparing dinner. Her father would be in his study. He had reclaimed the manuscript of his book when he had visited her, and would probably be working on it.

Once in the black and white flagged hall, Nan walked along it to the garden door, trying to make as little noise as possible. She had no idea of what she was going to do. She had no plans, either to leave or to stay. But where could she go? Who would give her refuge? She had thought for a moment of going to Sam and asking him to help her, but she also shrank at the thought of the scandal it would cause if she did. She only knew that she wanted to be out of her prison and in the open.

The garden door led to a path which ran down by the side of the back lawn, through flowerbeds bright with summer blooms. There was no sign of the gardener—he was probably drinking tea in the kitchen at this hour.

Then she walked through the paddock and the gate which led to the path through the wood and the scrub which Brandon had taken earlier. Did she hope to meet him? If so, what would she say? Still in a dream, as though she were lying on her bed, Nan walked on. Shock and distress held her in thrall.

The wood was shady and cool. She followed the path until she reached the small clearing where Brandon had found her up a tree, trying to free Chaz's kite. She supposed that she ought to think of him as Charles now that her father had belatedly taken charge of his family again.

Tiredness overwhelmed Nan. She had slept badly on the previous night, and poorly on many nights before that. She walked slowly to the back of the clearing, out of the sun, to a small hollow with a bank of grass where bluebells grew in the spring. To lie there and sleep. . . to forget—perhaps to dream that she was hand in hand with Brandon, for Randal had gone, her home had gone, and she was alone, and might please herself.

Out of the sight of man and beast, free from reproach, Nan lay down and, released from servitude, slept sweetly among the summer flowers.

Brandon had loaded his pistol and had thrust it into the sash which he wore beneath an old-fashioned half-coat which would cover it. It felt large and clumsy, and his one prayer was that he would not have to use it.

He was now worrying about Nan as well as the coming confrontation with Desmond. When he had called at the Rectory he had asked Jackson if he might speak to her, and Jackson had begun some talk of her being unwell when Caleb Fielding had arrived in the hall to ask testily, 'Yes, Jackson, what is it?'

'Mr Tolliver is asking whether Miss Fielding is at home——'

Caleb Fielding had interrupted him, his voice frosty and indifferent. 'Neither of my daughters is able to entertain you, Mr Tolliver, Miss Jane Fielding because she is visiting the Aldens, Miss Fielding because she is unwell; she has a low fever.'

For some reason Brandon did not believe him. There had been something in Parson Fielding's manner which he did not care for, some hint of something wrong. But what? Only his intuition, finely honed by many years of hard bargaining, told him this; he had no real evidence. Perhaps it was the way in which her father had uttered Nan's name. . .

He had bowed. What else could he do? 'You will convey my sympathies to her, I trust?' he had said politely. 'And I hope that she will soon be well.'

Remarkably for a man who always insisted on conforming to the most exact protocol of social life, Parson Fielding's only reply had been a mannerless nod before he had turned away and entered his drawing-room again. Nothing to do for Brandon, then, but to go home and brood a little, and eat his dinner, while he waited for the hour to arrive when he might offer himself as a target for his cousin's villainy.

Sighing, he rose, and put his head round the drawing-room door to tell Lydia that he was about to take his after-dinner constitutional. Then he set off down the path through the wood to the clearing where he had encountered Nan Fielding that fateful day—which might be a good omen or a bad one; only time would tell, and that time was upon him.

He was in the clearing before Thorpe and his two accomplices sprang at him. For a moment or two Thorpe managed a determined-looking scuffle on Desmond's behalf, the latter emerging from the trees to watch, half hidden, the villainy being carried out for him. The sham fight was realistic enough for Brandon to collect a few bruises—he told Thorpe afterwards that he ought to deduct a guinea of his pay for each of them!

It was ended by the arrival of a fourth man, whom Thorpe had hired as a look-out, who came running from the opposite direction to Gillyflower Hall, shouting, 'Run! We are discovered!'

Brandon had wondered how Thorpe would contrive to entangle Desmond and leave him behind while he and his untrustworthy cohorts fled. He did it by the simple expedient of catching Desmond round the waist as he ran by him and throwing him bodily towards Brandon, shouting, 'There's your man, master!' before disappearing down the path and into the wood, his part in the evening's work over.

Desmond's sudden arrival nearly took Brandon to the ground, but he steadied himself, caught Desmond by the throat, and snarled at him, 'So, cousin, not Luddites, nor Jacobins, but my own kinsman thought to hire bravos to kill me!'

Desmond recoiled. Here was a Brandon whom he had never met, someone quite different from the easy, genial man whom half the county thought that it knew. A man with the face and demeanour of a man of power, a man to be frightened of.

'No, cousin, you are quite mistook,' he gasped, half choking under Brandon's grip. 'I came upon you by accident, was about to help you——'

'Oh, damn that for a tale,' roared Brandon, now shaking Desmond as though he were a terrier. 'Those men you hired were mine, sent out to trap you. Their leader has worked for me for years, and has disposed of more than one piece of filth for me. I ought to have let him dispose of you, but you are my cousin, and I don't want your blood on my hands, even if you didn't mind soiling yours with mine.' He threw Desmond from him, and his cousin, holding his damaged throat, fought for breath.

It was useless, quite useless, thought Desmond bitterly. Brandon knew. *How* only the devil Brandon obviously was could have told him. 'Oh, damn you, damn you,' he choked hoarsely. 'To have everything while I have nothing. To be ousted by someone who has come up from the gutter—yes, I know that to be true; you have only attained respectability recently. . .'

'If you're respectable, then God save me from respectablity,' was Brandon's tart reply. 'I ought to hand you over to the constables for arrest and trial, but, God help me, you *are* my cousin, and I don't want the scandal of a trial, or your hanging on my conscience. If you promise to behave yourself in future, and leave me in peace, then I'm willing to overlook what you have repeatedly tried to do to me. I want your word on it, mind.'

He saw his cousin's face change. Saw the hate on it, and sighed. Common sense told him to hand him over to the law, but even if blood counted for something a quiet life counted for more. He saw Desmond's inward struggle before, still clutching his bruised throat, he managed to mutter ungraciously, 'Very well; you leave me no choice. I will leave you alone in future, but don't expect me to be other than sorry that I failed.'

It would have to do. Brandon sighed, shut his eyes for a moment, and then said, 'That could have been better expressed, but it is better than nothing. Remember that I have Thorpe and his men as evidence of your villainy. That should stop you from further nonsense of this sort.'

He wondered afterwards if it was the last contemptuous sentence which caused what happened next. Desmond had been half turning away from him as he had begun to speak, but as Brandon finished he swung round, dragging a pistol from underneath his coat to point it at Brandon. He too had been secretly armed, and now he was using his weapon to intimidate, perhaps to kill. Brandon's concealed pistol was of no help to him, since it would take too long for him to draw it and try to counter his cousin's last desperate move.

'Damn you,' Desmond snarled, 'I'd rather swing than live to endure the contempt of such as you. Tell me why I should not kill you here and now, and let the law take its course. I've nothing left to live for. You've even taken Nan Fielding from me.'

The black hole at the end of Desmond's gun stared at Brandon as he contemplated death. What a fool he had been! He had misjudged the lack of mental balance of the man before him, and was about to pay the price for it. He stood quite still, head high as Desmond cried desperately, 'Beg, damn you, beg; I'd as lief you died on your knees as on your feet so long as you die.'

But Brandon shook his head, refused to speak, either to beg or to argue—for he could see that Desmond's sanity was poised on a knife-edge—and tried to stare his cousin down.

CHAPTER SIXTEEN

NAN'S brief sleep was ended by noise and shouting voices. She stood up unsteadily, leaned forward to peer through the bushes and branches before her to find out what could be happening.

She saw the end of the attack on Brandon. She saw Thorpe throw Desmond at him, and heard what followed. It all happened so quickly. Time seemed to have speeded up. She was behind Desmond and could only see Brandon plainly. She was not surprised by his power for she had always known that he possessed it. At one point she thought that she might show herself, but the sheer enormity of learning that Desmond had deliberately set out to murder his cousin held her still. Besides, it was something which the cousins must settle between themselves; it was not for her to intervene.

Until Desmond drew his pistol and threatened Brandon. At that point she climbed through the scrub, and on Desmond's last words she called at his back, 'Stop it, Desmond, stop it immediately!' as though she were a teacher in a dame school admonishing an unruly child. Afterwards she shuddered. Suppose the sudden sound of her voice had caused him to fire the pistol? Suppose. . .?

As it was, Desmond, surprised and alarmed, swung around to face her, the pistol hanging lax in his hand. Brandon, with the pistol no longer trained on him, jumped forward in order to catch Desmond by the arm which held it, to wrench it from him, to fire it into the air, at the same moment that Nan appeared in the clearing.

In some strange way Nan's arrival seemed to unman
Desmond. All of his desperate desire to destroy his
cousin leached out of him. He made no attempt to stop
Brandon from overwhelming him, knocking him to the
ground, and placing his booted foot on his breast. Only
then, when all was safe, could Brandon look at the
white-faced Nan, an expression of mixed joy, pride and
gratitude for his salvation on his face.

'Thank God, my darling! Had you not come I was
done for. But your father said that you were in bed,
ill. . .' His voice trailed off at the sight of her sad face.

Below him Desmond writhed and coughed, until
Brandon removed his foot and allowed him to sit up.

Only for him to meet Nan's indignant stare. 'For
shame, Desmond! Brandon generously spared you, and
the thanks you gave him were that you again tried to
kill him! You deserve to hang for that alone!' This
forthright declaration had Desmond avoiding her eyes
and hanging his head. His shame was doubled because
Nan had been a witness of his treachery.

Brandon had drawn Nan to him and, his arm around
her, the pair of them confronted Desmond as he rose,
slowly and painfully, from the ground, a caricature of
the cool and self-righteous man he usually presented to
the world.

His head still sagging, his manner distraught, for
Nan's arrival had restored him to common sense and
normality, he ground out painfully, 'I suppose Nan is
right. It was the act of a cur to try to take your life
when you had just given me mine back. I think that
I've been light in the attic ever since you came to
Gillyflower Hall.'

It was as though for the first time he was struck by
the enormity of what he had been doing. To sit alone,
allowing hate to fester and boil inside him, to hire men
of straw to help him to kill his cousin was one thing—

but for Nan to discover what he had been doing was quite another.

He stretched his hands out to her, wordlessly pleading for understanding, and when she shook her head at him he muttered painfully, 'I thought that I had lost everything—the lands, the Hall, and you.'

'Your honour, Desmond,' Nan cried passionately. 'You were still left with that, and now you have thrown it away. And you never had me, any more than you had Cousin Bart's lands. You simply thought that you deserved them, as you deserved me, without doing anything for them. I am sorry that you did what you did, sorrier still that you descended into murderous self-pity when you should have been thinking about the future of the lands you *do* own, which you have allowed to fall into a sorry state.'

Brandon was hard put to it to stifle a grin as Nan came out with this typically Nan-like piece of sound and down-to-earth common sense. It was plain that Mrs Brandon Tolliver would never allow her husband's fortune to diminish. She would soon put him back on the right track if he strayed from the straight and narrow. In the same fashion she had practically and robustly found a means to restore the fortunes of her family. Marriage to her might have saved Desmond, but she would never have married a weak man, and Brandon thought that like Jane, despite his cousin's attempt on his life, Desmond was basically weak rather than wicked.

'Go home, cousin,' he told him gently. 'Try to forget what has passed here today. Be sure that Nan and I will say nothing of what happened. It was not my fault that Cousin Bart wrote his will as he did, merely my good fortune—the first I ever gained without working for it, I do own.'

Desmond nodded. He was quite defeated. He knew

that he would never again attempt to harm his cousin, but the knowledge that he had tried to—and failed—would always be with him. His head sagged again as he muttered, 'I suppose that Nan is right—that I should thank you for sparing me, and that I will do now, but you would not expect me to be happy because I have given you yet another occasion to demonstrate what a kind and splendid fellow you are! Now I will go back home, if you will so allow.'

What more to do? Desmond would have to live with his conscience and both Brandon and Nan were aware that nothing that they could say or do would comfort him, or restore his lost self-respect. Later Brandon, hard-headed as ever, was to say to Nan, 'He should find a rich widow who will take him in hand, but I doubt that he ever will.'

Meantime they watched him walk slowly away, down the path towards the Rectory where he might regain the main Broomhall road. Nan suddenly shuddered and clutched at Brandon's arm. Too much had happened to her during the past twenty-four hours, and between relief that Brandon was still alive and distress at her own sad condition her head was swimming. She wondered if her flight had been discovered and what she would do now. Perhaps she could try to make her own way back to her room, and hope that her absence had not been noticed.

And after that, what?

But Brandon, having Nan almost in his arms again, was not about to let her go. Now that he could think clearly about something other than his cousin, and his own possible imminent death, he could see how pale and thin she looked. Her father had said that she was ill, was confined to her room, and if that was so how had she come to be wandering in the woods? Here was a puzzle he ought to solve immediately.

So when Nan released her grip on his arm and made to return to the Rectory, he caught her hand in his and turned her into his arms. 'No,' he told her, 'no. You must rest again. I can feel that you are shivering.'

Now that danger was over, Nan had begun to shudder, and the clearing was turning slowly around her. . . She had eaten almost nothing since her father had sent her to her room the day before, and exhaustion was beginning to claim her.

Brandon caught her as she fell, muttered an oath—what in the world had been happening to his beloved?—and lowered her gently to the ground, to strip off his coat, to fold it into a pillow and place it beneath Nan's head so that she might lie in some small comfort on the hard ground.

What to do to help his darling? He remembered Lydia dealing with a parlourmaid who had fainted. He tried to imitate her by kneeling down beside Nan and picking up her hands in order to chafe them gently. She was deathly cold, even her lips were white, so he put her hands down and carefully gathered her to him, to share his warmth, her heart against his, his warm cheek against her cold one. He began to kiss her gently, as though, like the Prince in the fairy-tale, he could bring Sleeping Beauty back to life.

Semi-consciousness had given Nan a new kind of beauty. Loss of colour only served to reveal the pure planes of her face, the elegant bone-structure which would keep her lovely even into old age when those whose looks depended on blonde curls and pink and white prettiness had descended into ordinariness. Oh, that she would consent to be his, his peerless love, neglected by the uncaring and unseeing who had passed over her gold in favour of base metal, leaving her for him to find. He would care for her, make sure that she would never again descend into the depths of suffering which he suspected that she was enduring.

'Oh, my love, my love,' he whispered into her tawny hair. 'Wake up so that I may tell you how much I love and worship you—not only for your looks but for the selfless way in which you care for those around you.'

She stirred a little, and to his delight, as he kissed her near her shapely mouth, Nan turned her head and gently kissed him back on the corner of his, so that his whole unruly body tingled with the joy of it, and began to make demands on him which, in honour, he could not fulfil.

Nan was in heaven. Warmth returning was bringing full consciousness back again. She was in someone's arms, and the someone was loving her as she had not been loved for years—if ever. The someone must be Brandon, and, if so, how had he come to be in her bedroom?

But once her eyes were open she found herself not in her bedroom but in the dim and shady green of the wood between her home and his, and, memory swiftly returning, she remembered all that had passed. Not even memory, though, could compel her to pull away from him, and the next time that he kissed her she first responded, and then whispered, pulling her mouth away from his, 'We should not be doing this, Brandon.'

To which his answer was, 'Why not? I am enjoying myself, aren't you?'

Somehow that wasn't the point. The point was that if she did not return soon she was sure to be missed, and so she ought to tell him. The mere idea, though, was distressing. She began to shudder again.

Brandon felt her change of mood from quiet acquiescence to unhappiness. He held her closer to him and murmured in her ear, 'What is it, Nan? What is distressing you?'

She tried to pull away from him completely, to avert her face, but he would not let her. In some way he must compel her to confide in him, but he must do it gently, without bullying her. He muttered into her ear again. 'Nan, your father said that you were ill, were confined to your room. But here you are, and you look ill, but not in the way his tone to me implied. You must have been fit enough to walk from the Rectory to the clearing—and, by the by, your collapse has prevented me from thanking you for my life.'

This brought an immediate response. Nan turned her averted head, looked at him earnestly, and said, 'I don't think that Desmond really meant to kill you—though he might have done so accidentally, I do admit, by disturbing the hair trigger of his pistol. He was merely playing at villainy.'

While secretly acknowledging that this might be true, Brandon returned, his mouth twitching slightly, 'Well, if what he was doing was play, then I hope never to see him in earnest. He would have made fricassee of me by now!'

Nan, without thinking, put a hand over his mouth. 'Oh, do not say so,' she cried. 'It was bad enough to see you threatened—but to think of him succeeding. . .' And she shuddered again.

'No, we won't think of that,' Brandon agreed. 'Let us talk of other things. What is wrong at the Rectory, Nan, that you should be in such a state? Was it because your father discovered that you were the author of *Sophia*?' He saw by her expression that he was right.

'Yes, but how did you know? Oh, not that you knew I wrote *Sophia*—Sam told me that he thought that you had guessed some time ago. Can you read minds that you knew that, and know that something is wrong?'

'A little,' he said gravely. 'People give themselves away, Nan, in many ways. With their eyes, their bodies, their hands as much as their tone of voice. Tell me what has happened and I will help you. How you shall know in a moment, but we need to speak of what is distressing you before we go on to more pleasant things. What did your father do when he found out?'

Nan averted her face again. She could not tell him for very shame. To be sent away as though she were a criminal! But the nearness of Brandon, the scent of him, so secretly and deliciously male, the kindness in his voice, his kisses, his. . . She was growing maudlin. Yes, she would tell him; she would.

'He went a little mad, I think,' she said slowly. 'I fear that he saw it as an insult to him. I had no idea he resented me so. He said that he would rather we all starved than that we should live well on what I earned. . .'

Brandon ground out an oath which made him sound like a wolf howling. The slightly feral quality in him which Nan, if no one else, had scented had never been plainer. She fell silent.

'And?' he asked. 'There must be more to it than that. What did he do?'

Yes, she must tell him, but only if she held her face away from him. 'He ordered me to my rooms, to remain there locked in, until I was sent, like a parcel, to be a companion to my old aunt Smithson in North Yorkshire. He said that he would instruct her never to allow me to have ink and paper so that I could not disgrace him again by writing another novel.'

It was, after all, easy to confess, once one began. Perhaps that was why Roman Catholics set such store by it. One felt purged.

'Kelsey brought me my food. Either she forgot to lock the door or she left it unlocked deliberately, and so I decided to take a walk before I was shut away forever.'

Brandon uttered another oath, beneath his breath this time. It was a good thing that Parson Fielding was not near by. The wolf would have made short work of him.

Once started Nan could not stop. Besides, there was something else which she must confess to him.

'What made it worse was that Jane had just told me that she had stolen the letter you sent to me.'

The memory of it was suddenly so strong that Nan stopped. . . Then, 'Your letter,' she murmured brokenly. 'Your dear letter, the only true love letter I was ever sent, and she took it. If she hadn't had a fit of conscience I might never have been able to read it. . . and then Father came in and said. . .and said. . .' And she began to rock herself, her knees drawn up to her chin, her head bent, her glorious hair, once more undone, streaming about her.

Brandon said nothing of the part he had played in Jane's change of heart. Instead he put his arms around Nan's shoulders to lift her against him once more. 'What did the letter say, Nan? Tell me that.'

'It said——' and now the drowned turquoise eyes were looking straight into his loving silver ones, pleading for mercy '—it said that you loved me and wanted to marry me.'

'Yes, Nan, and that is no less than the truth. You will marry me, Nan, won't you? There's no need for you to worry about being sent into exile; you shall be the Queen of my heart, and wherever I am there shall your kingdom be.'

He had had no notion that he would say anything half so romantical, but it had flown out of him, a statement of love quite unlike anything the cynical and hard-headed man he had been until he came to Broomhall would ever have said.

'Oh, what a lovely thing to say to me, but. . .' And

now the tears began to fall in earnest, for Nan was finding that the emotions and pains of the last few weeks were turning her into the kind of watering-pot which she most despised. 'But, oh, Brandon, I love you so dearly, and I can't marry you, I can't, I can't.'

She burrowed her head into his chest as she cried out these words, and the sobbing grew worse, for oh, she loved him even more than she had loved Randal, for that had been a child's love, and now she was a woman and loved him with her heart and mind, her body and her soul—but she could never be his.

Brandon stroked her hair, lifted her head away from his chest, tipped his hand under her chin and murmured as gently as he could, 'Why should you not marry me, Nan, when we both love one another so much?'

'Oh. . .' wailed Nan, trying to look away from him and failing. 'I am not fit to marry you, or any man. I am a fallen woman,' she wept at him. 'Chaz is mine, not Father and Mother's.'

'I know,' Brandon told her simply. 'I know that he is yours, and it makes no difference to me, truly. What happened in the past, when you were only sixteen, means nothing to me, except that I would willingly be a father to Chaz—if I could.'

Nan swept on unheeding. 'Oh, that's not all. The worst of it is that I don't regret what I did—which makes me doubly fallen, and consequently unfit to marry anyone.

'I met Randal secretly on the last night before he left for the Army—our parents had forbidden us to have anything to do with each other—and somehow we both knew that it was all that we were ever going to have. It seemed inevitable when we made love, although I never thought at the time of the possible consequence for me, because I loved him so much—but even if I had I wouldn't have behaved any differently,' she added with a defiant sniff. 'At least Randal had that before he died, even if he never knew about Chaz.'

Her sobbing redoubled. 'To save my reputation, as well as the family's, Mother arranged everything. She was quite different in those days. I think that she used what I had done to compel me to be her servant so that she could have the life of the lady which she had always wished to be.

'I was never sure, until yesterday, when he reproached me with it, that Papa knew what we, she and I, had done. She said that it was she who was with child, and went into the country for her health, taking me with her. And Chaz was such a dear little baby. They wouldn't let me hold him or feed him when he was born. They bound my breasts up to stop the milk from coming.

'If he had been a girl, Mother would have given him away, but she and Papa had always wanted a boy so she took him home as hers, and we left Frensham Major for fear that the Scotts might find out the truth. They hated us all because Randal was in love with me and they wanted him to make a grand marriage. Which in the end was just as well, because Chaz has grown up to look exactly like Randal did when we were children together.'

She drew several gasping breaths. 'And Chaz has never been mine, even though I am the only one who really cares for him. He's not a bit like the boy Papa wanted—someone meek and scholarly, like himself. If any man ever showed an interest in me, Mother always reminded me that I was a fallen woman and could never marry a good man.'

During her sad recital she had, without willing it, clung closer and closer to Brandon, who tightened his own grasp on her, kissing the top of her head gently, and when at last she fell silent he murmured, 'There,

there, my darling, you shall have as many babies as you wish, and I promise you that you shall feed all of them. And I am not a good man, so you may marry me as soon as I can arrange it.'

Even as he spoke he was remembering how she had clutched Mrs Blagg's baby to her that day on the Soar, and her transfigured face as she had petted it. He knew why her father and mother had behaved as they did—to save her—and themselves—from shame and disgrace—but he also knew that as a result of it they had exploited her and blackmailed her unmercifully, turning her into the family's drudge.

Nan had been so preoccupied in telling her sad story to Brandon that his acknowledgement that he already knew that she was Chaz's mother had almost passed her by. Remembering now, she looked up at him with great drowned eyes and stammered, almost reproachfully, 'Y-you s-said that you knew that Chaz was mine. How could you know?'

'My darling, he is so unlike you all, and you love him so, when it is quite patent that no one else in the family does, and that made me curious, as did several other little things, including the way in which your parents used you so unmercifully. My agent had told me that you came from Frensham Major to Broomhall, and I wondered why your father had left a rich living for a poor one. So I visited Frensham and the Scotts on a pretext which was not quite a pretext, and there I saw Randal's portrait, and, yes, Chaz is the image of him.'

'So now you know, and you know why I can't marry you, and there's an end of it.'

Brandon gave a short laugh and shook her gently. 'My darling love, you have been a martyr to your family for so long that you have forgotten how to be anything else. Didn't you hear what I said to you about babies? I want to marry you, Nan, so that you can give me the babies we both want, free you from drudgery, and allow you to write your novels in the day and not in the middle of the night. You see, I mean to be the husband of the author of *Sophia*.'

'Oh,' cried Nan, her eyes suddenly starry. 'You cannot mean that, knowing what I did, and that I am not ashamed of it.'

Brandon held her away from him for a moment to look deep into her eyes. 'Oh, Nan, I have just told you that I am not a good man, and I know that I am not quite a gentleman and never will be. If we are to judge one another and condemn each other for our past sins, then how can *you* bring yourself to marry *me*? My whole life, or at least the life the county thinks it knows, is a lie. I never went to grammar school, except for one half-year, and I was never articled as a clerk, never made my way diligently up a reputable counting house to make my fortune by hard work and honesty.

'No, indeed! My father, the younger son of a younger son, gambled away what little we had on the Stock Exchange and in the gaming halls around the Haymarket. The bailiffs turned us out of our small house in Chelsea when I was ten years old, and we ended up in a tenement near the Docks, where my father drank himself to death and my mother died of shame and despair.

'Lydia, who is several years older than I am, went for a lady's maid, and I. . . I worked for the biggest fence and thief in London doing any job he cared to give me so that I might not starve—I had no trade, you see. When I had saved enough to start a little business of my own, I tried to make money honestly, or at least reasonably honestly, seeing that I had no desire to hang—which my old master did, soon afterwards.

'I had a talent for being a merchant and broker, and soon had enough capital to set up a decent home of my own, and save Lydia from servitude by sending for her to come and run it for me. By hook or by crook—and crooked some of it was—I made myself a fortune with the help of a wealthy India merchant who saw me as the son he had untimely lost. He married Lydia, and I suppose that he was the piece of luck which we all need if we are to succeed in life with only our wits to help us.

'You see, Nan, I was a user and a manipulator of men—and the succession of women whom I set up as my mistresses, until I grew bored and pensioned them off. I was a liar and a cheat, and when I grew rich enough I awarded myself an invented life to replace the one I had lived, first in the underworld and then in the *demi-monde*—a life of respectability when, in truth, Lydia and her late husband were the only claims I had to it—that and Cousin Bart's unexpected bequest which made me a country gentleman.

'When I met Jane I thought that she was exactly the kind of wife I wished to have. Someone young and charming, a kind of trophy for the poor boy who had risen from the gutter. Someone to whom I need make no real commitment, who would be compelled to let me go my own way, in exchange for being the mistress of a noble establishment.

'And then I met you. It was like a thunderclap. For the first time I met a woman whom I desired beyond reason, but also to whom I could talk as I had never talked to a woman before—as I could never talk to Jane. A woman who gave and never took, who lived her hard life uncomplainingly and with pride. A woman whom I wanted as the mother of my children. I saw how empty my past life had been, and I wanted to fill it. I never thought that I could love anyone as I love you.

'It is *you* who will be honouring *me* if you become

my wife. Marry me, Nan, and save me from nothingness.'

He had released her, made no claims on her by touch, made no effort to make love to her, to persuade her to do as he wished. All the arts he had practised on men and women to gain what he wanted from them were laid aside. If she came to him, here and now, after he had placed the truth of him before her, as she had placed her own truth before him, then he knew that they would be blessed indeed. True love and true lovers needed nothing of compulsion.

They were kneeling now, facing one another, as they might kneel in church before the priest who married them. Nan put up a hand to touch his face. 'You were so brave—to survive your dreadful beginning. Whatever you say of yourself, you are honourable as well as brave—else you would not have told me the truth of your past.'

She stroked his face, and saw a smile begin to dawn on it, but still he said nothing—everything had been said. Or, perhaps, nothing needed to be said. Since the first moment when they had met in the pantry they had been one soul, not two. Only time had been needed to bring the two halves permanently together.

Her hand still on his cheek, Nan leaned forward to kiss him on the lips, a gentle kiss, a chaste kiss, a kiss to which for the first time he did not physically respond, except that as she withdrew his eyes dilated as hope dawned in them.

'Of course I will marry you, Brandon, as soon as you wish.'

He gave an exultant cry before he took her into his arms. 'Oh, my dearly beloved—for that is what you are, Nan—I can scarce wait to say the words "till death us do part!" I remember the parson saying them when

Lydia married Henry, and they made no real impression on me then. . .but now. . .'

They were both shaking as the emotion of the moment swept through them. Slowly Brandon lowered her to the ground to hold her in his arms there, still refusing to do more than kiss her gently, though every fibre in his body demanded consummation. But that must wait. He would honour her by waiting; he would not fall on her hugger-mugger to remind her of what love, heedlessly fulfilled, had once done to her.

Nan felt the same. She could not really remember what it had been like to make love on the one and only time when she and Randal had clung together, in desperation rather than passion, before he had gone from her forever.

I am reborn, she thought, I who had never hoped to find love again, and warm in Brandon's arms, her head against his chest, happiness working on her, she slept. Afterwards she thought with wonder that almost from the first she had felt so secure with him that sleep had come easily to her—she who had always found it difficult before.

Once Brandon would have mocked a man who, with his willing love in his arms, held off, and was happy to cradle her as she slept. What a waste, would have been his sardonic comment on such an ass.

But they had all the time in the world, and he would let her rest before he took her to Gillyflower Hall, for he had no intention of allowing her to return to the Rectory, to reproach and exploitation. If Nan's parents had discovered that she had gone, then let them worry a little over what might have befallen her.

Twilight was all about them before Nan woke. Lydia would begin to worry—would already be worrying as to why he had not returned—might even be fearing the worst. But that did not matter. Nan's face, now rosy,

because she was loved and treasured, was turned trust-
ingly to him.

'What do we do now?' she asked him, her voice
trembling a little.

'We go home,' Brandon said, holding out a hand to
help her up.

'To Papa?' Nan shivered, her rosiness fading a little.

'No, I said *home*. To Gillyflower Hall. Lydia will
chaperon you. My only worry is that I have exploited
her too. She needs a husband and a home of her own.'

Nan could almost see him thinking this over. He
shook his head and said abruptly, 'No matter; time to
deal with that later. You shall not go back to the
Rectory until I have arranged matters for you there. I
shall begin by asking for your hand.'

Nan shivered again.

'What is it, my darling? What troubles you?'

'Chaz,' she said. 'Oh, how could I forget him? I can't
leave him to Papa; he will punish him for my sin. He
has been punishing him for it all his short life. My
happiness will be built on his misery.' Her face
crumpled at the thought.

'Yes, I see that.' Brandon was thoughtful. 'No
matter. There is a way out. Do not worry. Trust me.'

Yes, she would trust him.

The walk to Gillyflower Hall was a slow one, for Nan
was tired, and when they entered the last stretch of it,
on the gravelled sweep, he gave a short exclamation at
the sight of her white face, and the great blue smudges
beneath her eyes. 'This is no way to enter your future
home, my darling,' he said, and swept her into his
arms, to carry her up the steps and into the Hall.

He walked past the astonished butler who opened
the door, and past the astonished Lydia, who had come
out of the drawing-room to greet him. He carried his
burden in—to stare at Sam Stone who sat comfortably

there, before the tea-tray, with a footman at the far door to make matters proper.

Brandon gave a crack of laughter and announced enigmatically as Sam rose, 'Well, this seems to have settled one matter happily enough,' for both Sam and Lydia were giving off the aura of a pair of children caught in an orchard stealing apples.

He had no need to explain himself. Sam and Lydia's expressions told all, and Nan was busy thinking, as she peered at them over the shelter of Brandon's arm, how splendid for Sam that he has found someone suitable at last. And Lydia too, of course.

'What in the world. . .?' began Lydia as Brandon gently sat Nan down in a big armchair before telling the footman to bring more tea, and something for Miss Fielding to eat.

'Miss Fielding,' announced Brandon, once the footman had gone, 'has just done me the honour of accepting my proposal and consenting to be my wife. Her papa being rather exercised over his discovery that she is the author of *Sophia*, my future wife has appealed to me for temporary asylum—something which I need not dwell on, and the details of which will be confidential to us all.'

This grandly ambiguous statement had Nan coughing, Lydia looking startled, and Sam starting to his feet and exclaiming, 'The ungrateful old devil! I feared this. My dear,' he said, turning to Nan. 'He has not turned you out, I hope?'

Nan decided to be slightly more truthful than Brandon, but no less ambiguous. 'No, indeed. I suppose, in a sense, I have turned myself out. But not for long, I trust.'

'And you, my dear Lydia,' Brandon addressed his sister, still in the same grand manner which he had employed earlier, as though he were conducting a board meeting, 'will consent to be my future wife's chaperon, I hope.' He decided that he rather liked saying 'my future wife'. It gave him great pleasure and made Nan blush in the most charming way.

'Of course, Brandon!' exclaimed Lydia warmly. 'But we are being most remiss. We have not congratulated you on your news. I cannot tell you how happy I am to see you fixed at last, and with such a suitable wife.'

She walked over to Nan and kissed her. 'Welcome, my dear,' she said.

Her good wishes were followed by Sam's, who took the opportunity to say quietly but sternly to Brandon, 'You will look after her properly, my dear fellow. No one has ever done so before, and she deserves the best, the very best, from life.'

Brandon bowed to the only true friend whom Nan had possessed before he and Lydia had arrived in Broomhall. 'And she shall have the best, my dear sir. I promise you that. As I have promised her.'

Tea arrived, and sandwiches and cake, and then Lydia insisted that Nan retire. 'For, my dear, you are looking very tired, and I know that my brother, however much he loves you, has so much energy himself that he sometimes fails to recognise that other people may not always be so blessed.'

The two lovers looked at one another. Joy reigned on Nan's face, but those with her could not but see that excitement, pain and even the knowledge that she had reached harbour at last had taken their toll of her.

She whispered to Brandon. 'I don't want to leave you.'

'We shall have all our days together soon,' was his answer to that. 'Tonight I shall send word to the Rectory that you are safe at Gillyflower Hall and that I hope to see your papa tomorrow, and then we may be married in as short a time as possible.' He stopped, and had the grace to blush. 'You see, my love, I brought a special licence back from London with me, so that once you had accepted me we need not wait.'

All three of them reacted in their own way to this piece of supreme impudence. Nan said faintly, 'Oh, Brandon, were you so sure of me?'

And Lydia said, 'For shame, Brandon, before you had so much as asked your future wife!'

And Sam said, 'By God, Tolliver, Nan's fate was sealed once you had arrived in Broomhall. You leave nothing to chance.'

'I never do.' Brandon was brief. 'Come, my love.' And he escorted Nan to the bottom of the stairs where the lovers clung together and kissed, before the maid allocated to Nan arrived with a candle to escort her to her bedroom where she found herself lapped in the kind of luxury which she had never encountered before.

Downstairs, Brandon walked back into the drawing-room to be confronted by both Sam and Lydia.

'Now, Brandon,' cried his sister imperiously, 'the truth, if you please, of your and Nan's goings-on.'

But he shook his head at her, and quoted the late Francis Bacon, '"What is truth? said jesting Pilate; and would not stay for an answer."'

No more did Brandon.

CHAPTER SEVENTEEN

Nan woke up refreshed, to greet a glorious morning. Not a glorious dawn, for it was already past ten of the clock and she had been allowed to sleep on.

The little maid came in with fresh undergarments, and a dress of Lydia's, for which, she was informed, her new chaperon had no further use. Breakfast was in the dining-room at the back of the house.

Could it be true? Was she really to marry Brandon? It seemed that she was. Lydia, who had breakfasted much ealier, was waiting for her, and Nan ate her largest meal in years.

There was no sign of Brandon. 'He has already gone to see your papa,' Lydia told her, joining her in a cup of coffee. 'To ask for you hand, and for him to marry the pair of you as soon as may be.'

'Papa *will* be surprised,' returned Nan, with the sort of giggle which she had left behind over eleven years ago, before Chaz's birth. Accepting Brandon seemed to have given her her youth back.

Lydia privately thought that the whole of Broomhall, Highborough and the surrounding district was going to be surprised, but sensibly did not say so. Instead, putting her head on one side, she remarked, 'That dress suits you better than it ever did me. We are much of a size, and I thought that you would prefer something a little fresher than the gown you arrived in.'

She might have added that Nan's dress looked as though she had been crawling through half the undergrowth between the Rectory and Gillyflower Hall, but that was another thought she did not voice.

It was strange to be idle and waited on, to be doing nothing in the middle of the morning, when by now, at the Rectory, her duties would have been in full flow. Even stranger to have Lydia say briskly to her, as they chatted happily on the lawn below the terrace in comfortable chairs which had been carried out for them by the footmen, 'Now that I have come to know you, I am so glad that Brandon is marrying you and not one of the witless girls who have been chasing him. You will be so good for him. He needs a wife as strong-minded as he is. You will never bore him.'

A little later Nan saw the man she would be so good for striding towards them along the terrace. He looked particularly splendid. He had put on his London finery to visit Parson Fielding and had taken the chaise to go to the Rectory by the long way, taking the main road which ran towards Broomhall and which passed Gillyflower Hall's gates. He had been determined to arrive at the Rectory in full command of himself.

He was arriving back in that state, too. His coat and breeches were charcoal-grey, his shirt spotlessly white. His cravat was an extravagant dream. His hat, which he still held under his arm, and then threw on the grass beside the chair which was already set out for him, was from a hatter's heaven. His boots were like mirrors, so shiny were they. He had never, Nan decided, looked so stunningly and alarmingly handsome.

Nothing was said of his visit until Lydia, after a few moments' conversation with him, rose and said, 'I think that you are old and serious enough to be left on your own for a little. I have duties to perform, so I will leave you.'

'Good,' Brandon replied. 'We have several things to discuss, Miss Fielding.' He offered Nan his arm. 'You will allow? A quiet walk would do miracles for both of us, I think, and remove us from the gaze of the house.'

Nan took his arm and they walked away, down the slope, towards the tiny lake and the small gazebo where they had been private together once before. He handed her on to the marble bench where he had found her then, before sitting down beside her.

'Now, Miss Fielding,' he said. 'Allow me to tell you that your papa is on his highest ropes at the prospect of having Mr Brandon Tolliver as his wealthy and well-connected son-in-law. He told me so himself, and he will marry us when we wish, although he is a little perturbed that the unthinking might consider the haste with which we are marrying a trifle odd. But no matter. If that is what we wish, then it shall be so.'

Nan was bemused. 'Oh, Brandon, whatever did you say or do to make him so amenable? Whatever did you promise him? I vow that I was fearful that he would insist that I was a fallen woman, and therefore not worthy of you.'

Brandon began to laugh whole-heartedly. 'Oh, my love. I can see that we shall never be dull if you understand so quickly the way in which I operate! Of course, I bamboozled him into doing whatever we wanted. Before I left London I arranged with an old friend that if you accepted me your father would be given the rich living of a parish near Oxford where he will be able to use the Bodleian Library whenever he wishes, and meet again the many old friends whom he has lost sight of since coming to Highborough. He would have given me the Crown Jewels after that, never mind your hand!

'I told him that I was aware of what a treasure you were to the family, and that only by offering him such a prize could I compensate him for taking you away.'

He did not say that before the bribe had been offered her father had tried to blow upon her reputation, and that he had answered him in his most arrogant manner,

'You will, of course, say nothing against Nan to me, sir. She is the woman I love and mean to marry, come what may.' That had silenced the parson.

'And then,' he went on, 'we came to Chaz. I said that seeing that he was the child of your father's middle age, and consequently looking after him must be something of a trial, we were prepared to have him visit us on a regular basis, to relieve his burden. Of course, I said, Charles would shortly go on to Eton and then to Oxford, and I would be only too happy to bear the expense of him doing so, for, I told him, what were riches for but to enable us to make our friends and relatives happy?'

He drew her into his arms. 'So, you see, you have not lost Chaz. I think that he will be ours, for your father has, I regret to say, little feeling for any of his children, and none for Chaz.'

Enthusiastic kissing, stroking and moaning followed, until, his clothing in some disarray, Brandon sat up and gasped, 'For God's sake, Nan, I wanted you to arrive at the altar in three days' time untouched—or at least not touched vitally. But at this rate we shall not last the day. We had better sit a little apart and contemplate the view.'

Nan, lacing up her bodice, was inclined to agree. 'Oh, by the by,' he added, 'your papa was gaining plenty of practice in dealing with future sons-in-law. Your sister Jane accepted George Alden the other evening, and today he was there before me! The Reverend Caleb and Mrs Fielding will be a happy pair now that they have lost all their encumbrances.'

'Oh, that is of all news the best,' Nan said, smiling. 'Jane and George are well-suited and neither of us will sit about thinking that we have cheated Jane in any way by falling in love with one another.'

'No, indeed,' replied Brandon lazily, watching her

straighten her hair, which had, as usual, come down during their last bout. 'There is only one young woman to whom I wish to be "*most* particular", and that is the future Mrs Brandon Tolliver who is sitting by me. I can't wait to see you in Broomhall Church. Your papa has most particularly asked for us to be married there.'

'And Lydia has spent all morning deciding what I am to be married in,' Nan said happily. 'Oh, Brandon what a good thing it was that you lost your way and found yourself in the pantry!'

'Even more that I saw you up a tree,' Brandon announced naughtily. 'I have been longing for another look at the most splendid pair of legs I have ever seen, and now I have only a short time to wait. But I want to see you in your wedding-dress first.'

And so he did. And he and all Broomhall were agreed that no one would have thought what a handsome bride Nan Fielding would make, and small wonder, if he could cause her to look like that, that Mr Brandon Tolliver had decided to marry her.

And her legs were every bit as beautiful as Brandon had thought they were. . . .

Christmas Journeys

4 new short romances all wrapped up in 1 sparkling volume.

Join four delightful couples as they journey home for the festive season—and discover the true meaning of Christmas...that love is the best gift of all!

A Man To Live For - Emma Richmond

Yule Tide - Catherine George

Mistletoe Kisses - Lynsey Stevens

Christmas Charade - Kay Gregory

Available: November 1995   **Price: £4.99**

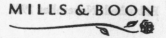

MILLS & BOON

Available from WH Smith, John Menzies, Volume One, Forbuoys, Martins, Tesco, Asda, Safeway and other paperback stockists.

MILLS & BOON

CHRISTMAS CRACKERS

*A cracker of a gift pack full of
Mills & Boon goodies. You'll find...*

Passion—in *A Savage Betrayal* by Lynne Graham
A beautiful baby—in *A Baby for Christmas* by Anne McAllister
A Yuletide wedding—in *Yuletide Bride* by Mary Lyons
A Christmas reunion—in *Christmas Angel* by Shannon Waverly

Special Christmas price of 4 books
for £5.99 (usual price £7.96)

Published: November 1995

*Available from WH Smith, John Menzies, Volume One, Forbuoys, Martins,
Tesco, Asda, Safeway and other paperback stockists.*

GET 4 BOOKS AND A MYSTERY GIFT

Return the coupon below and we'll send you 4 Legacy of Love novels and a mystery gift absolutely FREE! We'll even pay the postage and packing for you.

We're making you this offer to introduce you to the benefits of Reader Service: FREE home delivery of brand-new Legacy of Love novels, at least a month before they are available in the shops, FREE gifts and a monthly Newsletter packed with information.

Accepting these FREE books and gift places you under no obligation to buy, you may cancel at any time, even after receiving just your free shipment. Simply complete the coupon below and send it to:

MILLS & BOON READER SERVICE, FREEPOST, CROYDON, SURREY, CR9 3WZ.

No stamp needed

Yes, please send me 4 free Legacy of Love novels and a mystery gift. I understand that unless you hear from me, I will receive 4 superb new titles every month for just £2.50* each postage and packing free. I am under no obligation to purchase any books and I may cancel or suspend my subscription at any time, but the free books and gifts will be mine to keep in any case. (I am over 18 years of age)

2EP5M

Ms/Mrs/Miss/Mr _____

Address _____

_____

_____ Postcode _____

Offer closes 31st May 1996. We reserve the right to refuse an application. *Prices and terms subject to change without notice. Offer only valid in UK and Ireland and is not available to current subscribers to this series. Readers in Ireland please write to: P.O. Box 4546, Dublin 24. Overseas readers please write for details.

You may be mailed with offers from other reputable companies as a result of this application. Please tick box if you would prefer not to receive such offers. ☐

MILLS & BOON

By Request

Bestselling romances brought back to you by popular demand

Don't miss our December title...
Just Add Children—the perfect
mix for a spicy romance!

Two complete novels in one romantic
volume by **Catherine George** and
Emma Goldrick.

Available: December 1995   Price: £3.99

*Available from WH Smith, John Menzies, Volume One, Forbuoys, Martins,
Tesco, Asda, Safeway and other paperback stockists.*